Mack Bolan smiled grimly; the enemy was using frags

If they had incendiaries or gas, it would get ugly very quickly. A second salvo of rifle grenades flew through the shattered windows and detonated overhead. Metal fragments hissed down and scored the surface of their shields.

He forced himself to yawn to clear the ringing in his ears. Outside he could dimly perceive the sound of many boots hitting the concrete. The sound of automatic rifle fire was all too clear.

"I need you, Jack!" the Executioner shouted into the microphone in his collar.

"Inbound, Striker!" The pilot's voice sounded reassuringly near.

Bolan quickly scanned his team. No one was hurt. His voice rose above the din of autofire with the unmistakable thunder of command. "Now!"

MACK BOLAN®

The Executioner

DON PENDLETON'S
THE EXECUTIONER®
TARGET COMMAND

THE
POWER
TRILOGY
BOOK I

A GOLD EAGLE BOOK FROM

WORLDWIDE®

TORONTO • NEW YORK • LONDON
AMSTERDAM • PARIS • SYDNEY • HAMBURG
STOCKHOLM • ATHENS • TOKYO • MILAN
MADRID • WARSAW • BUDAPEST • AUCKLAND

First edition June 1998
ISBN 0-373-64234-2

Special thanks and acknowledgment to
Chuck Rogers for his contribution to this work.

TARGET COMMAND

The desire of power...caused the angels to fall;

—Sir Francis Bacon
1561-1626

Power, like a desolating pestilence,
Pollutes whate'er it touches;

—Percy Bysshe Shelley
Queen Mab

Those with a hidden agenda will discover that they can't sit back and manipulate players with an unseen hand. I'll ferret them out, then they'll have to face my brand of justice.

—Mack Bolan

THE
MACK BOLAN®
LEGEND

Nothing less than a war could have fashioned the destiny of the man called Mack Bolan. Bolan earned the Executioner title in the jungle hell of Vietnam.

But this soldier also wore another name—Sergeant Mercy. He was so tagged because of the compassion he showed to wounded comrades-in-arms and Vietnamese civilians.

Mack Bolan's second tour of duty ended prematurely when he was given emergency leave to return home and bury his family, victims of the Mob. Then he declared a one-man war against the Mafia.

He confronted the Families head-on from coast to coast, and soon a hope of victory began to appear. But Bolan had broken society's every rule. That same society started gunning for this elusive warrior—to no avail.

So Bolan was offered amnesty to work within the system against terrorism. This time, as an employee of Uncle Sam, Bolan became Colonel John Phoenix. With a command center at Stony Man Farm in Virginia, he and his new allies—Able Team and Phoenix Force—waged relentless war on a new adversary: the KGB.

But when his one true love, April Rose, died at the hands of the Soviet terror machine, Bolan severed all ties with Establishment authority.

Now, after a lengthy lone-wolf struggle and much soul-searching, the Executioner has agreed to enter an "arm's-length" alliance with his government once more, reserving the right to pursue personal missions in his Everlasting War.

PROLOGUE

Storm winds lashed against the window. The young man gazed outward as the violent winds and sleeting rain obscured the glare of the city lights below.

"So. It is decided." It was a statement, not a question.

"Indeed," the older man grunted. Despite his advanced age, he sat perfectly erect behind his massive oak desk. "The board has voted. The plan is to go into effect at once. We are placing you in direct command."

The young man restrained a smile. That was already known to him. He was obviously the most qualified man for the task. He grimaced. The execution of the mission would make or break him. It could quite possibly make him one of the most powerful men in the world within his lifetime, but the risks were astronomical.

"We are risking war with the United States and her allies."

The old man snorted derisively. "I do not believe so. Neither do the board members. The United States has shown itself remarkably reluctant to act on such matters. Think of the airliner that was destroyed over Lockerbie, Scotland, the attack on their Marine base in Beirut. Militarily the United States is indeed the most powerful nation on earth, but the freedom they regard so highly also weakens them. Politically they lack the ruthlessness necessary to react against our plan. They will second-guess themselves endlessly before they act, and if they try to counter us, it will be a fragmented effort after the fact. Even then, they will never know who their true enemies are."

The young man nodded. What the old man said was quite possibly true. A direct military attack on the United States and her allies by any power in the world would be suicidal. But the methods the old man was commissioning him to use were far more insidious. The militaries of the allies would be helpless to stop the atrocities. They would leave the United States and her allies helplessly reeling, economically disrupted and politically divided.

Then the new order would be established.

The young man watched the rain. Still, the task was daunting, but the rewards of success would be immeasurable, and he was an extremely ambitious man. He turned and looked at the old man. "Very well. I accept."

The old man nodded. "Good. Plans are already in place for our first action. It only remains for you to take active command."

"I will fly out tomorrow."

The old man nodded again. The die had been cast, and he was confident of victory. He suddenly smiled uncharacteristically at the younger man. "Do not worry. Who is there who can stop us?"

1

Libya

Mack Bolan, the Executioner, moved through the frigid desert night, a shadow among shadows in the inky darkness. The night sky was overcast, and there was no moon. It would have taken sophisticated viewing devices to detect the soldier, and even they would be hard-pressed to find and identify him. The fabric of the mottled battle clothing matched the infinite shades of dark gray of the sand and rock. The only trace the Executioner left were his footprints in the desert sand, and the hard, cold wind obliterated them moments after he had passed.

The soldier stalked the night like a phantom. Only the cold steel of the weapons he carried made him more than a mirage in the middle of the Libyan night. In his hands he held a highly modified silenced 9 mm Colt RO-636 submachine gun. The weapon had been developed for the DEA's fast-reaction teams, and it looked for all the world like an M-16 that had been sawed off to the foregrip. Unlike the standard silenced Colt used by the DEA teams, the Executioner's weapon had an M-203 40 mm grenade launcher mounted beneath the barrel.

Bolan crouched in a wasteland that was infinite shades of gray and green in his night-vision goggles. The desert formed a shallow, mile-wide bowl and then leveled off again as the sands of the Rabyanah Sahara stretched toward the rocky foothills of the Al Kufrah Mountains, and beyond the mountains to the desert sands of Egypt. Directly south, the Al Kufrah

Mountains and the Tibesti Mountains to the west formed a vast corridor of desert that led into Libya's southern neighbor, Chad.

The Executioner's point of interest was more localized. In the middle of the desert bowl was an encampment of military tents. Other than the camouflage webbing that stretched over the narrow alleys formed between the tents, the camp had almost no visible defenses. It didn't need them.

Hundreds of miles of the northern Sahara Desert in all directions was as formidable a defense as one could ask for. Libyan revolutionaries seeking to attack the camp would have to travel hundreds of miles across searing desert sand where the temperature could climb up to 125 degrees Fahrenheit with no cover from patrol aircraft. The only real military enemy nearby was Chad, and its government was terrified of Libyan aggression. Only the iron hand of France had prevented the Libyans from reducing Chad to a vassal state long ago. However, the French military posture was almost purely defensive. An armed incursion across the border was unthinkable, particularly if an energy-poor France wished to continue buying Libyan oil at favorable prices. Even in the event of such an unlikely military occurrence, such an incursion would be detected and intercepted by fighter-bombers and helicopter gunships long before it could ever reach the camp.

Observation satellites could monitor the camp, of course, but the Libyans paid a great deal of money to be kept abreast of the surveillance windows of observation satellites that orbited over their territory. When the satellites passed over, all they ever saw were tents and netting. Whatever activity went on in the camp was purely a matter of speculation, and would remain so. The camp didn't need minefields, fences or watchtowers. The only way in and out of the camp was by helicopter. Libyan air defenses watched the sky, and the Sahara Desert was an anvil beneath the hammer of the sun. The idea that a single man might walk up and take a look for himself on foot was sheer insanity.

Mack Bolan peered at the camp.

It was fairly large, but there were a number of anomalies. Bolan had circled the camp twice. There were no spent shell casings, blackened patches of sand from explosives or evidence of practice targets outside the camp. If the encampment was a training base for terrorists like a number of other deep-desert encampments in Libya, there seemed to be no training going on with small arms or explosives. Still, military helicopters flew in frequently and at extremely odd hours, often avoiding the surveillance windows of Western satellites. Any activities going on in the camp coincided with these same windows of satellite immunity, as well. It made one wonder what exactly was going on in this camp.

Bolan would just have to go in and find out.

A brilliant point of light blossomed under the camouflage netting as the single sentry lit a cigarette. Bolan's night-vision goggles were light enhancing, and had snap-on three-power lenses attached. He could see the sentry very clearly, and the man looked extremely bored. He carried a slung AK-47 assault rifle, and his night-vision equipment consisted of a flashlight that was clipped to his belt. His sentry duty was probably a token formality, or possibly some form of punishment, and the man seemed to be treating it as such. The camp's real sentry would be the radioman who would be monitoring for emergency reports from the Egyptian or Chadian borders or the Libyan air-defense command. It was quite apparent that the camp didn't expect any kind of conventional attack.

The Executioner flicked the safety off the silenced Colt submachine gun and moved down the gentle slope toward the camp. Given the prevailing overcast and wind, he doubted the lone sentry would be able to hear him, much less see him, until he was standing right next to him.

By then it would be much too late.

Bolan approached the sentry from the side and waited in a crouch at five yards. The tip of the cigarette pulsed brightly as the sentry dragged on it and stared up at the black sky.

The Executioner moved as the sentry raised his head.

Bolan loped forward and whipped the knife edge of his right hand into the mastoid process behind the sentry's right ear. He would have used his rifle butt, but the M-16 family of weapons kept their main springs in the buttstock, and the weapons had proved themselves notoriously fragile in bayonet fighting. The blunt ax of Bolan's hand was more than enough.

The man hunched and staggered forward with the force of the blow. Bolan caught him by the hair as he started to fall and yanked him around. The Executioner brought his knee up into the sentry's jaw and nearly stood the man back up on the tips of his toes, grabbing him as he collapsed and easing him down onto the sand.

The Executioner surveyed the sentry critically. His jaw was broken, and at the very least he had a mild concussion. Bolan had few moral objections to violating a Libyan sentry's civil rights, but until he at least knew what was going on in the camp, he would try to avoid killing anybody. He quickly bound the man and dragged him ten yards outside the camp. Bolan moved back under the camouflage netting spread between the tents, crouching as he heard voices above the moaning wind.

People were arguing.

A man was shouting in heavily accented English, which frequently broke down into his native tongue. Bolan understood enough Arabic to know the man was swearing profusely. Bolan started slightly as a voice answered in a parade ground bellow.

"Not bloody likely!"

The words and accent were distinctly Irish. The other man's voice dropped to a growl Bolan couldn't make out. The other man's voice lowered, as well. "We don't take commands from your lot. I've told you that before."

There seemed to be some dissension in the ranks. Bolan moved through the darkness on to the next tent. Light blazed between the edge of the tent and the sand where cables snaked out to a covered generator, which hummed quietly. Bolan moved around to the rear of the tent and listened intently.

A pair of voices was murmuring to each other. Bolan couldn't make out what they were saying, but he could faintly make out the patter and pecking of someone using a computer keyboard. The cables on the other side of the tent told him he was probably to one side of the operator. The soldier moved around the corner of the tent, hoping that he was now behind them. With luck, both men would be facing away from him and looking at whatever they were doing.

That side of the tent was sheltered from the wind. It was possible he could make a silent entrance. Bolan drew his combat knife and bent over one of the tent stakes. The razor edge sliced through the mooring rope, and he caught the edge of the tent. He slid the knife back in its sheath, then pushed his night-vision goggles onto his forehead. The soldier blinked in the near total darkness, sank to one elbow as he raised the edge of the tent and slithered inside.

The interior was lit by a pair of single-bulb lamps hanging from the ceiling. A glowing metal heater rested against one wall, and against the other was a folding table. Two men sat in front of it on metal chairs, their AK-47 rifles leaning against the table within easy reach. Both men were gazing intently at a computer monitor. The man working the keyboard suddenly stopped and looked up with a shiver of his shoulders. Bolan grimaced. He had let in a draft of the cold night air.

The man's dark eyes widened as he looked around and found himself staring down the muzzles of the Colt submachine gun and the 40 mm M-203 grenade launcher mated to it.

Bolan brought a finger to his lips in the universal sign to be quiet.

The man gulped and didn't move. The other man continued to peer at the screen a moment, then looked around. He was a blond man with a very dark tan, and he strangled a gasp as he saw Bolan. *"Santa Maria!"*

One of the Executioner's eyebrows raised almost imperceptibly. An Italian. He mentally filed that away. "Which one of you speaks English?"

The two men continued to stare mutely at the muzzles of the weapons facing them. Bolan smiled and spoke conversationally. "I'm going to fire this grenade launcher now."

"I speak English," the blond said quickly.

His companion, who appeard to be an Arab, nodded vigorously. "I speak English also."

"Good." Bolan kept his finger on the submachine gun's trigger. "I want you to eject your software, and then give me every disk you have."

The two men looked shocked.

"I have a white-phosphorous grenade loaded," Bolan told them. "Do it, or die burning."

He rose from his crouch as the two men started to turn back to the computer. They froze as he spoke again. "Do it slowly. Don't even think about deleting any data."

The blonde spoke English fluently, but with a heavy accent. "I was about to receive a transmission. Do you wish this information? And do you wish me to download the hard drive? I believe whatever you want would be found there."

It was a tempting offer, but the Executioner knew it was a trap. The man was counting on his being a soldier and knowing little about computers. It could take half an hour to download the hard drive, and the man could manipulate an encrypted transmission any way he wanted. Without knowing the codes, the man could send a message back right under Bolan's nose.

The Executioner raised the carbine to his shoulder and sighted at the man's face. "Eject the disk. Now."

The man flinched and punched a command into the computer. "As you wish." The computer clicked and made a whirring noise, and the disk popped out of its slot.

A blast of cold air blew through the tent as the flap was

hurled open. Bolan whirled around and found himself facing a wet, extremely well-built woman.

"Enzo! The hot water is down again...." The woman's voice trailed off as she gaped at Bolan.

The Executioner whipped around as a metal chair clattered behind him. The Italian had dived for one of the AK-47 rifles. The big American put a 3-round burst into his chest and tracked the Arab. As the other man's hand closed around his own rifle's pistol grip, the Colt whispered. The Arab shuddered, and his finger spastically clamped down on the rifle's trigger.

The snarl of the AK-47 rifle firing on full-auto was deafening within the tent. Bolan put a second burst into the man, and the rifle fell to the ground. The man sagged in his chair, but the damage had been done. Bolan could already hear yells from the other tents.

Bolan whirled at the high-pitched scream behind him, meeting the woman's attack. Her long dark hair streamed behind her, and her hands curled like claws. Her blue eyes were pinpoints of fury.

The Executioner stepped into her rush and whipped the butt of the Colt across her jaw. The woman's head rocked on her shoulders, and she fell to the floor of the tent in a heap. Bolan snatched the disk from the computer and slid it into a slit pocket of his blacksuit.

It was time to get out of Dodge.

He turned and put half of the remaining bullets in the magazine into the computer screen. Sparks flew from the ruptured monitor, and he burned the remaining rounds into the computer itself. The Executioner quickly slipped a fresh magazine into the Colt and rolled out of the tent the way he had come in. His eyes slitted as lights began to blaze into life all around the camp.

Bolan spoke grimly into his throat mike. "This is Striker. Mission accomplished. Enemy alerted. Breaking contact. Need immediate extraction. Expect hot pursuit."

Barbara Price's voice sounded as if she were right next to him across the satellite link. "Understood. Extraction on its way."

"Striker out."

Bolan pulled his night-vision goggles over his eyes and loped out into the darkness. Screams and shouts broke out as chaos ensued in the camp. He fixed his eyes on the dark masses of the mountains in the east and broke into a full sprint across the sand. The soldier redoubled his effort as he heard the roar of a military jeep's engine snarl into life. He wasn't too worried about being tracked through the darkness. It was during extraction that he would be the most vulnerable.

The Executioner ran on, covering the four kilometers to his extraction point with a long, ground-eating stride. In the three-power magnification of his goggles a dark lump appeared in the sand due east, which resolved itself into a pair of air-droppable cargo bags.

Bolan clicked his throat mike to his designated radio frequency. "This is Striker. Am at primary extraction site. Beginning extraction procedures."

Jack Grimaldi's voice spoke across the radio. "Roger, Striker. This is Mother ship, inbound. ETA five minutes to extraction site."

"Roger. Striker out."

Bolan reached the bags and began to pull out their contents. He unrolled one bundle and stepped into an insulated coverall. He adjusted the coverall's internal harness, then zipped it up and cinched the hood over his head. Pulling out a coil of nylon lift line and what looked like an oversize sleeping bag, he rolled out the bag evenly across the sand into a shape that looked like a small, flattened zeppelin. Bolan hooked the lift line to the balloon, then to the D-ring on his harness. He drew out two high-pressure helium bottles and attached them to the balloon's inflation valves. Helium hissed as he threw the valve wheels and the balloon began to slowly inflate. Bolan stepped on the lift line to moor the balloon and waited while it inflated.

Peering back, he could see the beams of searchlights combing the desert. They were still more than a mile and a half away and had no idea which way he had gone, but as with all military actions, it wasn't the actions themselves that caused problems, but rather the transitions.

For the next few minutes Bolan would be very vulnerable.

The balloon was filling rapidly, and as it inflated, the lift line tugged at Bolan's boot as the balloon strove to rise. It was eight feet in diameter and twenty-three feet long, and nowhere near large enough to raise a full-grown man laden with weapons and gear. But that wasn't its function. Bolan examined the needles on the pressure bottles. The balloon was inflated to optimum pressure. He shut off the valves and released the balloon. The silver shape bobbed and rose up into the desert night. Bolan payed out line smoothly as it gained altitude.

The lift line went taut at five hundred feet, and Bolan spoke into his mike. "Balloon deployed. Am activating infrared strobes now."

He pushed a button on the remote control in his harness. To the unaided observer the balloon was invisible five hundred feet up in the desert darkness. In the infrared spectrum a pair of strobes attached to the lift line began to pulse rapidly.

"Roger, Striker," Grimaldi said. "We have two strobes on our infrared. Altitude five hundred feet. We are inbound on your signal. Be advised, we have satellite confirmation of helicopter gunships launching from Al Kufrah."

"Confirmed." Bolan cocked his head as a distant droning rose over the moan of the wind. "I hear your engines, Mother ship."

Grimaldi's voice became jovial. "All right, Striker, assume the position."

Bolan sat in the sand and hugged his knees. "Ready."

The drone of the MC-130E Hercules Combat Talon grew louder as it roared approximately five hundred feet above the desert sand. "Striker, we have a vehicle, gun jeep configuration, heading your way. Less than half a mile."

Bolan craned his head around. The jeep was racing his way, and in the three-power magnification of his goggles he could see a heavy machine gun mounted in the rear of the vehicle. The faces of both the driver and the man in the passenger's seat were obscured, and they didn't have to get closer for Bolan to figure out they wore night-vision goggles. It would be older, Russian gear, using the infrared spectrum. It wouldn't have the range and sophistication of Bolan's ambient-light-amplification equipment, but it would be more than enough to see and aim a heavy machine gun at a C-130 Hercules flying overhead at five hundred feet, and they would have to be blind not to see the pulsing beacons of the infrared strobes flashing from the balloon's lift line, a balloon that Mack Bolan himself was roped to.

The transition had just turned ugly.

"Roger, Mother ship. Will take action."

Bolan flipped up the ladder sight for the M-203 grenade launcher. The jeep suddenly ground to a halt 250 yards from his position, and the three men in the vehicle were pointing at the balloon. In their infrared goggles the balloon's flares had to have appeared as small blinking suns in the night sky. A moment later one of the men whipped around and pointed in the other direction.

The C-130 Hercules came roaring over the bowl of the desert without lights. Through his night-vision goggles Bolan could see a V-shaped pair of metal guides like huge insect antennae projecting from its nose. The Hercules flew straight at the lift line, aiming its nose between the two blinking infrared strobes.

The weapons operator on the gun jeep yanked his heavy machine gun around on its pedestal and swung the muzzle into the air toward the approaching aircraft. The Hercules was flying low and slow, and the heat from its four turboprop engines would light up the plane in the infrared spectrum and make it a target few machine gunners could miss. Bolan moved the grenade launcher's sights slightly to his left to allow for the desert wind and fired.

The M-203 recoiled against his shoulder brutally, and yellow flame suddenly lit up his position. Bolan opened the breech on the launcher and reached for another grenade even as the first projectile arced toward the target. The grenade looped down, landing almost underneath the gun jeep's bumper, and detonated. The desert erupted in flame and light as the white-phosphorous grenade sent streamers of burning metal and superheated smoke into the sky like the Fourth of July.

The Libyans dived from the jeep. The engine block had saved them from most of the grenade's effect, but the front of the vehicle was now blazing with incandescent white fire. Orange fire strobed as the Libyans fired their rifles on full automatic. Bolan had to give their commander credit. They were ignoring him and concentrating their fire at the plane. Green tracers streaked toward the Hercules as it swooped overhead. Three AK-47 rifles were unlikely to shoot down a C-130, but they could damage it, and the border was still miles away.

Bolan racked a fresh grenade into the M-203's breech and fired at the Libyans' muzzle-flashes. The high-explosive fragmentation grenade hurtled down in the middle of the triangle formed by the attackers. The riflemen had abandoned the jeep and were in open desert without cover. The frag grenade had a lethal radius of fifteen yards, and as the grenade detonated in a flash of muted orange fire, the rifles fell silent.

The Hercules stormed over Bolan with a roar, and there was a sudden tug on the lift line. "We have you, Striker," Grimaldi said.

Bolan uncoiled his legs and ran along with the tug of the lift line. The tug gained speed, and suddenly the soldier left the sand. He watched the desert as it slowly receded beneath him, and he began to pick up speed and altitude. He slung his carbine and cinched the sling tight around his shoulders. As the plane increased speed, he found himself being pulled parallel beneath the plane. There was very little for him to do but dangle. Beneath him the burning jeep was a blossom of white fire surrounded by the winking stars of scattered, burning phosphorous. Above him Bolan saw the balloon rising into the night. Its breakaway cables had released as the locking device in the C-130's nose had clamped the line, and the balloon was now free.

Bolan kept his body arched like a sky diver to keep himself from tumbling. He looked up as sudden light flooded from the rear of the plane when its rear ramp opened. A hook descended from the rear of the aircraft, and a few moments later it clamped the lift line. Bolan rose upward as a winch in the cargo hold began reeling him in. He was drawn toward the open ramp, and he grinned as he saw Gadgets Schwarz flanked by a pair of airmen from the Eighth Special Operations Wing.

The Fulton Surface To Air Recovery system was a highly complicated, highly unusual and highly expensive method of recovering a single individual, but then again, after already deploying a B-2 Stealth bomber for Bolan to do a high-altitude, low-opening parachute jump into the Libyan desert, using a STAR system extraction had simply been par for the course. Bolan pushed up his night-vision goggles as Schwarz grabbed his hand and yanked him up onto the ramp.

"Evening, Striker! Find out anything interesting?"

Bolan unzipped the STAR system coverall and reached into his web gear. Schwarz raised an intrigued eyebrow as the soldier handed him the computer disk. "You tell me."

The rear ramp began to close, and the C-130's intercom crackled in the cargo bay. "Sealing rear ramp. Striker, Gadgets, you might want to come forward."

Schwarz pressed the intercom button. "Roger that."

The two men went up to the cockpit. The Combat Talon was a Hercules turboprop aircraft, distinguished by its extensive banks of radars, imaging equipment and a massive electronic-warfare suite. Schwarz took a seat at the electronic-systems operator's station. Bolan stepped out of the coverall and harness and shrugged out of his web gear as he took the copilot's seat.

Grimaldi grinned. "Glad to have you aboard, Mack."

"Glad to be here, Jack. What's the deal with those gunships coming out of Al Kufrah you were telling me about?"

"They can match our speed, but we have over a hundred-mile head start. Them I'm not worried about."

Bolan knew all too well what was on his old friend's mind. "Fast movers?"

Grimaldi nodded. "Frankly I'm surprised we haven't detected any yet."

Schwarz spoke from the electronic-warfare suite. "Don't be."

"What have we got?" the pilot asked.

"It looks like several airborne radars at long range. We have bogies coming in from the north."

"Any kind of ID?"

Schwarz peered at the screen. "The radar-warning receiver says we have a pair of High Lark radars, operating in the search mode. That means MiG-23s."

"Do they have a lock on us yet?"

"No, but they know approximately where we are, and they're closing in on our general vicinity at speed."

Bolan glanced out at the black horizon. "How bad is it?"

Grimaldi shrugged. "Could be worse. The MiG-23 isn't the latest-model Russian fighter, and I doubt the Libyans have the latest upgraded versions, either, but it can easily do Mach 2, and more on afterburners. In standard interception mode they can carry a pair of long-range radar-guided missiles, a pair of short-range heat seekers and a Russian 23 mm twin-barrel automatic cannon that can tear this heap to shreds. It's standard equipment on all models."

Bolan regarded Grimaldi dryly. "Any chance we can make the border before they intercept us?"

"Oh, no. No way in hell."

Schwarz leaned back in his chair. "Our bogies have changed course. They're now directly behind us and are closing in at high speed."

Grimaldi's eyes narrowed. "Roger, Gadgets. Stand by for electronic and infrared countermeasures." He glanced at Bolan. "Hold on, we're going to take her down to the deck."

The Hercules's nose suddenly dipped as Grimaldi shoved the control wheel forward. Bolan's safety harness cinched into his chest as the aircraft plunged toward the desert floor. A panel chimed from Gadgets's control console, and he peered at the display. "Our friends have gone into target-acquisition-and-tracking mode. They're trying to get a radar lock on us."

Grimaldi continued the dive. "They've gone to missile mode, Mack. They aren't going to try to force us down. They're going to take us out."

Bolan folded his arms impassively. "So do something."

Grimaldi almost managed to look guilty. "You know, activating countermeasures over foreign airspace could be legally construed as an act of war, but what the hell. Gadgets, all systems active. Electronic countermeasures now!"

Schwarz threw his switches, and the electronic-warfare suite blazed into life. To a human observer the desert sky remained pitch-black, but in the radio-frequency spectrum, the sky had gone mad. The Combat Talon now flew in an ocean of false targets, dazzling radar pulses and blinding electronic noise.

Bolan glanced back at Schwarz. "How are our friends?"

Schwarz listened into his headphones. "Extremely irritated. They're chattering at each other and their radars have gone back to search mode. They've lost us for the moment, but they know our approximate heading, and the closer they get to us, the less effective our electronic countermeasures become. They're closing fast."

"Going to emergency war power." Grimaldi leveled off the plane and shoved his throttles full forward.

The big transport vibrated as the four turboprop engines roared into the redline. One of the Combat Talon's greatest assets was its highly advanced forward-looking infrared imager and its terrain-following radar. It allowed the Hercules to almost fly nap-of-the-earth like a helicopter. Grimaldi seemed to be ignoring his flight instruments and flying the plane by watching a small black-and-white television screen. Bolan peered at the numbers on the screen. Grimaldi was flying 366 miles per hour eighty-five feet above the sand.

Schwarz's voice rose over the roar of the engines. "Radars on target-acquisition-and-tracking mode!" A buzzer sounded unpleasantly from his console. "They have a lock! Two missiles, incoming!"

Grimaldi snarled. "Countermeasures! Now!"

The fuselage shook as the chaff dispensers fired and clouds of radar-reflecting filaments filled the sky behind the Hercules. To the enemy radars the clouds were impenetrable, like flashlights in fog. Bolan watched as a radar-guided missile flew by underneath the Combat Talon as it lost lock and exploded into the sand ahead. The second missile streaked off to the right and sizzled away over the desert.

"They'll go to heat seekers next," Grimaldi stated.

"I don't think so." Gadgets shook his head as he stared at his radar screen. "Our bogies are diving hard, directly behind us at full speed. They know we have countermeasures, and I think they're tired of playing our game. I think they're going to use their guns, Jack. I think they want to finish this up close and personal."

Grimaldi chewed his lip and peered fixedly at the black-and-white screen of his thermal imager. "Mack, you see that sand ridge off to the right?"

Bolan stared at the screen. A dark gray mass rose off to the right of the aircraft, several thousand feet ahead. "Yeah, I see it."

"I'm going to try something, a trick I've heard Israeli fighter jocks have used."

Bolan's eyes narrowed. If Grimaldi said he was going to try

something when he was behind the joystick, it was best to tighten your flight harness. "What's that?"

"I'm going to fly right at the ridge and pull out at the last possible moment."

Bolan frowned. "You think they'll fly into the ridge?"

Grimaldi shrugged. "It's a possibility. Our terrain-following radar is a hell of a lot better than theirs, and I can actually see the ground and they can't. They might just get target fixation and screw the pooch. But I wouldn't count on it."

"Okay..."

Grimaldi looked at Bolan helplessly. "Mack, I've got four uprated T56-A-15 turboprop engines on full emergency war power, each one generating over 4500 horsepower. When I yank this bird out of a dive forty feet off that ridge, I'm going to send a couple of metric tons of sand into the air."

Bolan nodded decisively. "Do it."

"Hold on!" The nose of the aircraft dipped sickeningly as Grimaldi dived straight at the sand ridge. The collision alarm suddenly started yammering in shrill protest.

Schwarz's voice rose. "Bogies are three thousand yards and closing! Two thousand! One thousand. They're within cannon range."

Bolan saw streaks of green tracers shriek over the right wing, and the Hercules suddenly rattled and shuddered. Warning lights blazed on the instrument panels.

Schwarz snarled. "We're hit!"

Grimaldi's voice rose to a parade-ground shout as he yanked the stick back. "Hold on!"

The entire fuselage shuddered and groaned as the flaps went up and the big cargo plane desperately yanked itself back up into the sky. Warning lights and buzzers blinked and howled as the engines screamed in protest. Bolan held on grimly as the G-forces rammed him back in the copilot's seat. He gritted his teeth and looked out into the black through the windshield. A dark shape screamed beneath them, and the Hercules shuddered as its jet wash passed over them. Bolan watched the

MiG-23's tailpipe as a pulse of fire strobed from the afterburning engine and the plane flamed out. A jet engine simply couldn't suck in and spit out hundreds of pounds of sand and keep on running. The MiG's engine had seized and died at Mach speed less than a hundred feet off the ground.

The second MiG swerved past clearly out of control, and a moment later its cockpit exploded with yellow fire as the pilot ejected. The first MiG yawed and tumbled, then slewed downward toward the sand. The pilot failed to eject as the plane struck and exploded into the desert floor at nearly a thousand miles per hour. The second MiG-23 flew on without its pilot for another thousand feet, then punched into the sand a few moments later.

Grimaldi took the Hercules back up to 150 feet. His grin was in place, but it was shaky. "Well, that was closer than I thought. I had intended to pull up at forty feet."

Bolan didn't want to ask. Grimaldi shrugged. "We cleared it by about ten."

Schwarz's voice was as calm as ever. "We have more company. Fast movers, coming in from the south."

Grimaldi's voice was suddenly all business. "Can you give me an ID?"

Schwarz watched his screen. "I've got a pair of Cyrano IVM radars, which means Mirages, F-1s. They are closing fast."

Bolan glanced ahead into the darkness. "Who flies Mirage F-1s around here?"

Grimaldi eyebrows knitted. "The Libyans and the French."

"How close are we to the border of Chad?"

Gadgets consulted his screen. "Close, but Colonel Khaddafi disputes the border."

Grimaldi held a finger up to his headset. "We're being challenged."

Bolan flipped the switch on the cockpit intercom. A heavily accented voice spoke in English. "I am Lieutenant Phillipe Gudraux of the French air force. You are in direct violation of Chad airspace. I am empowered by the sovereign governments of France and Chad to shoot you down if you resist. You will adopt an altitude of one thousand feet and follow our heading to Faya-Largue airbase, where you will surrender to authorities. You will switch to the following radio frequency.''

A burst of code flashed across Schwarz's screen, and he switched to the corresponding frequency. The intercom crackled and Phillipe Gudraux's voice suddenly took on a jovial air. ''Excellent flying, *monsieur. Magnifique!* I salute you! Welcome to Chad!''

Chad

At the French embassy Mack Bolan watched the morning sun
rise over Chad in a blazing red ball. There was a cool breeze
coming through the balcony window, and the coffee and croissants were excellent. Gadgets Schwarz and Jack Grimaldi were
helping themselves to seconds when a massive man in full
French Foreign Legion regalia strode into the plushly ap-
pointed salon and saluted sharply.

"*Bonjour,* gentlemen. I am Captain Paul LeClerc. I trust
you find your accommodations adequate."

Bolan smiled diplomatically. "The coffee is excellent.
Please, have some."

The French captain removed his cap and smiled back. "Ah,
well." He poured himself a cup, then looked at Bolan with
mock severity. "I regret to inform you that Lieutenant Phillipe
Gudraux of the French air force shot you down last night in
Chadian airspace when you attempted to break away and escape from your fighter escort on the way to Faya-Largue airbase. You and your entire crew died in the crash."

"How terrible."

The legionnaire nodded solemnly. "Indeed."

Bolan raised an eyebrow. It was unlikely the Libyans would
believe such a pat story without some kind of evidence. "Was
there anything left from the crash?"

The Frenchman's eyebrows knitted. "Well, there was some

scattered wreckage several miles within the border of Chad. From the looks of it, it appears to be some kind of transport. A Hercules C-130, or perhaps an old DC-3 fuselage that some unscrupulous individuals dragged into the desert and blew up with explosives early this morning. Who can tell?'' The captain shrugged his indifference in an extremely French fashion. *"C'est la vie."*

Bolan nodded in agreement. "What's going to happen to us?"

"'Us'? Who is 'us'?" The captain shook his head tiredly. "I appear to be talking to myself again. Perhaps I have been in the sun too long. Perhaps a transport will be leaving for Cairo in an hour, then fly on to Israel. I do not know. It is all very confusing. Good day."

The captain spun on his heel and walked out of the room.

Grimaldi poured himself more coffee. "Well, that went easier than I expected."

"I suspect when the French contacted Washington last night, someone very important was waiting up to tell them what good people we are." Bolan shrugged. "Besides, the French military is a pretty bloody-minded bunch. When you downed two Libyan MiGs with a Hercules transport, I bet they all cheered."

Grimaldi nodded sagely. "It was a good piece of flying." He glanced out the window as the red sun slowly turned golden as it rose over the desert. "So, where to next, Mack?"

"It seems there's a transport heading to Cairo in an hour, then on to Israel. Maybe we should pay Katz a visit."

THE ATMOSPHERE in the penthouse office suite was very tense. "Impossible."

The younger man shrugged. "Nevertheless, it has happened. The camp was attacked."

"What is the damage?"

"Undetermined. Two men were killed. Both of them the camp's computer specialists, a Libyan named Hafez Malik and an Italian named Enzo Sabbatini. A sentry was incapacitated, as well as the German woman.''

The old man shook his head irritably. ''What was the damage?''

''The camp's computer was destroyed. The damage to its memory is irretrievable. That is in our favor, I think.''

''And what of the possibility that information was extracted before its destruction?''

The young man chewed his lip in meditation. ''I do not believe that the memory was downloaded. There was no time.''

''What of any other information?''

The young man cleared his throat. ''According to the camp records, there is one computer disk missing.''

The old man almost hissed. ''What kind of information?''

''Extremely sensitive.'' There was a moment of long silence. ''However, all information was encrypted by the most talented computer men in our organization. Breaking the codes will be an extremely difficult operation, if not impossible.''

The old man looked very unconvinced. ''What do we know of the attackers?''

''Little. The two computer specialists are dead, and the guard never saw who attacked him. The woman says only one man was in the computer tent, armed and equipped like some sort of special-forces operative. A jeep that was sent out after the attackers was destroyed, and the three soldiers manning it were killed.''

The old man looked incredulous. ''So one unknown man just walked into the camp, took what he wanted and then disappeared without a trace?''

The young man shifted uncomfortably. ''Not quite. We have a number of clues. Almost coinciding with the attack, Libyan air-defense radars picked up an unidentified aircraft in their airspace in the vicinity of the camp. The Libyan air force dispatched two interceptors. According to radio transmissions, they intercepted some kind of transport plane.''

The old man leaned forward. "So, the intruders were killed?"

"No. It seems both of the Libyan jet fighters were downed."

The old man was silent for a moment. "So the plane escaped?"

"No, the plane was picked up by French fighters in Chad and was reportedly destroyed when it attempted to break away from its fighter escort."

The old man's eyes narrowed. "You do not believe this."

"No, I do not. Such an operation could only have been successfully completed by two possible powers, Israel and the United States. We have no reason to suspect that France would not help them if it was in her interests."

The old man nodded. "I agree. What are your conclusions?"

The young man took a deep breath. "I do not believe that the United States or her allies could have found out about us so quickly. I believe they simply wanted to know what was going on at this base deep in the desert. I believe my predecessor was too secretive, and this attracted their attention. If they have the missing computer disk, I do not believe they have any idea of what they have. Our contacts tell us that a transport plane left Chad from Faya-Largue this morning, stopped briefly in Cairo, then flew on to Tel Aviv."

"Then the situation may still be containable."

"Perhaps."

"What do you recommend?"

The young man's voice hardened with steely resolve. "I have operatives standing by. With your permission, I will have the transport's pilots abducted and tortured, and get descriptions of their passengers and their itineraries if possible. We will then use our contacts in Israel to have these individuals killed, and the disk retrieved if it has not left Israel."

The old man nodded. "Do it immediately."

Tel Aviv

"HEY, KATZ, how's retirement?"

Yakov Katzenelenbogen failed to suppress a smile as he stood in the private plane terminal. "Retirement be damned! I feel a lot younger than you look at the moment."

Bolan grinned. It had been a long, hard forty-eight hours, and despite his age, Katz looked as lethal as ever. Since he had stepped down as the team leader of Phoenix Force, the Israeli had been dividing his time between working as a tactical advisor at Stony Man Farm and living in Israel. The Middle Eastern sun had given Katz a dark tan, and his pale blue eyes glittered from under heavy brows. His gray hair and casual clothes did little to hide the fact that he could be an extremely dangerous man.

"You're right," Bolan replied. "We could all use a decent meal and eight hours of sack time. We've been running on croissants and coffee since dawn." He jerked his head at the bags of gear they were carrying. "Do we need to check these with anybody?"

Katz snorted. "You're with me." Even though Katz worked for the Farm, he still had open ties with Israeli Intelligence. "What did you do with the plane?"

"The air force boys stayed with it in a military hangar at Faya-Largue," Grimaldi replied. "They'll fly it out of Chad in a few days when the Libyans aren't looking."

Katz nodded as he led Bolan, Schwarz and Grimaldi out of the air terminal toward to a dark Citroën sedan. "Brognola only gave me a short briefing on the operation. What did you find?"

"We recovered a computer disk."

"Ah." The Israeli gunned the engine as they loaded into the car. "What else?"

"Nothing you can put your finger on. There didn't seem to be any real weapons training going on that I could ascertain at the camp, and the population of the camp seemed awfully cosmopolitan."

Katz raised an intrigued eyebrow. "Oh?"

"I was only inside for a matter of minutes, but I found Arabs, Italians, Irish and Germans. It was like a convention."

"Interesting. I can see one or two small groups of terrorists collaborating or training together, but what you describe does seem odd. Perhaps this disk of yours will tell us more."

Schwarz spoke up from the back of the car. "I ran it through our laptop on the flight. The information on the disk is coded, and whoever encrypted the information did one hell of a job."

Katz sighed. "Well, we have to pay the Bear to do something."

Bolan looked at him shrewdly. "Any thoughts?"

Katz frowned. "Until the code on the disk is broken, anything is a shot in the dark. However, given the international scope of the people you found in the camp, a good place to start may be Berlin."

"How do you figure?"

Katz grunted. "Since the Wall fell between East and West Germany, Berlin has become the new Dodge City of Europe. It is the nexus of crime and terrorism between East and West. Many former East German special-forces soldiers and secret-police operatives are out of work and selling their services to the highest bidders. Criminal gangs are running out of control, and it is very international. Everyone wants a piece of the pie. I have seen reports of blatant activity by the Italian Mafia, the Russian *mafiya*, the Colombian drug cartels and African slave traders. Berlin is the nexus for trade in guns, military weapons, drugs, blondes and even nuclear materials. The city has always been a center of intrigue, but within the last year or so it has gotten completely out of hand. The German police feel they are outnumbered and outgunned, and they fear there may soon be open warfare between the various factions in the streets. Given what you have told me, I might be tempted to start looking there first."

Bolan mulled this over as the car headed into the low hills around Tel Aviv. Katz pulled up to a small, blindingly whitewashed house of Spanish architecture. Orange trees rose up over the clay walls. "Nice house."

"Yes, I'm considering buying it."

Katz led them inside. The small house was Spartanly furnished, but the furniture was mostly antiques and of impeccable taste. One look at the intricate tile mosaic on the floor told Bolan that Katz had cut and laid it himself. Carpentry tools and paint cans lay neatly in the corners.

The Israeli waved his hand casually. "Make yourselves comfortable."

Bolan's face grew serious. "Katz, I need you to find out anything you can about that encampment in the Libyan desert."

"Hasn't the U.S. government already communicated with Israeli Intelligence on the matter?"

"That's through official channels. I want to find out if any of your old friends might know anything or have any ideas. Anything anomalous or strange that might have a tie-in with the camp. Use the Berlin angle you mentioned. I'm willing to take personal opinions and wild speculation at this point."

Katz nodded. "I can do it, but it will take a little time."

"You've got about twenty-four hours. Meanwhile, I'm going to download the disk's contents over the satellite link with the Farm and see what Aaron can make of it. Tell your cronies I'm going to see about getting permission to hand over a copy of the disk to Israeli Intelligence."

Katz grunted. He was used to tight timetables, but a copy of the disk would help speed up matters. "All right. There's beer and food in the refrigerator. I'll go and see what I can do. I may be gone an hour or so." He glanced around his house with false misgivings. "Try not to destroy anything."

3

Mack Bolan sat cross-legged on Katz's back porch and opened the suitcase containing the satellite link. He had to give Katz credit. The house was small, but the location was ideal. Most of Tel Aviv was fairly flat, but Katz had gotten himself a house on one of the low hills that looked out over the ocean. The patio deck and railing smelled of new wood. The small yard had three tall orange trees bearing fruit, and there were fresh holes in the ground where Katz was going to plant flowering lemon trees that sat in pots along the wall. Unlike most dwellings in the area, the house itself didn't butt up against another house but actually had back and side yards. Despite its size, the house had to have been very expensive to rent. In the crowded city of Tel Aviv, its buying price would be astronomical.

Then again, it would be a somewhat conservative statement to say that Yakov Katzenelenbogen had connections.

Bolan connected the transmitter to the tiny satellite antenna array and adjusted his earpiece and throat mike. He punched in his identification code, and a moment later Barbara Price's voice spoke in his ear.

"You're in Israel, I assume."

"At Katz's house. We recovered a computer disk from the encampment. Have the Bear prepare to receive a download."

"One moment while I get you hooked up."

Bolan slid the disk into a laptop that had been extensively

modified by the Farm's cybernetic team. Bolan connected it to the satellite link and waited.

Aaron Kurtzman's voice spoke from a pickup in the Farms cybernetic center. "All right, Striker. Ready to receive your transmission."

"Transmitting now." Bolan pushed the transmit button, and the coded information on the disk began to shoot up into space. Twenty-three thousand miles above the earth's surface the transmission from Israel was received by an orbiting satellite and then bounced back down to Stony Man Farm in Virginia.

"We're receiving your transmission, Striker."

Bolan watched the small screen of the laptop as the disk's contents were downloaded into space. The rapidly scrolling lines of letters, numbers, words and characters meant absolutely nothing to him. "Gadgets said at first glance the encrypting job seemed excellent."

Kurtzman whistled. "You'd better believe it."

Bolan raised an eyebrow. When it came to computer encryption, Kurtzman was hard to impress. "Oh?"

The computer expert snorted with grudging admiration. "Striker, this stuff looks like it was written by aliens. I've never seen anything like it."

"So the Libyans couldn't have done this?"

"You know I don't think the Russians could have done this, and that's where the Libyans get most of their military technology."

"Well, now, that's very interesting."

"Very."

"Do you think you can break it?"

There was a moment's pause on the link. "Hmm. How much more is there?"

"It's a high-density disk, about two megabytes of information. You have about a third of it. It should take about another two or three minutes to finish the transmission."

"Well, there's no getting around it. This is going to a fun

one. I'll get the team on it immediately. Anything else of interest?''

"Yeah, as a matter of fact. In the camp itself—'' Bolan broke off as something made a soft thump in the dusty soil off to his right. A hand grenade sat next to the trunk of one of the orange trees.

Bolan whipped his Beretta 93-R pistol from his shoulder holster and fired. Long hours of training had made the weapon almost an extension of his will. He could put every round from the magazine into a playing card at fifteen yards on rapid fire. However, shooting a live Russian-made RDG-5 antipersonnel grenade was slightly more nerveracking than blowing a hole through the ace of spades.

Sparks shot off of the grenade's fragmenting outer steel casing as the 9 mm hollowpoint round struck it and sent it skittering deeper into Katz's miniature orchard. Bolan tracked the skidding grenade and shot it again, then threw himself flat as the bomb rolled over the edge of one of the empty planting holes. The grenade detonated with a piercing crack, and the orange trees rustled and hissed as a storm of metal fragments blew upward through their branches. Bolan roared a warning to Schwarz and Grimaldi inside.

"We have company!''

A pair of hands and a foot hooked the top of the wall as someone began to vault over. One hand clasped a Skorpion machine pistol, and a head masked by a brightly striped white kerchief and sunglasses followed. Bolan put a 3-round burst between the lenses of the man's sunglasses, and the assassin fell back out of sight. Behind him Bolan heard the rending crash of the front door splintering inward and the sudden snarl of gunfire.

Kurtzman's voice yelled in Bolan's ear. "Striker! What's going on?''

"We're under attack. Will continue to transmit. I'll get back to you.''

Three more grenades arced over the wall into the garden.

Three were too many to try the skeet-shooting trick. The Executioner abandoned the satellite link and let it transmit on its own as he dived into the house. Bolan slammed the back door and stayed low as the grenades began to detonate one after the other. Glass fell around him as the back-door window and the window in the kitchen shattered under the lethal hail of steel fragments. Screams broke out from the neighboring houses on the hillside.

"Gadgets! Jack!"

Schwarz's voice rose above the sudden ripping noise of Grimaldi's .45-caliber Ingram M-10 submachine gun. "Two down! We're unhurt! Here! Think fast!"

Bolan's black nylon gear flew down the hallway between the kitchen and the living room and clanked to the tile floor. The Executioner snagged the bag and pulled out his silenced Colt submachine gun and mated grenade launcher.

Schwarz suddenly yelled at the top of his lungs. "Mack! Get down!"

Bolan rolled away from the hallway and flattened himself against the wall. A whooshing hiss sizzled into the hallway, then the whole house shook as orange fire flared into the kitchen. He grimaced at the familiar sound.

The enemy had an RPG-7 rocket-propelled grenade launcher.

The Executioner rose as he racked the M-203 grenade launcher closed around a fragmentation grenade. Two men had clambered over the back wall and dropped into the garden, both of them clutching Czech-made Skorpion machine pistols. A third man was pulling himself over the wall with an AK-47 strapped to his back. All of them wore sunglasses and kerchiefs as masks.

The M-203 boomed, and Bolan dropped below the level of the kitchen window as the grenade detonated at point-blank range against the garden wall. He rolled to the back door and swung up the muzzle of his submachine gun. One man twisted and moaned in the red dirt of the garden. His companion lay unmoving. The man on the wall had disappeared.

Gunfire continued from the front of the house. Bolan shouted down the hallway. "I'm taking the high ground! Keep them busy!"

Schwarz and Grimaldi responded with long bursts from their weapons.

Bolan stepped onto the patio railing and vaulted to the red tile roof. He crouched as he moved up the shallow incline and peered down at the street in front of the house. Four men were positioned behind a beige panel van and an old Renault sedan. Two of them were busy pouring sustained fire from AK-47 rifles into the front of the house. The other two were reloading an RPG-7.

The Executioner flicked the selector on his submachine to semiautomatic and took aim at the man holding the RPG. The Colt whispered rapidly four times, and the man fumbled the rocket launcher and fell. His loader suddenly drew a pistol and looked around in a panic as he sought the shooter. As the man looked up and saw Bolan on the roof, the Executioner put two rounds into his chest.

The riflemen continued to exchange fire with Schwarz and Grimaldi. They hadn't heard the whisper of Bolan's weapon above the din of their own weapons. The two men had good cover behind the thick clay walls of Katz's house, and they continued to keep the riflemen occupied.

The Executioner took aim and fired. One of the riflemen collapsed across the hood of the car he was using for cover as he was drilled in the neck and chest. The second gunman managed to look up and see Bolan, but he was already too late. The 9 mm subsonic hollowpoints from the Colt hammered the assassin to the ground.

Bolan stayed in a crouch with his weapon at his shoulder as the gunfire suddenly ceased. Dogs barked, and muted screams of panic came from some of the neighboring houses as the soldier surveyed the scene. He spoke in a low, clear voice. "You two all right?"

Grimaldi spoke up. "We're all right. Gadgets got cut up a bit by some shrapnel. We have two dead in the doorway. What have you got?"

"I've got four down out front, two in back. Sit tight." Bolan moved to the roof eaves and leaped the four feet to the wall at the side of the house. He moved along the wall until he could see the dusty, narrow road behind the house. A man lay dead behind the wall. His shattered sunglasses and stained kerchief hid the red ruin of his face. The big American frowned as he looked down the little road to the alleys below. He was missing a body. The fourth man coming over the wall had avoided his grenade. "I've got one down behind the house. One got away. I don't see any movement."

Grimaldi shouted back. "We're still clear out front. No movement."

Bolan dropped back into the garden as Schwarz came out the back door, a kitchen towel wrapped around his wrist and hand. The soldier surveyed the scene. The wounded gunman was still alive but bleeding badly. He didn't envy the man the interrogation he would receive from Israeli Intelligence. Bolan's eyes slitted as he looked back at the porch.

The satellite link had seen better days. Five grenades had been detonated in the garden, and the link had been out in the open on the patio. Its aluminum casing was rended and torn from shrapnel. The laptop that Bolan had linked to it had been smashed to pieces.

Schwarz frowned. "Mack, we may have a problem."

"Tell me you made a copy of the disk."

Sirens began to howl in the distance as Schwarz gave Bolan a hurt look. "Of course I made copies of the disk. Unfortunately they were all in my bag on the coffee table during the attack."

Bolan raised an inquiring eyebrow, and Schwarz held up a floppy disk in his hand. A bullet had punched a perfectly round hole the size of a dime through the disk. Bolan asked even though he was afraid he already knew the answer. "And the other two?"

"You'd need tweezers."

"Well, we're just going to have to hope that Aaron got the whole transmission before the link got blown. Is the spare link still intact?"

Schwarz nodded. "Oh, it's fine."

Grimaldi came out onto the back porch holding his M-10 submachine gun loosely in one hand. Broken glass crunched under his feet. "You'd better get hold of Barbara pretty quick. I bet she's pretty upset right about now."

That was probably true. Bolan looked at Grimaldi as he glanced around the back yard. Shrapnel from the grenades had defoliated Katz's orange crop and pocked and gouged the whitewashed walls of the garden. The new wood of the back porch was ripped and scored. Bolan didn't even want to think about the inside of the house.

Grimaldi grinned. "Man, and Katz specifically told you not to destroy anything, too."

4

Mack Bolan sat on Katz's bullet-riddled sofa. The white-washed walls were blackened with smoke and drilled with bullet strikes. The doorway to the hall had been radically expanded by the RPG-7's five-pound warhead, and much of the furniture was smashed. A full colonel of the Israeli Defense Force sat on one of the few surviving chairs and gazed narrowly at Bolan and the men from Stony Man Farm sitting on the couch. Despite the man's advanced middle age, he looked as solid as a brick wall and carried himself with the trained ease of a special-forces soldier. He wore no special unit markings on his rather plain uniform, but Bolan would have bet a month's pay the man was from Sayeret Mat'kal, which was the IDF's main response to dire national threats. They were rumored to have done everything from leading the raid on the Entebbe airport to assisting Mossad hit teams in Europe. Katz's house was surrounded by heavily armed men in very plain uniforms.

The colonel turned an unforgiving gaze on Katz. "I am told by my superiors, Mr. Katzenelenbogen, that you are responsible for these individuals."

Katz looked at the man seriously. "Yes, that is true."

The colonel sipped at a glass of water. "How do you explain this disturbance in your home?"

The former leader of Phoenix Force considered that for a moment. "Well, they're Americans. What can you do?"

The colonel nearly strangled on his water. He took a moment to regain his composure and smiled ruefully. "Well, you have me there." His smile thinned slightly. "I am aware of your status with military intelligence, and I am informed that these gentlemen have had working relations with our military intelligence in the past. However, you must understand my position. Within two hours of these men's arrival in Israel, they were attacked in your home by heavily armed terrorists. Other than the fact that some of these men were involved in an operation in Africa, our intelligence was not given complete information. We certainly did not expect that they would be bringing the aftershocks of their operation with them onto Israeli soil."

Katz spoke soothingly. "I can understand your irritation."

The colonel suddenly gave Katz a sheepish grin. "I was told to be stern with you for at least five minutes before I offered you my complete cooperation."

"It is an unusual situation," Katz replied understandingly.

"I understand you wish to know about any unusual activity in Berlin."

"That's true," Bolan stated. "We found a camp in Libya that seemed to be more of an intelligence headquarters than a training camp, and the locals were awfully cosmopolitan. I need anything that might point to what could be going on there. Mr. Katzenelenbogen thought Berlin might be a good place to start looking."

The colonel nodded. "That is not a bad idea. I am authorized to tell you this, though whether it has anything to do with your mysterious camp I don't know. There does seem to be some strange goings-on in Berlin, but it is all rather vague, and it's hard to tell if any of it is connected."

"What kind of goings-on?"

The colonel frowned. "Money. Lots of it. One would expect this in such a criminally wide-open town. But there are rumors that there are purchasers, backers and suppliers with more money than is normal. There are feelers out for weapons and people. Some terrorists have been found with sophisticated weapons and equipment, and it's hard to understand how they could have gotten hold of such gear.''

Bolan frowned, as well. "I hear you can get anything you want in Berlin.''

"That is true. As I say, it's hard to put one's finger on, but our intelligence service, as well as the German authorities, have the feeling that something significant may be going on.''

"Anything on our guests this afternoon?'' Katz asked.

The colonel snorted. "Well, your friends killed most of them. However, we have identified the survivor as one Razi Malla. He is known to have connections with Hamas.''

Bolan considered this. Hamas was a particularly violent anti-Israeli group located within Palestine itself. They certainly had reasons to want to see Katz dead, and if they ever found out who Bolan actually was, they had more than enough reason to want to kill him and anyone from Stony Man Farm, as well. It was possible they had been tracking Katz already when he picked up the Stony Man team at the Tel Aviv airport, but Bolan didn't buy it. If they'd had Katz under surveillance, they would have wanted to find out who Bolan and his men were instead of attacking immediately. It also seemed hard to fathom that the Libyan secret police could have tracked them so fast. It was beyond their sophistication. Unless, of course, they'd had help.

Bolan rose. "Colonel, with your permission I would like to make a call.''

"By all means.''

The Executioner took the spare satellite link and went into the backyard. With heavily armed Israeli soldiers surrounding the house, he suspected his call wouldn't be interrupted this time.

Barbara Price answered immediately. "Striker!''

"Alive and well.''

Price took a deep breath. "You had us worried there for a while.''

"Some unexpected guests dropped by.''

"Anyone hurt?"

"Gadgets got cut up a little bit, but he'll be fine. Did the transmission get through?"

"Most of it, but not all. We heard gunfire and explosions across the link, then it went dead. The information was about three-quarters downloaded when the satellite lost contact with you."

Bolan sighed. "We lost the disk and the copies Gadgets made in the firefight. I'm afraid that what Aaron managed to get out of the transmission is all we've got."

Barbara sighed, as well. "Aaron won't be pleased. Without a complete copy, we can't be sure of all the variables in the code. Do you have anything else to report?"

"Tell him that Israeli Intelligence IDed our attackers as Hamas."

"Hamas? How did they get onto you that fast?"

"That's a good question."

"What do you intend to do now?"

"We don't have much to go on, just rumors and hunches, but it seems our road may lead to Berlin."

"How do you want to play it?"

Bolan had given the matter some thought. "Have Gary meet us in Berlin. He speaks decent German. McCarter's in London at the moment. I'd like you to have him link up with us in Berlin, as well. I'm thinking that the two of them can pass themselves off as South Africans or ex-Rhodesians looking for work or looking to buy."

"What are you, Jack and Gadgets going to pass yourselves off as?"

"Oh, I don't know, how about Americans?"

"If they got onto you that fast from Libya to Israel, they must have your descriptions."

"That's possible, but if so, then we might draw enough attention to make our friends show their hand. Either way, I see Berlin as the next move."

"The mission was officially over once you got out of Libya,

but I don't think Hal will have too much problem clearing you to do some fact-finding in Europe. Go ahead and head to Berlin at your convenience. I'll have a full load of gear waiting for you and the team at the American Embassy. If it falls through, we'll just fly you home out of Berlin.''

"I'm going to leave Katz here to work the Israelis for whatever we can find. I also want him to have clearance to share all information about the Libyan mission with Israeli Intelligence except for details about Stony Man and its personnel.''

"I can have that cleared within the hour.''

"All right. I'll contact you from Berlin. Striker out.''

The Executioner rose. The Israeli colonel had promised them his complete cooperation. It was time to see if he could sneak them out of Israel without being noticed.

THE YOUNG MAN looked coldly at the decoded communiqué in his hands. "Hamas have failed us in Israel. We must assume the worst.''

"We must assume that our opponents have downloaded the information from the disk,'' the old man corrected. "I have a great deal of faith in our cybernetic team and its abilities. I don't believe our opponents will be able to decode it overnight.''

"We still don't know who exactly our opponents are.''

"It is a narrow list of possibilities, and I think our opponents will show their hand quickly enough. If not, something can be arranged to help them betray themselves. I believe nothing has changed other than our timetable.''

"You wish to go ahead with the European phase of the plan?''

The old man nodded. "Indeed, with an enemy in possession of the disk—and, I assume, feverishly working to decode it— speed is now of the essence. We must drive ahead, complete preparations and then strike before they can take any kind of countermeasures.''

The young man nodded grimly. "The board agrees?''

The old man smiled uncharacteristically. "Indeed. They have full faith in you. What else does the report say?"

The young man peered at it. "Nothing that was not to be expected. The Hamas soldier who escaped confirmed that the man he saw in the backyard of the house in Tel Aviv matches the description of the man who attacked the camp."

The old man peered into space meditatively. "This man appears to be very talented. Was there anything else?"

"One of the Hamas men was wounded and taken into custody."

The old man shrugged. "He has nothing of value to tell Israeli military Intelligence, either voluntarily or under interrogation."

The younger man nodded. "Also the Hamas soldier who escaped reports that he heard the man who matched the description of the attacker in the Libyan camp shouting several commands. They were in English."

"Could he determine an accent?"

"He is a soldier, not a field agent, but he thought he sounded like an American, as opposed to an Englishman or an Australian."

"Hmm." The old man frowned slightly. "This proves nothing, but have our operatives assume that our opponents are Americans, and that American Intelligence is now in possession of the information on the disk and actively decoding it."

He fixed the young man with a steely gaze. "Begin the European phase of the operation immediately."

5

Berlin, Germany

The Executioner entered the security briefing room in the American Embassy in Berlin followed by Schwarz and Grimaldi. It had taken the three men forty-eight hours to get out of Tel Aviv, then travel on to Berlin. That was longer than Bolan liked, but there was no way he could fault the extraordinary measures Israeli Military Intelligence had taken.

Bolan took a chair. Gary Manning and David McCarter were already seated. Next to them sat a short and extremely powerful-looking man in the dark green uniform of the German border patrol. Arms like firehoses were crossed over his massive chest as he sat in his chair. Just above the massive arms, Bolan noticed jump wings over the straining breast pocket of his uniform.

Manning motioned toward him. "Mack, I'd like you to meet Captain Dieter Radtke, GSG-9."

Bolan almost raised an eyebrow. Grenzschutzgruppe 9 was Germany's elite antiterrorist unit. They were the equivalent of America's Delta Force, and were one of the most highly-trained and effective special-forces groups in the world. Katz had been right. The German government was indeed very disturbed by the developments in Berlin. The man sitting at the table with them was ample proof.

Radtke stood and saluted. He was a head shorter than Bolan,

but his command presence was palpable. He spoke excellent English.

"Hello. I am to be your liaison with the German authorities."

"Pleased to meet you, Captain. 'Radtke' is a Polish name, isn't it?"

The captain blinked and his smile widened. "Yes. 'Radtke' is a Polish name. My father escaped Poland when it fell to the Communists after World War II. He married a German woman he met in Munich. I was born there." He folded his arms across his chest again and raised a challenging eyebrow at Bolan. "I warn you. I am a German military officer with a Polish last name. I have heard all of the jokes."

Bolan grinned. He preferred to work with people who had a sense of humor. It helped a lot in his line of work. "I have a Polish background myself, and I'm more interested in hearing anything that might help us here in Berlin."

"I believe your friends have already made some progress in that direction."

Bolan glanced at Manning. "You've got something?"

"We just might."

"That was fast."

Manning agreed. "You're right, it was fast. David and I arrived in Berlin about thirty hours ago and made contact with the German authorities. They have a number of undercover operations going on here, and their operatives spread the word. We used the cover you suggested—out-of-work South African mercenaries. I guess the word 'Africa' punched all the right buttons with someone. The word got back to us within hours. Someone is very interested."

"What'd you get?"

"A telephone call at the number we'd given the German operatives."

Bolan turned to Radtke. "You traced it?"

The German shrugged. "Of course, and as you would expect, it came from a pay phone near the river."

Bolan nodded. "How did the call go?"

"My German is pretty good," Manning said, "but I wasn't sure if I could pass for a Dutch Boer with someone who would know the difference. A lot of South Africans speak British English, so McCarter took the call."

"Not bad thinking, Gary." Bolan turned to McCarter. "So, what can you tell me about your new friends?"

McCarter leaned back in his chair. "I talked with a man who spoke English with a German accent. He seemed rather excited that Gary and I were former South African Defense Force soldiers with combat experience. He wanted to know what we knew about the territory around East Africa."

"East Africa?"

"I know. It doesn't sound much like what we are looking for. However, I played along anyway and told him my associate and I had made some money poaching ivory around the border areas of Kenya and Tanzania. He asked if I knew the border area by Lake Victoria. I told him we were wanted criminals in that area, and he just about became my best mate on the spot. He wanted to know if I had more friends." McCarter grinned at Bolan, Schwarz and Grimaldi. "I thought of you blokes and told him I knew of several good men who were looking for work whom I trusted. I told him one of my friends was a pilot, and he was bloody pleased about that, as well. He wants to have a meeting with us. He says he knows some people who would very much like to employ military men with our qualifications."

Bolan frowned. "It's interesting, but it sounds like a poaching trip to me. Not exactly what we're fishing for."

"Did to me, too. But you said to keep an eye out for big money or the unusual."

"And?"

"And I asked him what kind of job it was and what it would pay."

Bolan leaned forward. "What did he say?"

"He said he couldn't say over the phone, but that the job

would be easy, a one-time shot. Easy in and easy out, very little resistance. Then he said the pay would be a million dollars per man. One and a half for me, of course, as the team leader.'' McCarter grinned smugly.

"It doesn't exactly sound like your average ivory-poaching excursion,'' Bolan stated.

McCarter nodded. "Too bloody right it doesn't.''

Bolan turned to the German. "What do you make of it, Captain?''

Radtke ran a hand through his close-cropped hair. "I am not exactly sure what to make of it. However, it is my experience that if someone offers you a million dollars to do something, you are either in show business or you are doing something illegal.''

There were murmurs of amusement around the table.

Bolan grinned. "That's been my general experience with these sort of things, as well.''

Radtke's expression became serious. "Listen. I know you have a specific mission here in Berlin, and I have been ordered to assist you. However, as you know, international crime is becoming endemic in Berlin. I admit that what we have discovered here does not seem to relate to your mission parameters, but as we have agreed, it smells highly illegal and it is being organized on German soil. My superiors and I would appreciate it if your men would continue with their cover story for another twenty-four hours and go to this meeting. With luck it may lead to some arrests, and my government would consider it a favor.''

Bolan considered it. Until Kurtzman managed to break the captured disk's code, they were shooting in the dark here in Berlin. They might as well do some good and score some points with a NATO ally of the United States while they waited.

Bolan nodded. "If my superiors clear it, it would be my pleasure.''

Radtke beamed. "Good. Excellent. With your approval, this is how I would like to run the operation."

MACK BOLAN SAT in an unmarked Volkswagen van while the team approached the meeting site. They were going in undercover to a supposedly friendly business meeting, which meant they could carry little in the way of armament and special equipment. Their ploy of posing as mercenaries left some leeway, but Bolan still felt woefully underequipped. Body armor and shoulder weapons were out. All of them wore business suits of good but not exceptional quality. McCarter had a 9 mm Browning Hi-Power in a shoulder holster and a second pistol holstered in the small of his back. Grimaldi carried a .45 Colt Officer's Model. Manning's weapon was a Ruger .357 Magnum pistol along with several speed loaders, and Bolan himself carried his 9 mm Beretta 93-R pistol and a pair of spare magazines in a shoulder rig. A snub-nosed .44 Magnum pistol was Radtke's choice. The weapon appeared to have seen extensive use. All of the men in the van also carried at least one knife. The hodgepodge of light armament certainly went along with their cover as mercenaries. They could be mistaken for a lot of things, but German policemen probably wasn't one of them.

A second van tailed them, and inside was an eight-man GSG-9 assault team in full body armor and equipped with automatic rifles and submachine guns. They would storm in when given the word. Bolan checked the Beretta's load one final time.

"All right. We do this one by the numbers, just like we planned it. David does all the talking. The rest of us keep it to yes and no answers and look happy to be getting employment. We make the bust on Captain Radtke's go. Gadgets will stay here in the van and monitor our wire and coordinate with the assault team. Any questions?"

There weren't any. McCarter took out a pair of reading

glasses with plastic frames. The team's wire was inside the temple. He whispered at the glasses. "How is my signal?"

Schwarz sat in the passenger's seat up front and wore a pair of headphones. He nodded as he adjusted a knob in the open briefcase in his lap and turned around. "Loud and clear. We're a go from here."

The van pulled to a stop, and the team got out by the train station. The meeting place was a warehouse four blocks away.

Bolan gave Schwarz the thumbs-up. "All right, you and the assault team go ahead and get situated. We'll be there in fifteen minutes."

Schwarz returned the thumbs-up through the window. "Roger that. We'll be ready."

Bolan glanced around at the early-afternoon traffic of Berlin. "Well, gentlemen, let's take a walk."

THE WAREHOUSE WAS in a run-down district of former East Berlin. Although the united Germany made a great deal of noise about unity and prosperity, the former East Germany lagged far behind its West German counterpart. Forty years of communism had left it a social, economic and technological poor relation. The wall had fallen, but the line dividing the former east and west was there for anyone with eyes to see.

The door to the warehouse was a blank sheet of steel. McCarter rapped on it with his fist.

A moment later a muted voice spoke from the other side. "What do you want?"

The Briton glanced at his watch. "It's bloody teatime, isn't it?"

There was a short barking laugh from the other side of the door. "Teatime. That is good. *Ja*, it is time for tea. Come in, come in."

Several locks turned, and the door swung open. A tall bald man with a badly set broken nose stood in the doorway dressed in an expensive-looking leather suit. Behind him stood two blond men as tall as he was, except they appeared to be twice as heavy. As the team entered, Bolan noticed the muscle kept their arms folded and their right hands inside their jackets.

The tall man shrugged. "Security. One cannot be too cautious." He gave them a sidelong look. "You would not object to being searched for wires, would you?"

McCarter shrugged. "By all means, let's get the formalities out of the way and get down to business."

"Good." The tall man was pleased. He jerked his head at one of the security men. "Karl, if you would."

Karl did a quick and efficient job of patting down the team as the men opened their jackets. He raised an eyebrow at Bolan's Beretta and Radtke's immense snub-nosed revolver, but reserved comment until he was through.

McCarter spread his hands. "One cannot be too cautious."

The bald man nodded. "*Ja*, this is true. Come. Come in. My name is Helmut. Let us get down to business."

The muscle stayed by the door as Helmut led the team through an empty area of the warehouse to a door where a portion of the interior had been partitioned. Through the door was a circle of couches and some chairs. Beyond was another partition with another door. Four more large men stood by the couches, holding 9 mm Heckler & Koch submachine guns and folding-stock shotguns. Helmut led them to the couches and took a seat himself. He smiled in a sincere fashion at McCarter. "So, you were soldiers in South Africa?"

McCarter nodded at Manning. "Me and him, we were in the First Regiment together in Durban."

Helmut perked an eyebrow. "First Regiment? You were reconnaissance commandos?"

McCarter smiled at the German's recognition. "That's right. We saw some action in Angola in '87."

The man's eyes narrowed, but his smile remained fixed. "May I inquire why you are now, how shall I say, available?"

McCarter's face turned grim. "With the election of Nelson Mandela, the South African army was downsized. This downsizing included many of the special-forces groups. Our unit was demobilized.''

Helmut nodded, and his face became equally grim. ''*Ja*, with the unification, much of the East German armed forces were also reduced or eliminated.'' His voice grew bitter. ''Our unit, the Grenztruppen, was eliminated, as well.''

Bolan filed that away. The Grenztruppen had been the special units of the former East German border guards. The Executioner could well understand why they had been eliminated. Officially their duty had been to stop incursions by NATO forces across the border. In reality their primary purpose had been to hunt down and kill anyone trying to defect to the West. During the decades of the cold war they had killed hundreds of German men, women and children who had tried to escape to freedom.

They weren't popular.

McCarter nodded sympathetically. ''Things are tough all over.''

''*Ja*.'' The East German suddenly smiled. ''But! New times! New employers! New opportunities for men like us! Come, you drink beer?''

The Briton nodded. The man turned his head toward the rear door and raised his voice. ''Heidi, bring our new friends some beer!''

A woman's voice called out through the door. ''Coming!''

The man looked at Bolan, Grimaldi and Radtke. ''And these men?''

McCarter nodded at Grimaldi. ''He's American. The pilot I was telling you about.''

Helmut nodded. ''He can fly a helicopter?''

Grimaldi flashed a winning smile. ''Been flying 'em since Nam.''

''Good.'' He peered at Radtke and Bolan speculatively. ''And these two?''

McCarter waved at Radtke and snorted. ''I grew up with

that bastard. He served his stint in the regular army. He's not recon, but I trust the stumpy little bugger with my life.''

Helmut laughed, and Radtke grinned ingratiatingly. Mc-Carter pointed at Bolan. ''Him, he's another American. He—''

A woman entered the room carrying a wide wooden tray laden with foaming, liter-sized beer steins. She and Bolan locked eyes, and the Executioner's blood went cold. Her hair was now short and blond, but there was no mistaking the intense blue eyes or the still visible yellowish green bruise Bolan had given her on the chin with his rifle butt four days earlier in the Libyan desert. The woman's eyes flared wide as Bolan's hand flashed to the grips of the Beretta 93-R. Without hesitation she threw the tray of heavy steins at the team and screamed at the top of her lungs.

''Kill them! Kill them all!''

The heavy beer steins flew through the air, streaming foam and beer. McCarter took one in the face, and another bounced off Radtke's chest. Grimaldi dodged his head smoothly and pulled his .45 automatic as one of the glass missiles sailed past over his shoulder. For a moment the former border guards were as startled as the rest of Bolan's team, and the Executioner used that fleeting moment to his advantage. He put the front sight of the Beretta 93-R on one of the security men as the German brought up his shotgun. The pistol spit a 3-round burst, and the man staggered backward. Bolan lowered his sights onto Helmut. The former border guard was drawing a large automatic pistol from inside of his leather coat as he rose. The Beretta snarled a staccato chatter as the Executioner double-tapped the trigger and Helmut sat back down on the couch with six bullets in his chest. His pistol clattered to the floor from his dead fingers.

Guns began firing in all directions, and training told the tale. The ex-Grenztruppen of the former East Germany were ruthless, highly trained hunters, but the men from Stony Man Farm and the GSG-9 man were some of the most experienced shooters on Earth. Even as the Germans brought their shoulder weapons to bear they were already targeted.

Grimaldi's .45 and Radtke's .44 Magnum roared in unison and knocked the other shotgun-toting man off his feet. Bolan had already tracked his sights onto another target, and a German fell as he was stitched by a 3-round burst. The fourth man tottered backward, spraying his submachine gun high and wide as Grimaldi, Manning and Radtke shot him simultaneously. Bolan took a long stride and aimed the Beretta around the couch on which Helmut lay dead.

The woman was gone. She had to have dropped behind the couch and crawled back through the rear door. Bolan ejected the Beretta's nearly spent magazine and slapped in a fresh 20-round magazine. "We've still got two by the front door. Jack, you and David cover our back here, the captain and I will go after the woman."

As Grimaldi nodded, there was a sudden burst of gunfire from the front and the thunder of boots in the warehouse. "I think the GSG-9 backup is here."

Radtke had picked up one of the fallen Heckler & Koch submachine guns and several spare magazines. Bolan jerked his head at the rear door. "Let's do it."

The Executioner strode up to the door and kicked it off of its hinges as the German captain covered him. Behind the door another part of the warehouse had been partitioned off, and a small kitchen area and a table dominated the area. There was a door in the back, but the room was empty. Beyond the door they heard the sound of another door smashing down and men yelling in German. Radtke roared something at the top of his lungs, and a moment later a voice shouted back.

The captain turned to Bolan. "I told them we were on the other side of the door."

The Executioner nodded and lowered his pistol slightly as the rear door swung open cautiously and a goggled man wearing a black helmet and black body armor peered in. The figure lowered his assault rife and saluted. *"Kapitan!"*

Radtke returned the salute as more GSG-9 men entered the room. He spoke in English to the lead trooper. "Rudolph, did you encounter anyone on entry? We are missing a woman, blond and well-endowed."

The GSG-9 man shook his head. "No. We encountered one man at the back door—he is dead. Front team reported two men at door, both down. No woman."

Bolan pointed at the table, and the two Germans followed the muzzle of the Beretta. The table and chairs seemed slightly askew. Beneath the table was a trapdoor. Radtke motioned at two of his men, and they overturned the table. Bolan spoke as they bent over the trapdoor.

"If that's their back door out of here, I'd think about booby traps."

Radtke scowled at the trapdoor. "Yes, good thinking. Rudolph, get the bomb team here immediately."

Bolan shook his head. "Let me get Gadgets in here. It'll be a lot faster."

"Gadgets...your man in the van?"

"The same. He's good at this sort of thing."

GADGETS SCHWARZ PEERED at the trapdoor speculatively, then eased a long flat piece of metal between its hinges. He suddenly raised an eyebrow. "All right, everyone stand back."

Everyone complied as Schwarz slowly lifted the trapdoor, then disappeared behind it. There were a few clicking noises, and his head reappeared. "Got it."

He brandished a stick of C-4 plastic explosive trailing broken duct tape and a pair of severed wires from its detonator. "Not a bad job. This one would have been enough to kill anyone opening the trapdoor without disarming it."

Bolan looked down the hole and sniffed. "The shaft drops into the sewer?"

Schwarz nodded and held up a short coil of knotted rope tied to a ring in the shaft. "You got it. The lady is somewhere in the Berlin sewer system with a ten-minute head start."

Radtke grimaced. "So. We have nothing."

Bolan smiled grimly. "No, we have something, all right. The woman didn't just want us dead for no reason. I've met her before, in the Libyan desert four days ago."

The captain's eyes widened. "So, this operation is indeed somehow connected with your objective."

"It seems that way, although at the moment I have no idea how." Bolan shrugged. "We also have two names and some bodies. Our friend Helmut said he was in the Grenztruppen. He also called the woman Heidi, and we all got a good enough look at her to generate a sketch your intelligence people can work with. It's a start." Bolan's eyes narrowed. "You're bleeding, Captain."

Radtke looked down at his jacket. There were three spreading stains on the left arm and shoulder. "*Ach*, shotgun pellets."

Bolan checked over the rest of his team. Half of McCarter's face was covered with blood from where the heavy beer stein had hit him in the eyebrow. His handkerchief was soaked through from mopping his face, and the Englishman would undoubtedly require stitches. He looked at Bolan sheepishly. Other than being covered with beer, the rest of the team was unhurt.

Bolan smiled ruefully at the captain. "Your superiors are going to smell us and figure we got drunk and shot everybody."

Radtke snorted and looked down at the bodies with disgust. "The Grenztruppen were little better than Nazis. I don't have to get drunk to shoot them."

Bolan nodded. "I think we should get a forensics team in here and search the place from top to bottom."

The German frowned at his bleeding shoulder. "Yes, I agree." He turned to his number-two man. "Rudolph, get an intelligence team here immediately. I want the warehouse searched top to bottom."

6

Mack Bolan sat in the secure communications room of the American Embassy in Berlin. The room had been swept for electronic bugs, and it was extensively shielded from any kind of external surveillance. Most embassies sent out classified information to their home governments, and since World War II the American Embassy in Berlin had seen its share of secure communications.

Alone in the windowless room, Bolan pressed a button on his satellite link-up panel and spoke into the intercom. "I've got a meeting in the conference room in five minutes, Aaron. What have you got for me?"

Kurtzman's voice was crystal clear. "We have a partial break in the code."

"Tell me about it."

The computer expert warmed to the subject. "It's a hell of a code, Striker, and as you know, we got interrupted in Tel Aviv and didn't get a complete downloading of the disk's information when you transmitted. That complicated things immensely, and it's still gumming up the works right now. It's hard enough to break a code when you have the complete message. If you're missing part of it, you don't have any idea what pieces of the pattern may be missing."

"But you think you have something?"

"I think so. As you could tell when you saw it yourself, the code was a cipher, all symbols, numbers and letters that stood for something else, and you can cipher, recipher, and then recipher your symbols again, each time according to different rules. On top of that, the information itself is coded. Even when you begin to break the cipher, the information revealed stands for something else, as well.

"It's like what happened in the Pacific in World War II. We broke the Japanese ciphered symbols before they attacked Pearl Harbor, but when our intelligence boys broke it, the revealed code simply read, 'Climb Mount Nihitaka.' That was a private signal between Admiral Yamamoto and Admiral Nagumo to go ahead with the attack. We had broken their cipher, but we had no idea what the coded phrase meant. Without a context, it could literally mean anything. You know the way it ended. We didn't find out what 'Climb Mount Nihitaka' meant until half of our Pacific fleet was already burning in Pearl Harbor."

Bolan understood all too well. "So, you're telling me you've broken the cipher."

"We believe so."

"And now what you've got is reams of meaningless hash without any context."

"Well, it's not quite that bad. Yes, we have reams of hash, but that works in our favor. As I said, a short, simple code phrase like 'Climb Mount Nihitaka' can mean just about anything, but a long code, one with pages of text like we have from the disk, starts to form patterns and have context. The more complicated the information you're trying to code, the harder it gets to make it impenetrable. If you're working with names, dates, schedules and geographic areas, then patterns arise. When we can plug in outside information that we already know, like a camp in Libya and meetings in Berlin, then you can start making headway and build."

"What have you built for me, Aaron?"

"Well, we haven't actually built much, but we think we've started to get some bits and pieces, mostly geographical."

"Give me something I can use."

Kurtzman paused for a moment. "We think we've isolated

Libya in the code, and Berlin, as well. Since we have your recent adventures to give us the clues, looking for them in the code was easier than if we were working the code cold. We believe we've also isolated a third geographical location out of the text.''

"Where?''

"Remember, we're not sure about this.'' Bolan could actually hear Kurtzman scratch his beard over the link. "I can't be positive until we break more context out of the code, or you can get more outside information to corroborate.''

"Where?''

Kurtzman let out a long breath. "Well, we think the code repeatedly refers to Moscow.''

BOLAN STRODE into the embassy's briefing room. Captain Dieter Radtke sat at the table in his dress uniform with his massive left arm in a sling. Several thick folders sat in front of him on the table, and despite his injury he looked pleased with himself. McCarter's left eyebrow had a bulging bandage taped over it. The rest of the Stony Man team sat around the table and looked up at Bolan expectantly. The Berlin CIA station chief sat at the head of the table, wearing the poker face typical of most CIA station chiefs Bolan had ever met.

The Executioner nodded at the CIA man. "Good morning.''

The station chief nodded as Bolan took the seat opposite to him. "Good morning, Mr....'' The chief peered at a sheet of paper on the table before him. "Belasko. I have received a communiqué from the Pentagon that I am to render you all assistance possible here in Berlin.''

The look he gave was another one Bolan was familiar with. The soldier had to admit he had a habit of dropping in on senior United States field operatives armed with clearances that went straight up the chain of command to the top and orders that he be given every assistance.

"I'd appreciate it. Have you and Captain Radtke had a chance to coordinate your resources here in Berlin?''

The chief nodded. "As a matter of fact we have. Captain?"

Radtke opened one of the files in front of him and slid it across the table to Bolan. On the top of the documents was a color photograph. The woman had shoulder-length hair that was a shade between dirty blond and light brown. She held her hands to her hair, and the low-cut sweater she wore left little of her ample measurements to the imagination. Her blue eyes were heavy lidded as she smiled winsomely at the camera. The last time the Executioner had seen her, she had hurled nearly ten liters of beer at him. There was another photograph beneath the first. The woman stood wearing an orange smock and held a placard with her name and a series of numbers. It was obviously a prison photo.

Captain Radtke spoke. "Heidi Hochrein. Born in Baden Baden. In the 1980s she became associated with the Red Army through a socialist boyfriend and a radical political group he belonged to while they both attended the University of Berlin. Her boyfriend died under somewhat mysterious circumstances. We believe she may have killed him because his politics were no longer radical enough, and possibly as a test of her loyalty by the movement's more fanatic elements. However, this is unproved. She did serve a year in the women's facility for possession of an unlicensed automatic weapon found in her car in 1987, but other than that she has never been convicted or positively connected to any specific terrorist act. We keep an active file on her, but she has not surfaced or been mentioned in any report since our nation's reunification."

Bolan skimmed the file. Someone had taken the trouble to translate the copy into English. "Any ties to Russia?"

Radtke frowned. "Yes, I believe she went to the former Soviet Union twice in the mid-1980s, and again in 1994 under tourist visas. Her exact activities there on any of these occasions are unknown to us. We believe she may have also been a guest of the North Koreans for a month in 1986, but that is unsubstantiated."

"How about our friend Helmut?"

The captain nodded and opened another file. "According to our military records, his story checks out. Helmut Schneck was a captain in the Grenztruppen." Radtke's face twisted with scorn. "His service record with the East German army was exemplary. He was decorated for numerous actions, and he had over forty-seven confirmed kills of East German citizens attempting to escape across the border. With reunification his unit was disbanded. Afterward he worked in his father's bakery. However, other than the daily atrocities that comprised his military duties, he has never been accused of any crime in either the former German Democratic Republic or in unified Germany. The men with him in the warehouse have been confirmed as fellow soldiers in the Grenztruppen, as well."

"What did you find when you searched the warehouse?"

"Very little." The captain shifted in his chair. "We found some guns other than the ones they were carrying. The shaft that connected the warehouse to the sewer was professionally dug. The sewers on the east side of Berlin are very old and not terribly well maintained, and the Hochrein woman left no discernible trail. With a ten-minute head start she could have headed in almost any direction and surfaced anywhere. The search teams found nothing. We have a bulletin out with the police for her arrest, but so far she has not been seen."

Bolan mulled this over.

The station chief's eyes narrowed. "You have an idea?"

"I have a few thoughts. I don't believe Helmut was a key player in whatever is going on. I believe he and his men were hired locally here in Berlin, to act as muscle and himself as a middleman. He talked of new employers and new opportunities, and he was acting as a recruiter when we encountered him. I doubt he actually knew the details of the job that was being planned in East Africa. I believe he was a cutout."

Radtke absently scratched his shoulder under his sling. "I agree with you about Helmut, but do you have any idea why these unknown employers of his would be hiring people for a job in Africa?"

Bolan frowned. "No. None at the moment."

"But you believe the connection to Russia is important?"

"Yes, I do." The Executioner gazed at the photo of Heidi Hochrein on the table before him and thought of what he and Kurtzman had discussed. "I have a hunch that with her currently being wanted in Germany, our Miss Hochrein may be headed to the former Soviet Union."

The station chief nodded. "With your permission, Mr. Belasko, I'll contact the Moscow embassy and have Miss Hochrein's dossier faxed over to them immediately."

"Thanks. That would be a big help." Bolan turned to Grimaldi. "Jack, see about getting hold of a plane and a flight plan."

Grimaldi folded his arms. "Moscow International?"

"You've got it."

Bolan addressed McCarter and Manning. "You two stick around here. Hochrein may just keep a low profile, waiting for us to leave the city."

Bolan closed Heidi Hochrein's file and turned to Radtke. "Captain, I'd like to take this copy of the file with me."

The German nodded. "Of course, but may I ask why?"

"I have someone in mind I would like to show it to."

7

Moscow, Russia

Valentina Svarzkova of Russian Military Intelligence turned arctic blue eyes on Mack Bolan as he entered her tiny office in the GRU building in Moscow. Bolan noted the light tan shoulder boards on the dark-moss-colored dress uniform that the Russian army refered to as "Tsar green." The shoulder boards now had one thin red stripe running down the middle with four tiny stars in a T-formation straddling the stripe.

Bolan grinned at the GRU agent and saluted sharply along with the two armed Russian soldiers who accompanied him. "Congratulations, Captain."

The Russian agent blushed uncharacteristically and returned the salute. "Yes, I have been promoted since we last encountered each other." She nodded at the two soldiers and dismissed them in Russian.

Bolan examined Svarzkova. She had changed since the last time he had seen her. The scar on her chin had lightened into a thick white line that cleft the point of her jaw, and her nose was very slightly askew from where it had been badly broken and reset. She had received the injuries by ramming a sedan into a jeep loaded with armed terrorists in the rural lanes of Arlington, Virginia. The massive wound she had received to her leg with a special-forces entrenching tool in Bosnia didn't seem to bother her as she rose, but there were circles under her eyes and her face was thinner, as if she had lost weight.

Her long blond hair was pulled into a severe military braid. She was still a beautiful woman, but the intervening year appeared to have put some hard miles on her.

Bolan's face became serious. "How are you, Valentina?"

The Russian agent's smile faded. "I am well."

Bolan raised an eyebrow at the Russian and she sighed. "With promotion comes more responsibilities." She shook her head at the mound of papers on the desk in front of her. "Things do not go well in Russia. The transition to democracy and a free economy is long and strewed with stones. The nation is politically divided, the *mafiya* has bought its way into the highest offices of power. Crime and corruption are everywhere. I am a trained Russian Military Intelligence field agent, and now I am little more than a policeman, using my skills against my own people rather than against enemies of the nation."

They were both silent for a moment, then Svarzkova suddenly smiled at Bolan ruefully. "Food shortages are still common."

Bolan grinned. Getting fed was one of the consuming passions of Valentina Svarzkova's life. While in the United States she had consumed a vast quantity of food for a woman her size. "You're still thinking about the mud pie I bought you back in Kansas."

Svarzkova's face became utterly serious. "It haunts my dreams." She smiled again. "I am told you need my help."

"Yes, I was surprised I was given access to you and your department so quickly."

The woman grinned and waved her hand around her tiny, windowless office. "Well, I am not the most important field agent the GRU has in its command, and your help, and your government's discretion, in the Baibakov affair are well remembered. The GRU does not forget its debts, and neither do I." Her face turned serious. "How is it I may help you."

"I have a problem. It's gone from Libya to Berlin, and I believe the trail leads here to Moscow."

A deep crease formed between the Russian agent's brows. "Libya is still ostensibly an ally of the Russian Republic. Even if we no longer support many of her positions, Libya is still an active trading partner of ours. Our economy is starved for hard currency. With her large oil reserves, the Libyan dinar is very strong, and she spends a great deal of those dinars on Russian weapons and equipment. I must warn you it may not be in the best interests of my country to assist you in this matter."

"I understand. All I ask is that you hear me out."

Svarzkova's frown stayed fixed. "Again I warn you. I am a captain in the GRU. Anything you tell me affecting the security of my government will be reported to my superiors."

"I wouldn't have it any other way." Bolan held out the file tucked under his arm. "Why don't you take a look at this file? I'll come back in the evening and pick you up."

Svarzkova eyed the file with suspicion. "Pick me up? Where are we going?"

Bolan shrugged causally. "Well, I'm on an expense account. I figured I would pick you up, then we could discuss the matter over dinner at the Metropole. I hear it's very good."

The Metropole was one of the fanciest and most expensive restaurants in Moscow. Located within the lavish Metropole Hotel, it catered almost exclusively to foreign diplomats and tourists with hard currency. The Metropole's international clientele ensured that it was unaffected by food shortages, and it was interesting to note that the fanciest restaurant in Moscow didn't accept Russian rubles. A GRU captain would have to take an entire month's pay and convert it into dollars on the black market just to eat a meal there, and that was assuming a GRU captain could get reservations. Bolan was hitting Valentina Svarzkova below the belt, and they both knew it.

Svarzkova's eyes narrowed. "You are the son of the devil."

Bolan grinned shamelessly. "Say, seven o'clock?"

The GRU agent snatched the file from Bolan's hand. "Yes. Seven o'clock will be excellent."

VALENTINA SVARZKOVA looked radiant. Some lipstick and a black cocktail dress had transformed her into an almost completely different woman. She didn't look at all out of place in the lavishly elaborate decor of the Metropole. She beamed as Bolan ordered oysters and champagne, and she looked positively giddy as he ordered the chicken Kiev for both of them along with cauliflower fried in butter and Hungarian white wine from Lake Balaton to accompany it.

As the waiter left, Bolan got down to business. "You had a chance to examine the file?"

Svarzkova nodded as she sank her teeth into a piece of bread slathered with butter. "Mmm."

"What did you think?"

"Very interesting." Her eyes narrowed slightly. "What is it that led you to this woman?"

Bolan decided to level with her. There really wasn't too much that was classified in the mission. He was operating almost entirely on hunches and circumstantial evidence. Other than Stony Man Farm's direct phone number, there was very little worth holding back.

"The woman was sighted at what we believed was some sort of terrorist camp in the Libyan desert. The camp itself was an enigma. There seemed to be no actual training going on. Information taken from the site indicated it might be a command-and-control center for some larger operation. The woman resurfaced in Berlin, and appeared to be involved in recruiting for some sort of illegal operation going on in East Africa. The recruiting operation was broken up by the GSG-9, but the woman escaped and we found little information. We have reason to believe she may have fled to Moscow."

The waiter arrived and they both waited for him to put down the champagne and oysters. Svarzkova nodded at Bolan as the waiter left again. "You are correct. The Hochrein woman is in Moscow."

"That was fast."

The Russian woman slid an oyster down her throat with practiced ease. "Heidi Hochrein is known to the former KGB. I have some connections there."

Bolan watched the Russian agent's face. "I was under the impression that the GRU and the KGB weren't exactly allies."

Svarzkova gazed at Bolan frankly. "The United States and the Russian Republic are not exactly allies, either. But we worked well together, didn't we?"

Bolan took a sip of his champagne. She had him on that one.

"As I am sure you know, the KGB was officially disbanded with the fall of the Communist government. It was extremely unpopular with the people. In reality, however, it was simply renamed and broken down into a number of smaller organizations. I have connections with what is now called the Foreign Intelligence Service. They have extensive records of past international operations during what you westerners call the cold war." The agent pulled a file out of her attaché case and handed it across the table. "Hochrein has worked for the KGB on a number of occasions in Berlin."

Bolan examined the file. It hadn't been translated into English, but it still told him a great deal. There were various identification photos of the woman, photostats of her fingerprints and reams of reports. There was also a series of photographs of the woman naked and actively engaged with various equally naked men.

"What kind of work did she do?"

Svarzkova arched a condemning eyebrow. "Various things. She is built like a cow, and some men like that. She seduced some married diplomats, acquired information, abetted the KGB in blackmail, set up meetings, acted as courier for sensitive documents and materials. There was also a black file on her that I was not given access to."

"A black file?"

Svarzkova nodded. "A black file is generally information concerning very sensitive operations. It is my personal suspicion that Hochrein may have participated in KGB-sponsored assassinations. Her regular file indicates she has received training in killing techniques using her hands, knives and poisons. She has also received at least rudimentary training with small arms and explosives.''

"And she is here in Moscow right now?''

"That is what I am told by reliable sources.''

Bolan frowned. "I assume some former KGB elements must be sheltering her.''

"That is an excellent assumption.'' Svarzkova's face became very serious. "I must warn you that there are still some very hard-line factions of the former KGB who are still active. They do not wield the power they once did, but they are fanatics and they are very dangerous.''

Bolan folded his arms. "And you believe they would help her, even if she was wanted by the German authorities?''

Svarzkova frowned. "It would depend. The Russian people are very frugal, even the KGB. We never throw anything away. However, if she was a liability, the KGB would simply kill her rather than chancing her talking to the authorities if arrested. But if she was still useful, there would be those who would shelter her. Particularly if she was currently active in some sort of operation.''

Bolan nodded. "And someone appears to be sheltering her.''

"Yes. It seems so.''

"Any idea exactly who?''

Svarzkova's frown deepened. "It could be almost anyone. As I say, the KGB was split apart into different divisions. During the cold war, KGB operations were Byzantine to say the least. Now, with their breakup, and the new ways in Russia, there are factions within factions, all with their own agendas.'' Her frown turned into a grimace. "I must warn you. I suspect my inquiry will not have gone unnoticed.''

Bolan nodded as the food came. Svarzkova watched him as

he accepted the wine and then dug into his chicken. "What do you intend to do now?" she asked.

Bolan grinned around his food. "Finish my meal and ask for seconds."

Svarzkova smiled and began to attack her chicken.

THE NIGHT AIR WAS WARM, and there was a breeze coming off the river. It was a beautiful summer evening in Moscow. Bolan glanced at the Russian GRU agent. She had the look of someone who had truly enjoyed herself.

"Thank you for the meal. It was delicious."

Bolan smiled. "It was my pleasure." It had been a very pleasant evening, but business was business. He locked gazes with the Russian. "Can you help me?"

Svarzkova averted her gaze and glanced into the sky. "I wish to help you. My superiors wish to help you. I told you, Russian Military Intelligence does not forget its debts. But I do not think my superiors wish to start a clandestine war with a faction of the former KGB, particularly when we have so little information." Svarzkova shook her head unhappily. "I admit the circumstances you present are intriguing, but you yourself admit you cannot specify what they mean. You cannot demonstrate a threat to the Russian Republic or the GRU. I wish to help you, but our debt to you goes only so far. If you had something more, something that would alarm my superiors, then I could try to help you. But…"

Svarzkova hunched her shoulders and stared off into space to avoid Bolan's eyes.

Bolan looked out at the lights of Moscow himself. He held no bitterness, but he couldn't help his frustration. He had come to Moscow chasing a mystery and run into a familiar wall, and he didn't relish trying to run an independent operation around Svarzkova and the GRU to attack the former KGB. It was the stuff that international incidents were made of. Bolan changed the subject. "So, Gimpy, how's the leg?"

"Gimpy?" Svarzkova stared at Bolan in mock anger. "Do not call me Gimpy, or I will show you how good my leg is."

Bolan folded his arms and looked at her dubiously. "Is that a threat?"

Svarzkova smiled. "The injury was extensive, but no major arteries were severed. The doctor recommended martial-arts exercise to help it heal and regain full range of motion. Martial arts are no longer suppressed in Russia and are practiced openly. I chose tang soo do, and have been practicing daily for nine months." She looked at Bolan very seriously. "It is the art of Chuck Norris, you know."

Bolan nodded gravely. "I know." Chuck Norris was considered a god in the former Soviet Union.

They walked down the steps of the Metropole Hotel toward the carport. Bolan's gaze narrowed as the valet took his tag. The man was sweating. It was a warm evening, but it certainly wasn't sweltering. Bolan smiled at the man and he smiled back, but every bodily clue the man gave off communicated fear. The Executioner took Svarzkova's hand. "Talk to me, act unconcerned."

Svarzkova's only reaction was to blink once as she turned to him. "What a lovely evening it is...."

Bolan watched the valet out of the corner of his eye. The man lowered his hand facing the street to his side, unobtrusively sticking out his thumb, then clenching his fist. The soldier took Svarzkova's face in his hands as if he were about to kiss her. "The valet just gave some kind of signal. You're armed?"

Svarzkova breathed in Bolan's ear. "Yes."

"There's a parked car down on the curb in front of us. It's our cover in case of trouble. Be ready."

Bolan's right hand was hidden from the street and he slid it up under his jacket and found the grips of the Beretta 93-R.

With her left hand, Svarzkova casually flicked open the catch of her purse, her eyes going hard as she looked past

Bolan's shoulder. "There is a four-door sedan coming down the street. It has tinted windows."

The soldier freed the Beretta from its shoulder holster but kept it under his jacket. "What is it doing now?"

Svarzkova's hand slid into her purse. "It is slowing down. Its windows are rolling— Guns!"

Bolan whipped the Beretta machine pistol onto line as Svarzkova drew a large automatic pistol from her purse. Two men were jockeying the stubby barrels of Kalashnikov carbines out the front and rear passenger's windows of a black BMW. A set of head and shoulders emerged from the sunroof. Bolan ignored the gunmen and fired a pair of 3-round bursts into the windshield. The car lurched and swerved as the windshield pebbled around the bullet holes.

Svarzkova had taken two long leaps down the stairs and slammed her pistol on top of the hood of the parked car in a two-handed hold. Her face was locked in a grimace as she discharged her weapon rapidly. The gunmen's car swerved drunkenly, and horns blared from oncoming traffic. The night was suddenly split with the long snarls of automatic carbines.

Bolan stood and fired. The gunman riding shotgun sagged as the Executioner put a 3-round burst into his face and neck. The head of the man standing in the sunroof suddenly snapped back on his shoulders as one of Svarzkova's rounds took him in the forehead.

The man in the back crouched below the window as the car swerved in a shallow turn into oncoming traffic and halted. Brakes screamed as other cars came to a stop and their passengers cowered as the area flared into a war zone. Svarzkova continued to fire into the body of the car. Bolan strode down to the car she was using for cover and crouched at the fender. In the BMW, the doors away from Bolan and Svarzkova flew open and two men burst out. Both raced down the street, sending unaimed bursts of fire from their carbines behind them. One of the men fell as Svarzkova put a bullet in his back. She cursed roundly as her 9 mm CZ-75 pistol clacked open on an empty chamber.

Bolan flicked the selector switch to semiautomatic fire and took careful aim through his sights. The remaining man screamed as his left leg was smashed out from under him by a 9 mm hollowpoint round. He collapsed onto the road, and his rifle clattered out of his hands ahead of him.

The Executioner rose from behind cover and kept his front sight squarely between the crawling man's shoulder blades. Svarzkova reached up under her skirt and made a yanking motion. There was a sound of tearing Velcro, and her hand came out from under her dress filled with a tiny Russian PSM 5.45 mm assassination pistol. Bolan and Svarzkova both scanned the street.

The woman nodded in satisfaction. "I think we are clear."

"Let's go check on our suspects."

Bolan checked the car while Svarzkova strode over to the wounded man and kicked his fallen weapon out of his reach. The white leather interior of the BMW was a mural of red ruin. The driver and the two gunmen inside the vehicle had all taken head shots. The soldier noted they all had the identical armament of short-barreled, folding-stock AKR automatic carbines. There were many worse weapons one could choose for a drive-by shooting.

He walked down the street and turned over the fallen runner. His eyes were glazed over, and a spreading red stain marred his gray sweatshirt around his solar plexus. The man was dead. Bolan glanced up. Svarzkova was standing over the remaining gunman, yelling as he writhed on the ground holding his wounded leg. The man howled in pain as she kicked him mercilessly while holding him at gunpoint.

"Captain, perhaps we should call for some backup. We also need to start a search for our valet. I believe he was an accomplice."

The Russian agent's head snapped up. "Yes. You are correct. I will do so immediately." Svarzkova reached into her purse and pulled out a portable phone while she continued to cover the fallen man with her pistol. She punched buttons with her thumb and began to speak rapidly in Russian. After a moment she snapped it shut again. "GRU personnel is on the way. I suspect Moscow police is already on its way, as well."

Bolan glanced down at the bleeding man. He didn't envy him. The GRU interrogation wouldn't be gentle. "Do you know any of these men?"

"No, but I will soon enough."

Bolan nodded. "Can you think of anyone else in particular who might want you dead?"

Svarzkova snorted. "I know many people who wish me dead. But very few would have the resources to know that I was having dinner here with you tonight."

Bolan didn't have to say what was on both of their minds. Svarzkova's voice shook with anger as her look turned feral. "If I can prove these men are agents of the former KGB, it will mean war in the streets."

Colonel Uri Ozhimkov of Russian Military Intelligence scowled out from under heavy brows. His head was nearly bald and his face was deeply lined, but he held himself erect, and his bearing belied his nearly sixty years of age. He spoke in heavily accented English. "This is a highly unusual situation."

A short, broad man with shocks of gray hair sitting next to the colonel nodded, but said nothing.

"I agree," Bolan said. "I assume your investigation has revealed something."

It took all of Ozhimkov's will to keep his shoulders from sagging. This situation was the last thing he needed. Things weren't going well. The colonel steeled himself, and his scowl deepened to the point his eyes were almost lost in shadow. "Your and Captain Svarzkova's assumption is correct. Your attackers were indeed the agents of the Foreign Intelligence Service."

Bolan's eyes narrowed. He'd had little doubt of it. Svarzkova's eyes flared with vindicated rage. "When do we attack?"

Ozhimkov grunted. Many things had changed in the former Soviet Union. He was still not used to beautiful blond female captains in combat. "I wish it was that simple, Captain Svarzkova."

The man next to Ozhimkov spoke, and his English was very

nearly perfect. "Your zeal is commendable, Captain. But perhaps somewhat rash."

Svarzkova, attempting to bottle her rage, was a sight to see. She locked her gaze with the man in civilian clothes, and her words came through clenched teeth. "The FIS scum must be made to pay."

Ozhimkov cleared his throat. "Captain Svarzkova, I would like to introduce you to our guest, Colonel Nikita Degederov of the Foreign Intelligence Service."

Bolan examined the incognito FIS colonel while Svarzkova flushed to the roots of her hair. Degederov kept a poker face as he spoke. "There is no need to apologize, Captain. I understand what it is like to be shot at. I often react to it with ill humor, as well."

The Executioner almost had to smile. He suspected an actual apology would've had to have been physically beaten out of Valentina Svarzkova, but the colonel had headed off a potentially embarrassing situation with aplomb.

Svarzkova kept her mouth shut. The FIS colonel looked at Bolan curiously. "I understand you were there during the attack."

"I suspect I was the main target of it."

The man nodded thoughtfully. "Likely you are correct."

Ozhimkov grunted. "There is no doubt of it in my mind, though I am disturbed that a GRU agent is considered a viable secondary target."

The FIS colonel nodded again. "I am disturbed by this, as well. Those responsible obviously had little qualms with starting a war between the GRU and factions of the former KGB."

Bolan folded his arms. "I'm assuming your branch had nothing to do with the attack."

"That is correct."

The Executioner turned to Ozhimkov, looked at him and said bluntly, "You believe him?"

Ozhimkov looked back at Bolan with frankness. "I have known Colonel Degederov for many years. In many ways his role in the FIS is a counterpart to mine in the GRU. We have been at odds many times. The enmity between our organizations is old and well established. However, I greatly respect his abilities, and I cannot believe he would be so stupid as to murder a decorated GRU captain and start a war in the streets of Moscow."

Bolan accepted the statement at face value and looked back at Degederov. "But you know who did."

"I have my suspicions."

"I would appreciate your sharing them," Bolan stated. "No one at this table would like any mistakes to be made in this matter."

The colonel's face stayed impassive, but Bolan's statement and all that it implied were very clear. The man nodded. "No. No one here would want any mistakes made in this matter. It is indeed a delicate situation." Degederov steepled his fingers in thought. "The KGB officially no longer exists, but its functions remain. Everyone here knows this. It has been broken down into a number of departments and renamed. My department is the Foreign Intelligence Service. Despite Russia's new status, international intelligence-gathering is still very important. My department has continued on much as it has in the past. However, many other arms of the former KGB have been decommissioned, reduced or reassigned. This has not sat well with many. There is much discontent."

Bolan nodded and said nothing. The man was telling him nothing he didn't already know.

"There are factions that call for a return to the old order. Many of those are factions who were assigned to internal security."

Bolan grimaced inwardly. "Internal security" was a polite way of speaking of the KGB paramilitary who were the iron fist of the Communist Party. Internal-security operatives had been directly responsible for crushing any kind of dissident movements. Bolan could well imagine that such men wouldn't be pleased with the shaky new democratic order in the Russian Republic.

Degederov continued. "I fear some of these factions are in great danger of becoming political terrorists in support of the Communist hard-liners."

The word *terrorist* touched a chord in Bolan's instincts, but he couldn't quite place what it was trying to tell him.

Degederov's instincts were keen, as well, as he peered at the Executioner. "You have had a thought?"

"Perhaps." Bolan gazed at the man levelly. "What are you prepared to do to help us?"

The colonel showed emotion for the first time in the meeting, and it was a weary sigh. "I cannot become actively involved."

"But you might let it slip where I can find Heidi Hochrein and who is assisting her."

"I might." Degederov examined the table before him. "But I warn you. You must be very careful in how you approach this. I have come here to avoid a war, but it is still a very possible repercussion."

Bolan's gaze narrowed. He understood all too well. "You're saying that despite the unsavory nature of this faction you're telling us about, they have supporters and sympathizers."

"That is true."

"And if Colonel Ozhimkov sends in an armed team of GRU field agents or a platoon of Spetsnaz soldiers, other former KGB factions will retaliate out of loyalty and fear they may be attacked next. It would be taken as a direct attack of the GRU against the KGB, and you would have the war you are trying to avoid."

"You have an excellent grasp of the politics of the situation," Degederov said dryly.

Bolan shrugged. "The Russian Republic doesn't have a lock on interservice rivalry."

Degederov almost smiled. "I am very pleased to hear that. I was genuinely starting to believe that we did."

"So, we are to sit on our hands and do nothing?" Svarzkova demanded.

"No." Ozhimkov leaned back in his chair. "Our superiors wish a war even less than Colonel Degederov, but the act cannot go unanswered, either."

Svarzkova sat at ramrod attention. "What is it you would have me do?"

Bolan saw what was coming. Ozhimkov turned to Degederov, and the FIS Colonel looked at Svarzkova appraisingly. "You are well-known to us, Captain. Your service record is exemplary. You and an American under your protection have been attacked. It would not be out of character for you to seek some kind of vengeance. It is also known to us that you have traveled to the United States and operated in conjunction with some kind of paramilitary operation in there."

Bolan finished the thought. "And if Captain Svarzkova went and sought vengeance on her own, backed by nonofficial 'mercenaries,' no one could point any fingers. If we succeed in capturing Hochrein and smashing this dangerous faction, the FIS and the GRU will both be pleased and a direct confrontation will be avoided. If we fail, we are expendable, deniable, and a direct confrontation is avoided. Either way, both the FIS and the GRU can sit back and watch with clean hands."

Ozhimkov folded his arms and scowled at Bolan's bluntness. Degederov sighed but nodded his agreement. "That is essentially correct."

The three men at the table looked at one another for a moment in silence.

Svarzkova beamed. "I believe it is an excellent plan!"

9

"You!"

Former Spetsnaz Major Pietor Ramzin, retired, nearly strangled on his vodka as he looked up and saw Mack Bolan standing in front of him in his favorite bar on the lower west side of Moscow. Ramzin half rose from his seat and looked back and forth between Bolan and Svarzkova. He quickly regained his composure, then sat back and refilled his shot glass. He glanced up at Svarzkova. "You, I expected to see sooner or later. Probably on the other side of a pistol." He tossed the vodka back, then peered up at Bolan in speculation. "However, seeing you here—this is unexpected."

"I'm here on business, Ramzin."

The former major leered somewhat drunkenly at Svarzkova. "And I thought you came just to get a taste of the flower of Russian womanhood. I always suspected you wanted Svarzkova."

Bolan was surprised that the captain merely smiled at the man. "How are you, Ramzin?" She looked at him in mock pity. "I understand you lost your job in the factory."

Ramzin lost his leer and stared with deep concentration into the half-full bottle in front of him. He spoke with cold bitterness. "I am Hero of the Soviet Union. I have medal and the scars to prove it." He glared up at Svarzkova in resentment. "I do not inspect light bulbs."

"Ah." She nodded sagely. "So, now you just sit about and drink up your hero's pension."

Ramzin's face tightened but he resumed staring at his bottle silently. Bolan looked at Ramzin appraisingly. The Russian was as tall as himself, and even more heavily muscled. Despite his present dissolute state, he appeared to be in decent shape. Finding the man hadn't been hard. Svarzkova's office kept tabs on the once renegade major, and he spent nearly every evening in this Georgian bar. Balalaikas and Georgian tapestries hung on the red-painted walls, and a pair of Cossack sabers hung crossed over the bar. It was a favorite haunt of many ex-military officers. Festive folk music played over a record player, but it wasn't a match for the mostly drunk and gloomy men who sat hunched over their bottles of vodka.

"How would you like a job, Ramzin?" Bolan asked.

The Russian grunted derisively and poured himself another glass. "Helping you hunt down more of my former officers, I suppose."

Bolan could understand the Russian major's bitterness. It had been Bolan himself who had broken up his smuggling ring on the Arizona-Mexican border and landed him and his surviving men in Leavenworth prison. Bolan later had him freed to help track down one of Ramzin's own men who was helping terrorists in the United States. The major had cooperated, but he hadn't been pardoned. He had committed far too many crimes in the United States. He had simply been released from prison, then deported back to the former Soviet Union, where he was just one more unemployed military officer living on a scant pension and scrounging for menial jobs. It was better than a life sentence in Leavenworth, but Bolan suspected the past couple of years had been hard on the former Hero of the Soviet Union. The lines on his face had deepened, and more gray had crept into his hair. Nonetheless, Major Pietor Ramzin had been an extremely worthy foe in the Sonoran Desert, and he had proved himself a worthy ally in firefights in Washington, D.C. Right now the Executioner needed a few good men.

"No, I have something much more to your taste in mind."

Ramzin rolled his eyes dismissively and raised his glass to his lips. "Keep your filthy job. I am not interested."

Svarzkova smiled pleasantly. "I see. You do not wish to assist us in fighting KGB paramilitary scum. Very well, then." She looked at Bolan and jerked her head toward the door. "We go."

Ramzin's eyes flared at the mention of the KGB, he stopped drinking in midsip. The wheels turned in his mind for only a moment, then he tilted the entire glass back decisively. The major pushed the bottle away as he rose from his seat. He looked at Svarzkova with a confused shrug. "Why did you not say this in the first place?"

CAPTAIN VALENTINA Svarzkova had only two rickety wooden chairs, a small table and an old couch that pulled out into a bed in her one-room apartment. She had given the seats to her guests and now sat on the counter of her tiny corner kitchen. She watched, grinning, as her guests devoured her carefully hoarded store of pot cheese, pickles, onion bread and beer. She didn't often have foreign guests, much less her own independent operation, and she was enjoying the situation immensely.

Pietor Ramzin stood by the bookcase and found himself frowning. He looked at Schwarz, Grimaldi, Svarzkova, then turned a troubled gaze back to Bolan. "How many more men are we to expect?"

The Executioner looked Ramzin straight in the face. "None. This is it."

"Ah." Ramzin looked around at his new team members again dubiously. "How many do we expect in opposition?"

Bolan folded his arms. "At least a dozen. Maybe more. Mostly former KGB paramilitary, perhaps some armed Europeans."

"Ah." Ramzin digested this information. "Do they know we are coming?"

Svarzkova smiled. She had no reservations about the operation at all. "They are not sure. My superiors have made it clear to the former KGB divisions that they do not wish a war, and will take no action in retaliation. Our opponents may expect me to try to do something, but even that would most likely be investigative or through channels. They will certainly not expect a direct attack, much less you, Major, or the Americans."

Ramzin raised an eyebrow. "So. This is to be private venture?"

Svarzkova grinned. "Officially, anyway."

The major found himself smiling ruefully. "With FIS and GRU turning a blind eye to results."

Bolan smiled. "You catch on fast, Major."

Ramzin turned his attention to the FIS photo of Heidi Hochrein in her seductive pose and then leafed through the packet of blackmail photos. "You wish the woman taken alive for interrogation?"

Bolan nodded. "If possible."

"It will be difficult."

"We have advantages."

Ramzin raised an eyebrow. "Oh?"

"Speed, surprise and firepower," Bolan replied.

The major snorted. *Speed, surprise and firepower* were the words beaten into every Russian buck private from his first day of conscription and every day after. It was the unofficial motto of the Russian armed forces, and Russian military doctrine stated that with these three elements victory was assured.

Ramzin grinned and shook his head in amusement as he heard these words come from an American, and he held up his beer in salute. "Well, then. Victory is certain."

MACK BOLAN GIRDED himself for war. His close-fitting raid suit was a shade of navy blue that bordered on being black. Threat Level III body armor encased his torso. The Beretta 93-R and a .44 Magnum Desert Eagle pistol hung locked and loaded in their respective holsters under his arm and on his hip. A 9 mm Smith & Wesson snub-nosed Centennial revolver was snug in its ankle holster, and a Tanto fighting knife hung upside down on the webbing strap on his chest. The skeletonized handle of a double-edged boot dagger peeked up from one boot top. Across Bolan's knees rested an M-4 Ranger carbine with its M-203 40 mm grenade launcher mated to its forestock. Bandoliers of ammunition crossed his body.

Bolan glanced at the rest of his team.

Major Pietor Ramzin was almost a Russian version of Bolan. His massive upper body was sheathed in titanium body armor encased in fiberglass. He carried a 9 mm Stechkin machine pistol in a shoulder holster, and across his knees rested an AK-74 carbine with a BG-15 30 mm grenade launcher attached. Thrust through his belt was a massive Kindjal dagger. The eighteen-inch double-edged blade was the universal weapon of the Georgian people of the Caucasus Mountains. In its size and shape the weapon resembled nothing so much as the ancient Roman short sword. Russian military equipment was even to this day extremely Spartan. The average Russian soldier was thought to require only his rifle and the will to win. However, Ramzin was a special-forces veteran of the Soviet war in Afghanistan. In the brutal fighting among the cliffs and caves of that rugged country, the Russian special forces had rediscovered the need for handguns and edged weapons. Bolan glanced appreciatively at the massive knife.

Ramzin had obviously gotten in touch with his cultural roots somewhere along the line.

Captain Valentina Svarzkova wore the same low-tech but effective Russian-made armor as Ramzin. Her Czech-made 9 mm CZ-75 pistol was strapped over her armor, and Bolan knew from past experience that a 5.45 mm PSM assassination pistol was secreted somewhere on her person, as well as an AK-47 bayonet with its handle scales and guard removed and the remaining steel tang wrapped in electrician's tape. Her main armament was more surprising. Standing up between Svarzkova's knees was a PPSh-41 submachine gun.

With its wooden rifle stock and drum magazine, the weapon was a museum piece. During World War II the Russians had manufactured more than five million of the weapons, and its high rate of fire had earned it the nickname of the "burp gun." The burp gun's rugged reliability, the high firepower of its 71-round drum magazine, and the magnum velocity of its 7.62 mm Mauser pistol chambering had endeared it to its users. By today's standards its technology was archaic, but its effectiveness couldn't be denied.

Svarzkova held the weapon with an easy familiarity.

Jack Grimaldi wore the same armor as Bolan and held a 45-caliber MAC-10 casually in his right hand, and a similarly calibered Colt Officer's Model pistol rode on his right hip. Gadgets Schwarz carried a 9 mm Heckler & Koch MP-5 submachine gun and carried a silenced 9 mm Beretta pistol strapped to his armor. Everyone carried a small assortment of grenades.

Their target was a dacha, a country house, in the woods outside of Moscow. The structure was a two-story affair, with a barn across the gravel driveway from the house. Bolan glanced at the aerial photograph that Colonel Degederov had provided. To his practiced eye, the dacha was obviously a safehouse. Trees close to the house had been removed and the underbrush cleared to give the occupants clear lanes of fire. The walls were made of stone and heavy timber and would resist small-arms fire. The windows on the first floor were few and small, while the upstairs windows gave commanding views around the house in all directions. The barn could probably house an entire platoon of security troops if needed.

Bolan and his team would literally be storming a fortress.

The Executioner examined a map of the area, and he didn't like the layout. A single road led up to the dacha, and it would undoubtedly be watched. As a safehouse for a faction of the KGB, the forest surrounding the area would most likely have intruder-detection systems, perhaps including lethal booby traps. Bolan considered the van they had appropriated.

He didn't like the idea of driving close and trying to sneak in. They were outnumbered and didn't know the terrain, which left too many advantages to the enemy.

"This won't work," Bolan stated.

"It was best I could do on such short notice. I don't know another way in," Svarzkova replied.

Bolan nodded. "I know. But we can't afford to go stumbling in and hope for the best. I want total surprise."

Ramzin scratched his chin. "I agree."

The Executioner studied the map again, then looked up at Grimaldi, who was grinning. They were both thinking the same thing. Bolan tapped his finger on top of the aerial photo of the dacha. "We need an air assault."

Svarzkova bit her lower lip in thought. "Helicopter?"

Schwarz frowned. "I don't like it. They're not expecting us, but they must at least be on a semi-state of alert. Planes fly overhead all the time, and no one looks up. Helicopters have a distinct sound, and they attract attention."

Ramzin nodded in agreement. "This is true. When I ran smuggling operation in Arizona, seeing or hearing helicopters always made me nervous. Even when they were far away. I believe our opponents will be in same frame of mind."

Bolan sat back in his seat. They had answered their own question. "Even if we insert by helicopter, we'll have to do it far enough away that they won't hear it. We still run the risk of trying to sneak through whatever security measures they have along the road or in the forest. I want to circumvent all that." Bolan stabbed his finger onto the dacha. "We're jumping in. Right on top of them. We need a plane."

Svarzkova blanched.

Ramzin frowned. "A good plan in theory. But after attack, many KGB factions will be investigating. The ears of the KGB are everywhere. If they learn we used a military flight, the cat will be out of the bag, as you Americans say. We could not get a military drop flight without direct GRU aid. The war the leaders fear between the GRU and the former KGB will become a reality."

Grimaldi frowned. "We could charter a flight."

Ramzin sighed. "You would be putting that individual in danger. KGB was famous for vindictiveness."

"Well, then," Bolan said, "we'll just have to hijack one." Valentina Svarzkova was as white as a sheet.

Bolan raised an eyebrow. "You don't like the plan?"

"No. It is excellent plan."

"You don't like the idea of hijacking a civilian plane?"

"No. It is very creative."

Bolan spread his hands. "Then what?"

Svarzkova looked at the tips of her boots and wouldn't meet the Executioner's eyes. "I have never parachuted from plane."

"Don't worry. You'll love it. Everybody does."

10

Stefan Artyshenko wasn't happy.

He sat in the cockpit of his Anatov An-2 Colt biplane and wanted desperately to wipe the sweat from his eyes. Artyshenko's problem was that he was too terrified to move his hands. He slid his gaze to the copilot's seat and swallowed with difficulty. The black muzzle of a silenced machine gun looked back at him, and over its sights, the American's insane grin shone out of the black greasepaint smeared over his face. Artyshenko shuddered as the thin man's eyes glittered at him.

"You know, Artie, this is a fine plane you've got here."

Artyshenko's voice shook as he replied, "Yes. I enjoy it very much."

Grimaldi was right. The Anatov An-2 Colt was indeed a fine plane. The Colt was the last production biplane-wing aircraft in the world. The lift from its twin sets of wings and rugged construction allowed it to take off and land from very short and very rough runways. Its spacious interior could easily carry a dozen passengers or a remarkably heavy load of cargo. In Russian and Russian-allied service, the single-engine biplane had been a light transport, paratroop trainer, target tug, observation plane, fire water-bomber, air ambulance and, in the war in Bosnia, the Croatians had even used it successfully as a light-attack bomber.

Stefan Artyshenko had flown An-2 Colts for the Russian air force in many of these duties. With the fall of the Communist regime, Artyshenko had convinced friends and family to help him lease a surplus An-2 from the government. With the new free-market economy in Russia, someone in Moscow always needed something shipped somewhere, preferably yesterday, and Artyshenko had found overnight light transport a lucrative business. He now owned the plane he had once leased, and was planning on buying another. In the course of affairs, he had been offered many illegal payloads, as well. He had always politely refused. Artyshenko loved flying, and the Russian *mafiya* was the kind of trouble he didn't need.

Heavily armed Americans hijacking him and his plane in the middle of the night was something he had never factored into the equation. Artyshenko considered his situation again nervously.

Once they had taken off, one of the Americans had very efficiently rendered his radio temporarily out of service. Two large men and a woman were back in the cabin, and all of the Americans were armed as if for World War III. The thin man sat with Artyshenko in the cockpit. The Russian couldn't help but notice the way the grinning man looked at the control panel and told him what headings to take. Artyshenko suspected with a high degree of certainty the man was a pilot, which wasn't good. It meant Artyshenko might be expendable.

Jack Grimaldi looked up above the control panel, and his eyes widened slightly. In a niche between panels, Artyshenko had wedged a well-thumbed copy of Richard Bach's *Biplane*, which his girlfriend had given him, and a cross that had been given to him by his mother.

"Hey! Artie! That's a great book!"

Artyshenko swallowed. Anyone who had read *Biplane* couldn't be all bad. He smiled with feeble hope. "Yes. I enjoy it very much."

Grimaldi glanced at his watch, then at the map across his knees. "All right, we have an ETA of five minutes. How are we doing back there, kids?"

Bolan glanced up from his task. "ETA five minutes. Roger that."

The Executioner went back to cinching straps. Once they had ascertained that Stefan Artyshenko was conversant in English, only Bolan, Grimaldi and Schwarz had spoken. With luck Artyshenko would think they were all Americans and report that to the police. With luck, that would be enough to save his life. The only person on the plane that looked unhappier than Stefan Artyshenko was Captain Valentina Svarzkova. She had gone from pale and sweaty when the plane had taken off to looking positively green.

She looked up at Bolan and spoke quietly but in abject misery. "I am not happy."

Bolan gave her a sympathetic smile. "I know."

The GRU agent looked very close to tears as she glanced around herself helplessly. "I do not want to jump out of the plane."

"I know."

Svarzkova looked down at her boots and shook her head. "I hate you."

"I know."

Bolan finished connecting the tandem jump rig to himself. "All right, turn around."

The captain turned woodenly, and Bolan began to strap the Russian woman into the tandem rig, back to stomach. He always liked to have at least one tandem rig anywhere he was having parachutes deployed for him. They were useful for jumping someone who was wounded, or for people who had never jumped out of a plane before. When he had been given the word to go to Moscow, Bolan had instructed Barbara Price to have a full complement of gear delivered to the U.S. Embassy. He tightened the straps and gave them a few test tugs.

He leaned forward and spoke in Svarzkova's ear. "Okay, remember, I'll control the fall. All you have to do is arch your back like I showed you until I hit the chute."

Svarzkova spoke in a condemned voice. "All right."

Bolan had never seen the Russian agent so subdued. "Oh,

one other thing. Try to stop screaming once we get below a thousand feet. The enemy may hear you."

Svarzkova turned her head and stared at Bolan, utterly appalled.

Bolan cleared his throat. "That was a joke."

She bowed her head and clutched the submachine gun strapped to her chest. "I won't scream."

"One minute!" Grimaldi called from the cockpit.

Schwarz and Ramzin rose from their seats. Grimaldi would be the jump master and leave the airplane last. Bolan and Svarzkova would go first, then the rest of the team would follow. Grimaldi checked his watch, then their speed as he navigated by instruments. Ramzin opened the door, and cold air blasted into the cabin.

Grimaldi roared over the noise. "We are over target! Go! Go! Go!"

Svarzkova gave one sharp whimper as Bolan stepped through the door, then they tumbled out into the black Russian night.

Ramzin stepped out after them, followed by Schwarz.

Stefan Artyshenko craned his head around as the thin man left the cockpit and quickly clipped his weapon to his jump rig. He strode to the door and flashed Artyshenko one last wide grin.

"Great flying with you, Artie!" Grimaldi dropped through the door backward and shot the dumbfounded Artyshenko the thumbs-up as he shouted the extreme-skydiving salute, "See ya!"

BOLAN PULLED the big tandem chute's toggles to adjust his course. The dacha was lit below him with several outside lights, and light streamed from several of the unshuttered upstairs windows. As good as her word, Valentina Svarzkova hadn't screamed, but she hadn't managed to arch her back, either. Once outside the door, she had yanked her arms and legs into herself and shuddered like a spider about to be crushed. It made maneuvering in free fall slightly more difficult, but when he had deployed the chute she had sagged in her straps and gone limp.

Bolan reached a hand up to his brow and pulled his night-vision goggles over his eyes. The grounds around the dacha lit up in the view of the light-amplifying lenses. No light came from the barn, and hopefully that meant it was unoccupied. An extra squad of ex-KGB paramilitary types might just ruin the whole evening. As Bolan examined the grounds from above he could clearly see the starlike pattern of infrared laser beams that protected the immediate area around the dacha. The beams would be invisible to the naked eye, and anyone passing through one would break a beam and set off the alarms within.

The Executioner angled his descent so that they would land within the perimeter of the dacha's external security measures. They would be landing nearly on top of the country house, and for the brief moments after landing, the team would be terribly vulnerable while they cut their chutes and drew their weapons. The M-4 carbine was strapped to Bolan's side, but he couldn't maneuver or release his gear with the double weapon in his hands. He reached down awkwardly to his left side and unholstered the Beretta 93-R. Svarzkova squirmed against him, then heard the click-clack of a weapon's bolt being racked.

The ground came up swiftly. No lights shone from one side of the house, and Bolan angled toward it, pulling back on the control toggles. He whispered in Svarzkova's ear. "Lift your legs."

The Russian agent lifted her knees into her chest as Bolan pulled the toggles full back and stalled the chute. For a second the two of them hung almost motionless a foot above the ground, then the chute collapsed and Bolan bent his knees as he took all of their weight. It was a textbook tandem landing.

Even as Bolan released Svarzkova from the rig straps, he heard the light flutter of another chute. The woman crouched with her weapon and covered the house as the rest of the team descended out of the night sky. Ramzin came to a running halt ten yards away, but still well within the infrared alarm beams. Schwarz came in almost on top of him. Bolan holstered the Beretta and shrugged out of his straps. He took the safety off his M-4 carbine as Grimaldi spiked a perfect landing behind Ramzin.

Bolan scanned the area. There was no movement or sound. Apparently they had landed undetected. They quickly wadded their parachutes and moved in a string to the back of the house. Light streamed from a thin horizontal window, and Bolan immediately detected the smell of coffee.

The kitchen would be as good a place as any from which to mount their assault.

The Executioner moved along the wall at a crouch and reached the back door, which he examined critically. It was almost medieval looking, with heavy oak timbers and reinforced with metal bands. The door would undoubtedly be barred from the inside, and it would probably take a satchel charge to blow it open. Fortunately it was an old-fashioned oaken door, and its heavy iron hinges were on the outside. With time, effort and proper tools, the hinges could probably be removed quietly. Bolan grimaced. Time was in short supply, and if there wasn't an alarm wire attached to at least one of the hinges from the inside he'd be surprised.

Bolan turned and jerked his head at Grimaldi and pointed at the door. The pilot reached behind his back and slid the "key-master" out of a sheath as he came forward.

Special-forces units had been using shotguns as entry devices for more than a decade. The usual method was a 12-gauge slug applied directly to the hinges of the door. It was a reliable method, but it was very noisy and sometimes took several tries.

As the resident weaponsmith at Stony Man Farm, it was John "Cowboy" Kissinger's duty to come up with solutions to these problems. Kissinger's answer had been simple—more power. He had simply taken a double-barreled 10-gauge shotgun and sawed the barrels down to the foregrip and removed all of the stock except for a vestigial pistol grip. Loaded with Magnum slugs, the key-master threw over 1.75 ounces of lead per barrel, which at 1280 feet per second delivered a ton and a half of point-blank muzzle energy into a stubborn hinge. Its recoil and muzzle-blast were horrendous, but the key-master was brutally effective.

A flexible linear charge would have been more efficient, but they were deliberately going in like a bunch of Yankee cowboys. Bolan waved Ramzin forward to enter with him. Grimaldi positioned himself to the side and pointed the key-master at the top hinge.

"Do it," Bolan said quietly.

The night lit up in a thunderclap of orange flame as Grimaldi fired the weapon, and the wrought-iron hinge twisted under the massive impact. The pilot took a step back from the recoil, then shoved the sawed-off shotgun toward lower hinge and fired the other barrel. Bolan and Ramzin threw their shoulders against the massive door. Wood shrieked as the mangled hinges tore out of their moorings and the door flew backward into the kitchen.

A man sitting at a small table had half risen out of his seat. He threw back the bolt of an AKR automatic carbine, and Bolan put a 3-round burst from the M-4 into his chest. The gunner toppled backward over the back of his chair. As Bolan and Ramzin moved forward, the big American shouted for Svarzkova to kill the lights.

The dacha was set up like a fortress. The power lines were buried underground, and the fuse box was inside. Like most such setups in Europe, the fuse box was in the kitchen. Svarzkova raised her machine gun, and the ancient weapon let out a snarl like ripping canvas as it poured fire into the metal door of the fuse box. Sparks shrieked from the panel, and the lights in the house pulsed and went out. The rest of the team pulled their night-vision goggles over their eyes.

The dacha was plunged into darkness. In the view of their night-vision equipment, the interior of the house was a flat, eerie greenish gray. For the occupants the house would be pitch-black. It gave Bolan and his team an ugly advantage, but their opponents were ex-KGB paramilitary soldiers, and they were harboring terrorists. There would be no quarter asked, and none given.

There were two doors, one on either side of the kitchen, and Bolan and Ramzin split to cover them. The Executioner moved through the far door at a crouch with Svarzkova covering him. Yelling came from the next room, and as Bolan rounded the corner a long wild burst from an automatic weapon stitched the wall and ceiling above him. Three men were in the room, and two held weapons.

The big American put his front sight on the man who was firing and sent a burst climbing up his chest. The man staggered back into one of his companions as Bolan shot him again. The third man saw the muzzle-flash and turned his weapon in the Executioner's direction.

From the far side of the room, Ramzin's rifle opened up on full-auto, and the man shuddered as he was hammered to the floor. The remaining man grabbed his wounded compatriot and held him in front of himself as a shield. Bolan raised his sights for a head shot. Ramzin apparently had the same idea, and the man and his shield collapsed as bursts of rifle fire tore through his head and shoulders.

There was more yelling toward the front of the house.

Bolan and Ramzin moved into the room as the rest of the team covered them from the doorways. Svarzkova suddenly yelled, and loosed a burst from her submachine gun. "The stairs!"

The Executioner tracked his muzzle upward. There were no actual stairs, but there was an upstairs balcony and a man crouched behind the railing. He held an automatic rifle with a long tube attached beneath the barrel, and the room suddenly flared with incandescent light. The man didn't have a grenade launcher. There was a powerful searchlight attached to his rifle, and the light-enhancing night-vision goggles made the beam seem as bright as the sun. Bolan couldn't see the man behind the light, but he could hear Grimaldi and Schwarz swearing and the curses of the Russians. The night-vision goggles Svarzkova and Ramzin wore weren't as state-of-the-art as his, and they had probably solarized. Bolan heard the rifleman on the balcony open fire.

The big American pointed his weapon directly into the brilliant ball of light and fired the 40 mm M-203 grenade launcher. The light on the balcony went out as the ex-KGB gunman took the full brunt of the lethal storm of lead.

Bolan blinked away the spots of light and quickly scanned his team. Ramzin swore and pulled off his goggles. The lenses had solarized, and they would be useless for the next several seconds. The Executioner's gaze moved to the Russian's side. On his left chest two holes had tufted the fiberglass sheath covering his titanium armor, and a dark stain was spreading on his left biceps. Svarzkova had shoved her goggles onto her forehead and was blinking and shaking her head. The men from Stony Man were up and ready.

The soldier spoke low as he reloaded another round in the M-203 and slipped a fresh magazine into the carbine. "Svarzkova, Ramzin's hit. Stay with him. The rest of you, come with me."

Schwarz and Grimaldi fell in behind Bolan. The Executioner jerked his head at the balcony. "Discourage whoever else might be up there."

Grimaldi removed a grenade from his webbing and pulled the pin. He lobbed the grenade up and over the dead man at the railing and into the darkness beyond. The team moved on as the grenade detonated and metal fragments hissed and tore through the air overhead.

Bolan pulled a frag grenade of his own and pulled the pin as they moved down a hallway. As the hallway opened up into a room, the Executioner tossed the bomb around the corner.

It hit the floor with a dull thump, and automatic weapons tore into the hallway just in front of Bolan's team. A second later the grenade detonated, and men screamed as metal fragments tore outward in a lethal arc.

The Americans moved into the room. Two men were down and moaning. A third staggered, a machine pistol waving drunkenly in his hand. The M-4 carbine rattled in Bolan's hands, and the man jerked and fell as he took three rifle bullets at point-blank range.

Suddenly the house was eerily quiet.

Bolan glanced back at the sound of footsteps coming down the hall. Svarzkova and Ramzin had their goggles back on. Ramzin's rifle was slung, and his left arm was tied to his chest with a field dressing. In his right hand he held his Stechkin machine pistol at the ready. Bolan nodded. Russian soldiers had a justifiable reputation for toughness.

He jerked his head at the stairs. "Ramzin, Svarzkova, follow me. Gadgets, Jack, clear the top floor."

Grimaldi moved up the stairs while Schwarz covered him. Bolan strode through the room and moved to the other hallway. There were two doors in the hall and one at the end.

Bolan nodded at Svarzkova. "Cover the hall."

The Russian agent moved ahead and covered the second two doors. Bolan and Ramzin moved to the first. The Executioner leveled his weapon and nodded at the former major. "Kick it."

Ramzin put his massive boot into the door and twisted to one side as Bolan entered and fired the M-203. The Executioner entered behind the swarm of buckshot and swept the room with the muzzle of his carbine.

The room was empty.

They moved to the second door, and again Ramzin kicked it and Bolan entered, this time on the heels of a frag grenade. The room was empty. Svarzkova kept her weapon trained on the door at the end of the hall. They moved toward the last door, and gunfire erupted from upstairs. A moment later they heard breaking glass. Bolan kept his weapon on the door and spoke into his throat mike.

"What's happening up there?"

"We've got two down," Schwarz replied. "Top floor is clear. One tossed a chair through a window and jumped." There was a moment's pause. "Our friend is up. He's dropped his rifle and is limping toward the woods. You want us to take him out?"

Bolan gave it a half second of thought. "No, shoot at him, but let him go. Make sure you yell at him in English."

"Roger that."

A moment later a pair of unsilenced handguns began to bark, and two voices started to shout. "Son of a bitch! Kill the Commie bastard! Get him!"

As Bolan kicked the door in front of him, Svarzkova tossed in a grenade. The walls shook as the bomb detonated, and the Executioner entered the room. Other than a fold-out bed and a few pieces of furniture, the room was empty. They had cleared both floors.

Heidi Hochrein was not to be found.

Bolan's gaze narrowed. "The barn."

He spoke into his mike. "Gadgets, Jack, get to an east window and cover the barn. Shoot anyone coming out."

"Roger that."

Svarzkova frowned. "Why would she be in barn?"

Bolan shrugged. "Why not? But I'm betting she wasn't until we hit this place."

Ramzin nodded grimly. "Ah, you suspect tunnel."

Svarzkova glanced about. "Where?"

The Executioner grabbed the edge of the fold-out bed and flipped it up with a yank. Beneath it the rug was huddled in a heap as if someone had been unable to spread it back in place. He kicked the rug out of the way, and a small square door was revealed.

"Ramzin, cover this hole, but don't try to open it. In Berlin the last hole we checked out was booby-trapped. Just shoot anyone who comes out of it.''

The former major nodded and positioned himself in a corner to cover the trapdoor with his machine pistol.

"Jack, get down here. We're going to take the barn. Gadgets, cover us from upstairs.''

Bolan and Svarzkova moved to the front of the house as Grimaldi came downstairs. Schwarz's voice rose slightly with urgency over the radio. "We have lights on in the barn.''

The three of them fanned out of the front door. Bolan pointed at the rear of the barn, and Grimaldi broke off to cover any escape from the rear. The Executioner loaded a grenade into the M-203 as he and Svarzkova spread out to put the big barn door in a cross fire.

"Be ready. I'm going to try and flush them out,'' Bolan said.

Svarzkova knelt behind a tree stump by the gravel driveway and put her sights on the wide double door. "I am ready.''

The M-203 thumped and shot out pale yellow fire as Bolan squeezed the trigger. The 40 mm grenade punched through the boards of the barn door with ease and sailed inside. The Executioner quickly reloaded and fired another round through the door. He slid a frag into the breech and waited.

Both CS rounds had penetrated the door and would now be spewing tear gas in thick clouds. Bolan could already see gas start to seep like fog from the cracks between boards in the walls of the barn. Without gas masks the interior of the barn would become unbearable.

The Executioner snapped his carbine to his shoulder as he heard the sounds of engines snarling into life. "They have vehicles! They're going to make a break for it!''

A powerful engine roared and gears ground inside the barn. The door buckled, and a Russian military troop truck smashed its way out of the barn in a cloud of gas. A man leaned out of the passenger's window and fired a machine pistol. The Executioner squeezed the M-203's trigger.

The 40 mm frag grenade hit the truck dead on and detonated in a flash of fire, but the hissing metal fragments weren't enough to disable the charging truck's engine.

Svarzkova rose into the middle of the gravel driveway and held her machine gun in the hip-assault fire position as she held down the trigger. The weapon cut loose a long stream of fire as the truck accelerated straight at her. The muzzle of her gun rose inexorably from the grille to the windshield as she stood grimly in front of the oncoming truck and burned the entire 71-round magazine into it.

There was no time to load another grenade. Bolan took aim and began to fire bursts from his M-4 carbine into the cab of the truck. The man in the passenger's seat sagged in the window, and the Executioner aimed past him for a shot at the driver. The man behind the wheel hunched below the dash and kept his dead compatriot between himself and his attacker. The truck wasn't stopping. Svarzkova dropped her spent submachine gun and drew her pistol. Sparks shot off the roof of the vehicle as Schwarz fired down on it from the upstairs window.

Bolan's carbine cycled dry, and he tossed it aside as he drew the .44 Magnum Desert Eagle from his hip and lunged onto the gravel driveway. The Executioner took the pistol in a firm two-handed hold and began to fire as fast as he could pull the trigger. The upper engine compartment and the dashboard were no match for the .44 Magnum armor-piercing rounds. The heavy, steel-jacketed conical bullets punched through iron and sheet steel and found the driver. Bolan continued to fire as the truck suddenly swerved toward Svarzkova.

The Russian agent dashed to one side and continued to fire her pistol through the driver's door. The truck slowed and slammed to a rebounding halt against a thick stump. Steam rose from the radiator, and nothing moved behind the shattered windshield.

Tires screamed inside the barn.

Bolan dropped the spent Desert Eagle and drew his 9 mm Beretta. A black Russian ZIL sedan with tinted windows tore out of the barn in low gear. He raised his weapon and fired a burst into the windshield, which caused the sedan to swerve and accelerate toward the truck. The Executioner fired again, and the driver put the truck between himself and Bolan's fire.

Svarzkova continued to shoot, but her pistol clacked open after three rounds. She clawed for her backup as she dived out of the way of the speeding car.

The sedan came around the truck with its accelerator floored. Bolan fired a string of bursts into the speeding car as it passed, but the vehicle didn't slow. The Beretta cycled dry, and Bolan ejected the spent magazine and reached for a spare. Svarzkova's tiny PSM assassination pistol spit futilely at the receding lights of the car as it sped out of the long gravel driveway and onto the road.

Bolan switched to semiauto and fired carefully aimed shots between the swiftly diminishing red taillights. The lights winked between the trees and were gone. He took a deep breath and let it out slowly, then spoke into his throat mike.

"Jack, any movement behind the barn?"

"I've got zip. Maintaining position."

Bolan glanced up at the second-floor window of the dacha. "Gadgets, any movement from your vantage?"

Schwarz's voice was as calm as always. "Nothing moving. Maintaining position."

"Ramzin, anything?"

"No. Nothing has moved." The Russian paused. "You wish me to maintain position?"

"Yeah. Stay in position. Once the gas clears, we'll check the tunnel and work our way up to you."

"Understood."

"Are you all right?"

Ramzin grunted noncommittally. "Bleeding is under control."

Bolan strode over to Svarzkova. "You get a look at the driver?"

"Yes. The glass was dark, but much of it was smashed out

by bullets. I saw the Hochrein woman and a man. I think you hit the man.''

The soldier holstered the Beretta and scooped up the Desert Eagle. He frowned as he picked up the Ranger carbine and loaded a fresh magazine and 40 mm grenade into the dual weapon. Heidi Hochrein was becoming an ongoing problem. "Check the back of the truck," he said to Svarzkova. "I'll check the cab."

The two men inside were dead. One hung from the passenger's window, and one was crumpled under the steering wheel. Svarzkova's voice suddenly broke out into a shout. "Come! Come quickly!''

Bolan rounded the truck with the Beretta in his hand. The GRU agent stood in the tailgate and looked inside the canvas-covered cargo bed. She vaulted into the back and followed her gaze.

Two six-foot-long crates were lashed down to cleats in the truck bed. Both crates bore a large marking painted on the tops and sides. The design featured a circle, and within it was a trefoil. The marking looked like a black propeller with three blades.

It was the international symbol for radiation hazards.

Bolan pulled his fighting knife and slit the belts that held one of the crates, then shoved the chisel point under the crate lid. He moved along the crate, and when he reached the end he bore down on the hilt of the knife. The crate lid popped free of its nails. Bolan tossed the lid and stared down. A long gray cylinder sat in a nest of plastic packing material. The radiation-hazard symbol repeated itself on both ends of the cylinder, and heavy steel bands sealed it shut. There was a small set of block letters next to the radiation-hazard symbol: PU-239.

The cylinder contained plutonium.

11

Mack Bolan sat in the briefing room of the United States Embassy in Moscow. Within the past twenty-four hours the situation hadn't improved. Valentina Svarzkova peered at the tabletop and thought her own thoughts. Major Ramzin wasn't present. He had protested, but his left biceps muscle had been severed by a rifle bullet and would require immediate surgery to be reattached. He might never regain the full use of his left arm.

Colonel Ozhimkov of the GRU and Colonel Degederov of the Foreign Intelligence Service were both present, and once again the ex-KGB colonel was in civilian clothes and had taken a circuitous route to the embassy to avoid detection. The CIA Moscow station chief looked around the table with a furrowed brow. He had only been let in on the situation a few hours earlier, and things still hadn't been explained to him to his satisfaction. He looked at the sketchy file that had been prepared for him.

"So, this Hochrein woman, she escaped?"

Bolan nodded. "That's correct."

"I see." The station chief wasn't sure that he did. Mostly he was aware that the United States operatives he had no files on had just run a paramilitary operation in conjunction with the GRU with help from the Foreign Intelligence Service. Their targets were ex-KGB internal-security troops who seemed to be harboring German terrorists. Worse, no one had seen fit to keep the station chief informed.

He peered at the photo of Heidi Hochrein. "Do we know where she is now?"

Bolan looked at Colonel Degederov, who shook his head. "No. I don't know where she is."

"Can you find out?" Bolan asked.

The colonel blinked, then his expression set into steely resolve. "I'm sorry, but I can be of no more help to you in this matter."

The Executioner held the man's gaze for a moment. Degederov had stuck his neck out for them. Bolan had few illusions about his motives. The colonel had done it to avoid a war with a rival service, a bloody war that his side might well have lost. The danger to Degederov and his organization was past, and an unsavory element had been struck down. The colonel's duty in the matter was finished in his own eyes. Threats and recriminations would have no effect on the man.

Bolan nodded. "I understand, and the government of the United States thanks you for your cooperation."

The soldier swiftly changed the subject. "How did our ruse go over with the internal-security types?"

Degederov seemed only too pleased to talk about something else. "Very well. According to my sources the pilot, Stefan Artyshenko, reported to the authorities that his plane was hijacked by armed Americans. I was also able to ascertain that one of the paramilitary soldiers at the dacha escaped, as you said. He reported to his superiors that he and his comrades were attacked by individuals speaking English and armed with Western weapons. I believe that the ruse has worked. I believe my counterparts from internal security will believe it was a retaliatory strike by Americans for the attack on yourself and Captain Svarzkova. I do not believe my branch will be implicated in assisting you. The war we feared between my branch and Colonel Ozhimkov's has been averted."

The station chief frowned. "But the Hochrein woman is still on the loose."

Degederov's eyes narrowed slightly. "Yes."

Bolan didn't want to engage in finger-pointing. "What can you tell us about the plutonium?"

Degederov shrugged. "I believe Colonel Ozhimkov can tell you more about that than I."

Ozhimkov cleared his throat. "Yes. Following Captain Svarzkova's radio report, we were able to run the serial numbers of the plutonium containers through our computers. The containers were manufactured in a plant outside of Omsk."

Bolan folded his arms. "The plutonium was stolen?"

Ozhimkov's eyes nearly disappeared under the dark shelf of his brow. "It is hard to say. According to our records it never existed."

"I thought all weapons-grade plutonium in Russia was closely monitored. I understand that some lots have been stolen and turned up on the black market, but by backtracking you should be able to determine its last location."

Ozhimkov nodded. "This is so. However, scientists in GRU employ were flown to the dacha last night after Svarzkova's radio message." Ozhimkov's look turned to one of puzzlement. "The plutonium in the canisters was not of weapons grade. According to our scientists, it was of low-purity industrial grade."

The CIA station chief scratched his head. "You're losing me."

Bolan wasn't a physicist, but he'd had more than one encounter with nuclear materials in his career. "It's a question of purity. Plutonium 239 doesn't exist in nature. People dig up uranium in mines and convert it into plutonium in nuclear reactors. To make fissionable materials out of it, which means to turn it into nuclear-weapons-grade plutonium, it has to be concentrated and purified, usually to at least ninety-five percent purity. To get that kind of concentration, you have to process it. Processing it is a difficult task. It takes a lot of very expensive machinery and scientists with teams of trained technicians who know exactly what they're doing."

The station chief didn't look any more enlightened. "How

would terrorists get access to the necessary scientists and machinery?''

"I believe such things are largely unavailable to them," Ozhimkov replied.

The CIA man shook his head in confusion. "So, Hochrein and her friends couldn't make a nuclear weapon out of the material that was recovered from the truck."

Degederov nodded. "It would seem very improbable."

"Well, if it's useless to them, why would they be carting the stuff around?"

Degederov smiled dryly. "That is a very interesting question."

"Well, maybe they're just boneheads and don't know any better."

A ghost of a smile passed across the Executioner's face. The fact that the average terrorist wasn't exactly the sharpest knife in the kitchen had always been a trump card in dealing with them. The smile died as Bolan regarded the station chief.

"I'm not willing to bet any lives on that. I'm betting they knew exactly what they had, and they had something very specific in mind for it," Bolan stated.

The CIA man looked at Bolan in exasperation. "Like what?"

"I don't know."

If Ozhimkov could have frowned any deeper, his face might have collapsed in on itself. "There is something else you should be aware of."

Bolan turned. "What is that?"

"GRU investigating agents found a manifest in the truck carrying the plutonium." Ozhimkov's shoulders sagged. "According to the manifest, two similar shipments of nuclear materials have already gone out of the Russian Republic."

"So Heidi got away?" Kurtzman sounded surprised.

Mack Bolan sighed as he spoke across the satellite link. "Yeah, she did."

The link between Moscow and Virginia was extremely sharp. Bolan could hear Kurtzman shuffling through the photographs of Heidi Hochrein that had been duplicated and sent to the Farm. He could almost hear the wheels in the man's mind turning, as well.

Kurtzman spoke with grudging respect. "She seems very resourceful."

"She'd have to be to still be around this long." Bolan looked at the file in front of him. "She's been active since the early eighties. That's a long career for most terrorists, particularly a female one. Most of the women operatives are sacrificed during operations by their boyfriends or killed as liabilities. The fact that we know so little about her activities tells me she's been clever and highly useful to people who are willing to protect her."

"Like the KGB."

"The ex-KGB."

"You think the point is important?"

"Maybe." Bolan mulled the word over in his mind. There was still something that was eluding him. "Think about the people she's been working with."

"Well, when you first ran into her, she was in a Libyan camp."

"That's right, and more recently she's been engaged in some very mysterious activities with ex-East German border guards and ex-KGB internal–security troops."

"With *ex* being the operative word."

Bolan tapped his finger on Hochrein's photo. "So, what do they have in common?"

"A lot of them are out of work. Both organizations were basically internal-security troops, both groups' primary military activities were targeted at their own people."

Bolan pictured the individuals he had fought recently in his mind. "How would you characterize those kind of people?"

Kurtzman cleared his throat diplomatically. "How about politically extremist fanatics?"

"And who else does that describe?"

Kurtzman saw all too clearly where Bolan was going. "You're comparing them to terrorists."

"State-sanctioned terrorists."

"Yes, but state-sanctioned terrorists no longer sanctioned by the state. We're talking about extremist fanatics who are out of a job."

"Exactly," Bolan agreed.

"Yes, I see. It would take very little to motivate such individuals to engage in all sorts of illegal activities, particularly if they were cloaked in a political cause. They would have no problem working with international terrorists. Hell, many of them actively trained people like Heidi Hochrein."

Bolan nodded. "That's what I'm thinking."

Kurtzman's voice turned somber. "Well, that leaves us with the question of what they were doing with low-grade plutonium."

"I was hoping you might have some ideas on that."

"Well," Kurtzman replied, "I can't imagine how they would get access to facilities that could process it into weapons-grade material. You can't just drive up to a nuclear plant with a couple of truckloads of the stuff and process it in the middle of the night. Even if you have people on the inside, the job would take days, and I can't see them either bribing or fooling the entire staff of a nuclear plant."

Bolan nodded. "Neither can I. It would be easier to try to buy a weapon on the black market or try to steal one from somebody's stockpile."

"You'd think."

The Executioner stared at Hochrein's face again. "What else is low-grade plutonium good for?"

"Well, not much. Low-grade plutonium is more a step in a process than an actual product. You can make reactor rods out of it for use in nuclear power plants, or for use in the engines of nuclear-powered ships and submarines. You can use low-grade plutonium to make nuclear-isotope power supplies. It's literally a small nuclear battery. It's a common power source used in satellites. The link we're using now has an isotope power supply, but..."

Bolan frowned as Kurtzman trailed off. "But none of those seem like things political terrorists would care about."

"I'm sorry, Mack, but I really can't think of what they'd want it for unless somehow they have access to a plant that can process it."

"All right, Aaron, I need a list of every facility that could process the plutonium into weapons-grade material. According to our information, two shipments have left the Russian Republic. To narrow it down, let's assume the shipments are somewhere in Europe."

"We're looking at half a dozen countries and probably five times that many facilities."

"You'd better get busy," Bolan suggested.

"What are you going to do?"

"Do you have anything more deciphered from the Libyan disk?"

Kurtzman sounded subdued. "It's being stubborn."

Bolan came to a decision. "Until you do, we're still playing hunches."

"And what's yours?"

The Executioner looked at the photo of Heidi Hochrein. "In the morning I'm heading back to Berlin."

MACK BOLAN SLID the Beretta 93-R out of its holster and flicked the selector switch to 3-round burst mode. He wasn't expecting late-night visitors to come knocking on the door on his last night in Moscow.

"Who is it?"

A familiar female voice spoke through the door. "Room service. You ordered vodka and blond woman."

Bolan lowered the pistol and opened the door. Valentina Svarzkova stood in the doorway. She was wearing her black evening dress again. It was probably the only formal garment she owned other than her dress uniform, but she still looked stunning in it. She stood in the doorway and admired the hotel room's plush decor. "I was surprised to find you were staying at the Metropole." She peered past Bolan again. "Your government is paying for this?"

Bolan shrugged. "They gave me a discount rate after I was attacked on their front steps. I also wanted to steal some of their towels."

Svarzkova narrowed her gaze at him. Bolan grinned. "Officially I'm not in Moscow. I don't want to be at the embassy any more than I have to. The Metropole is convenient to the airport and the embassy, and it has a high level of security."

"Ah." The woman's face grew serious. "I would wish to go to Germany with you. My German is nearly as good as my English. However, I must stay here and continue investigation in Moscow."

"I figured as much."

"I have Colonel Ozhimkov's authority to share any information in my investigation that does not compromise security of the republic. Anything I find out in my investigation, I will have communicated to American Embassy in Berlin."

Bolan smiled. He knew from long experience it was best to have Russian Military Intelligence on your side rather than the other way around. "I'd appreciate that."

They looked at each other for a moment in an awkward silence. Svarzkova stood in the doorway and tapped her foot impatiently. "So…"

Bolan folded his arms. "So, where's the vodka?"

The Russian agent made a great show of looking surprised. "Oh! It is not here? Perhaps you should call and order again."

"Well, I was thinking about taking a shower." The Executioner gestured expansively at the bed. "But the phone is on the nightstand, and I believe the Metropole has an excellent late-supper menu."

Svarzkova's eyes glittered. Without hesitation she shrugged

off the straps of her black dress, and the slinky garment slid down her frame and puddled around her ankles.

Bolan raised an appreciative eyebrow. Captain Valentina Svarzkova wasn't wearing underwear.

The Russian agent grinned up at Bolan. "Bathe later."

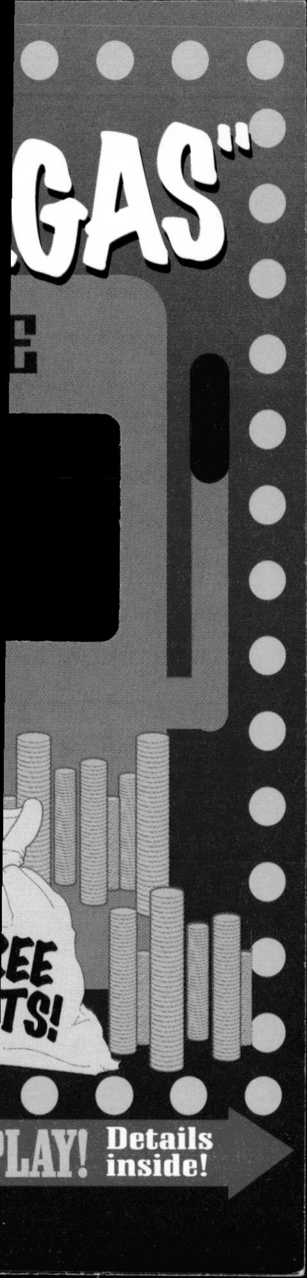
GAS"
PLAY!
Details
inside!

Play the

"LAS

3 FRE

FREE GIFTS!

1. Pull back all 3 tabs on t
   see what we have for you
   FREE!
2. Send back this card and
   never before published!
   they are yours to keep al
3. There's no catch. You're
   nothing — ZERO — for
   any minimum number of
4. The fact is thousands of r
   Gold Eagle Reader Servic
   they like getting the best
   and they love our discou
5. We hope that after receiv
   subscriber. But the choic
   all! So why not take us up
   You'll be glad you did!

Play the

"LAS VEGAS" Game

PEEL BACK HERE ▶
PEEL BACK HERE ▶
PEEL BACK HERE ▶

YES! I have pulled back the 3 tabs. Please send me all the free books and the gift for which I qualify. I understand that I am under no obligation to purchase any books, as explained on the back and opposite page.

(U-M-B-06/98)

164 ADL CGTA

NAME _____ (PLEASE PRINT CLEARLY) _____

ADDRESS _____ APT. _____

CITY _____ STATE _____ ZIP _____

GET 2 FREE BOOKS &
A FREE MYSTERY GIFT!

GET 2 FREE BOOKS!

GET 1 FREE BOOK!

TRY AGAIN!

Offer limited
to one per
household
and not valid
to current
subscribers.
All orders
subject to
approval.

PRINTED IN U.S.A.

▼ DETACH AND MAIL TODAY ▼

12

The old man stared coldly at the man he had placed in command. "The board is not pleased with the latest developments."

The young man returned the stare unflinchingly. "Neither am I."

The old man admired his subordinate's impertinence, but failure wasn't only intolerable; it would be disastrous. "What is the current situation?"

The young man steeled himself. The old man knew exactly what the situation was, but he wanted to hear it from the man he had personally recommended to take command of the operation. "Our operation was attacked in Moscow. We have lost one of the shipments of plutonium, and it is now in the hands of Russian Military Intelligence. The Hochrein woman once again managed to escape and report. The other two shipments are currently safe, and I will continue the operation, with your approval."

The old man's lips creased into a brief smile at an inner thought. "The German woman, she is very resourceful."

The young man was all too aware of the old man's predilection for large blond women. "Yes, she is a valuable asset."

"The attack in Moscow, Russian Military Intelligence was involved." The old man wasn't asking; he was stating a fact.

"It was, but I believe it was reacting to our attempt on the Russian woman agent we attempted to assassinate when she began investigating Heidi Hochrein's presence in Moscow."

"I have read reports that she was with an American at the time."

"Indeed." The younger man's frown deepened. "When she escaped from the safehouse outside Moscow, she reports she saw the same American who was in Libya and Berlin. He was shooting at her. She reports also that she visually confirms that the Russian woman agent, Captain Valentina Svarzkova, was there, as well. They also had several other accomplices of unknown origin. Other than that, they spoke English and carried Western weapons."

The old man scowled. "This is untenable. This man has tracked us from Africa to Europe and then into Russia. We must assume they have broken the disk's code."

"I disagree. If they had all the information off the disk, I believe they would have taken direct action."

The old man snorted. "I would call the attack on the safehouse a direct action."

"No, the American came to Moscow and received the help of the GRU in finding Hochrein. The American and the Russian agent survived our preemptive strike against them and counterattacked, I presume with the help of some branch of the former KGB. It is my opinion that our opponents have no real idea what is going on."

The old man's expression didn't change. "They have one of our shipments of plutonium."

"That is true. But low-grade plutonium is not all that difficult to replace."

An eyebrow rose on the old man's face. "Can you replace it swiftly enough to stay with the timetable?"

The commander of the operation frowned and shook his head. "Regretfully, no. However, we still have the other two consignments. We shall simply have to be satisfied with destroying two targets. I believe that the effect will be much the same, regardless."

The old man nodded thoughtfully. "The other two consignments are currently safe?"

"Yes, they are both in safe locations in Berlin."

"You will triple security."

The young man frowned and started to speak but the old man cut him off.

"Twice we have been attacked, in Libya and in Moscow. Twice we have tried to kill this commando and failed. Through luck or skill, he has managed to trail our operation. I will tolerate no more such interference."

The young man shook his head. "He does not know the consignments are in Berlin, much less where we are moving them to. Also, tripling security could draw attention."

The old man scowled. "Fool. The trail in Russia is cold. If I were he, I would return to Berlin. It is one of the great nexus points of Europe. I want you to assume he will go there. I want you to assume that he will have the aid of German Intelligence and the local authorities. Do not use the Grenztruppen again—we must assume such men will be watched by the authorities. Use other operatives. I want you to assume the commando is actively searching for us there. I want you to actively search for him, as well. In trying to locate us, he will undoubtedly be forced to reveal himself." The old man's voice dropped to a lower register. "When you find him, I want him killed."

The younger man controlled his anger and nodded. "I understand. I will continue the operation, and if the American is in Berlin, I will find him and have him killed."

Berlin, Germany

CAPTAIN DIETER RADTKE of the GSG-9 sat in his Berlin office and scanned the file he had been given. He looked up from the papers at Bolan and grimaced. "So. Hochrein escaped in Moscow?"

Bolan nodded.

The German shrugged, then winced as his shoulder moved. His left arm was slung against his chest where he had been hit with shotgun pellets during the firefight in Berlin. "She is a most slippery woman." He scratched absently underneath his sling. "You now believe she is back in Berlin?"

"It's a hunch."

Radtke nodded knowingly. Anyone who had survived active operations in special-forces units learned a deep and profound respect for hunches. "You say the Russians may have exported low-grade plutonium."

"We believe two truckloads. If they match the load we found outside of Moscow, they'll be in pairs of shielded containers, with each container holding approximately six hundred pounds of plutonium."

"You have a hunch that the plutonium is here in Berlin, as well."

The Executioner nodded. He had learned to respect his hunches, as well.

The GSG-9 captain's eyebrows drew upward in a quizzical expression as he looked at the file again. "What do you suppose they wish to do with low-grade plutonium?"

"I don't know. We're currently trying to establish a security net over the nuclear facilities in Western Europe."

Radtke snorted. "There are many such facilities in Europe, dozens in France and Germany alone. Even so, most of them already have extremely high levels of security."

Bolan was all too aware of this. "I know. It seems redundant. But at the moment it's the best we can do. What have you found from this end?"

The captain gestured at several files on his desk. "We have pulled the military files on all former members of the Grenztruppen and are having their current whereabouts and activities tracked. However, there were thousands of East German border-unit troops. It will be difficult to locate them all quickly, and perhaps impossible to watch all of them throughout Germany, even with the help of local police units. So, I am concentrating on those within the Berlin area."

The Executioner shook his head. "I think we should assume that our enemy knows that we are on to the Grenztruppen connection. I doubt they will use them actively in Berlin again, at least during whatever operation they currently have going."

The German put his chin in his palm. "You are undoubtedly right."

The Executioner had been in this kind of situation before. With little in the way of pursuable leads, his only real option was clear.

He was going to have to stick his head out and see who tried to blow it off.

"Excluding fanatical ex-Grenztruppen, who would you hire in Berlin if you wanted someone killed?"

Radtke chewed his lower lip speculatively. "Who do I want to have killed?"

"You and me."

HEIDI HOCHREIN SAT in a basement in a very bad part of Berlin. She had been rather intimately searched for a wire, and her Walther PP pistol had been taken from her. Twenty-five thousand deutsche marks had bought her an introduction to the man she now faced.

Under the light of a filthy single bulb hanging from the ceiling, she regarded the man in front of her in frank appraisal. He was huge. Massive arms and a broad chest strained the seams of his expensive silk shirt. His eyebrows formed a single, massive, hostile V-shape over black eyes that could only be described as sharklike. A thick, curled mustache drooped over a cruel mouth. Hochrein concealed a smile. If you had put the man on horseback in a turban and put a saber in his hand, he would look every inch the medieval Ottoman conqueror of southern Europe.

In a city with a large Turkish minority, Kemal Kose had the distinction of being known as "the Turk." Any Berlin police officer would know exactly who was being talked about if someone were to mention that moniker. Kose's status in the underworld of Berlin was taking on legendary proportions. In the past ten years, there had hardly been an illegal activity he hadn't engaged in to his profit in Berlin, and he had never been so much as cited for a parking violation.

The man's black eyes gazed down into Hochrein's almost expressionlessly. "You wish me to kill a member of the GSG-9?" His eyes narrowed slightly. "That is a very tall order, even for me."

"I also need you to kill an American commando working with him, and several possible accomplices."

"Ah."

Kose examined the woman. He didn't know her, but he liked what he saw. Her face and figure, particularly with the dark blue eyes, would fetch a high price in the Middle East white slavery market. He gazed at the low neckline of her straining sweater. She appealed to his own personal tastes, as well. She wasn't wearing a bra, and he had thoroughly enjoyed watching as his men had strip-searched her. He briefly ran the idea of breaking her to his will, then shipping her south to be some Saudi's pleasure slave. Kose enjoyed the mental image for a moment, then returned to the matter at hand. He considered himself a professional. Professionalism was what had kept him successfully in business for so long, and the woman had bought an introduction to him with a very substantial sum of German marks.

The woman herself also seemed very professional. She showed no fear in his presence, and no squeamishness at all while his men had searched her. Kose found the woman very intriguing, even if her proposal was outlandish. However, she seemed to be deadly serious about it, and he had yet to make up his mind about what he intended to do with her. He kept his tone reasonable.

"You understand, killing a member of the GSG-9 and some American soldier would not be difficult to arrange. However, the repercussions would be extremely serious, on both my business and myself. If it was learned that I was responsible, my career in Berlin, and probably all of Germany, would be over. Even if my complicity in the matter could not be proved in a court of law, I do not believe the GSG-9 would let the matter rest. If one of their members was killed, I believe they would seek private vengeance. I do not relish the idea of having to look under my bed every night for fear of having highly trained special-forces soldiers lurking underneath it with automatic weapons." Kose spread his hands. "To be honest, this is not the kind of trouble that I need."

Hochrein smiled and nodded. "Oh, I understand completely. Such an action would probably be your last in Berlin. You would undoubtedly have to leave Germany afterward." She turned up the wattage of her smile, and her deep blue eyes held Kose's gaze with their intensity. "You would have to be richly compensated."

Kose snorted. "I would have to be compensated enough to retire on."

The blue eyes veiled themselves demurely under heavy lashes. "And what kind of sum would that require?"

The Turk's black eyes widened slightly at the question. It was vaguely amusing to consider the proposition in the abstract, and for a moment he rolled the idea around in his head. "Oh, I should think at least five million in U.S. dollars, and that would be for myself alone, not counting expenses and the men required."

Hochrein leaned back in her chair. "Would five million U.S. dollars up front, and then five million more upon successful completion suffice?"

Kose leaned back, incredulous.

Hochrein's smile stayed warmly in place. "That does not include, of course, the money you would also receive in German marks for expenses and the hiring of men, as well."

The Turk swiftly regained his composure. "You are serious."

Hochrein's smile turned cold. "My employers are deadly serious."

The wheels in Kose's mind turned. "I would have to see the initial five million dollars before I did anything."

Hochrein nodded. "That can be easily arranged."

She watched as the Turk struggled to keep his poker face

as the idea of ten million dollars blurred his mind. She had done her research. It had been rumored that Kose had been thinking of getting out of the Berlin rackets, and she had also noticed how his eyes had crawled all over her body when she was being searched. She locked gazes with him, pulled her sweater over her head and tossed it casually to the floor. She noted with satisfaction the look that came into his eyes. She drew his eyes off her chest with her own and held his gaze as she ran a calculating tongue over her lower lip.

"What do I have to do to convince you?"

The Executioner covered the inside of the warehouse with his M-4 carbine. The selector was set on full-auto, and a 40 mm high-explosive grenade was loaded in the M-203 launch tube. Nothing moved in the flat grey-green tones of his night-vision goggles. He spoke in a tone so low it was almost inaudible.

"I don't like it."

Radtke crouched next to Bolan wearing full armor and cradling a Heckler & Koch VP-70 machine pistol with its plastic shoulder-stock holster attached to his good arm. His wounded left arm was slung tightly across his armored chest. With his night-vision goggles and "Fritz"-style helmet he looked like a giant mutant bug. He peered into the center of the warehouse and the truck that was parked there.

He shook his head. "No. I do not like it, either."

Bolan spoke into his throat mike. "Gary, what have you got?"

Gary Manning was on top of the building across the street. He surveyed the operation from above with the ten-power night-vision scope mounted on his M-21 semiautomatic sniper rifle. "I have no targets. Nothing is moving from my vantage."

Bolan frowned under the black greasepaint camouflaging his face. "David, anything?"

David McCarter and Jack Grimaldi were stationed by the back door of the warehouse. The Briton spoke softly across the radio. "No sound. No movement. No detectable heat signatures."

Bolan considered the situation. GSG-9 headquarters had received an anonymous tip that armed men were guarding something in a warehouse on Berlin's east side. Anonymous tips were a mainstay in regular police work. In the Executioner's world they always stank of a trap.

Gadgets Schwarz crouched behind the Executioner along with half a dozen heavily armed GSG-9 troopers. Schwarz peered down at what appeared to be a small laptop with several antennaes protruding from it. "I'm not getting anything. No devices are actively scanning the area." He cleared his throat softly. "But I wouldn't rule out the possibility of a radio controlled bomb."

Bolan nodded. The idea that they had been lured there to be blown up had occurred to him, as well. The Executioner lifted his head slightly as he breathed in the still air of the warehouse. He didn't smell any strong odor of diesel fuel, or the telltale smell of ammonium-nitrate fertilizer, which would indicate a home-made truck bomb. That didn't mean much. For all they knew, the canvas-covered bed of the military troop-transport truck could be loaded with a thousand pounds of sealed high explosive.

"I'm going to check out the truck." He turned and looked over his shoulder at Schwarz. "Do it."

Schwarz nodded and pressed a pair of keys in his laptop electronic-warfare suite. A green light began to blink on the panel, and all the team members had to turn down the gain on their personal radios as static yowled in their earpieces. In the radio-frequency spectrum the immediate vicinity of the warehouse had gone mad. Schwarz's "black box" was emitting a jamming signal that was sweeping up and down the civilian radio frequencies like a rolling wall of white noise. If there was a radio-controlled detonator in the truck, the destruct signal would have to pass through a hurricane of interference.

He gave Bolan the thumbs-up signal, and the Executioner

bent down under the rear wheel well and examined the bottom of the truck. There was no obvious tampering, and nothing appeared there that shouldn't have been present. Bolan checked the cab and under the hood, then moved to the back of the truck and looked inside the cargo area.

There were two long gray metal cylinders like the ones they had captured in the dacha outside of Moscow. Both cylinders were emblazoned with the universal-radiation hazard symbol, and both had PU-239 painted on them in block letters. The retaining straps holding down the cylinders had been cut. Both cylinders were open, and both were empty.

The Executioner stepped off the back of the truck. "Gadgets, bring the radiation detector."

Schwarz stepped forward, climbed into the truck bed and held a small plastic box over the opened cylinders. He nodded grimly as red numbers flashed across the tiny display. "I've got about twenty millirads."

"Which means?"

He shrugged. "Twenty millirads isn't dangerous to us standing here, but it's enough to confirm the cylinders recently held radioactive materials."

"Like low-grade plutonium?"

"Yeah, I'd say trace radiation of twenty millirads is consistent with low-grade plutonium in this kind of containment." He shone a flashlight into the containers. "I see trace dust, as well. I don't think we want anyone doing anything with these containers without protective suits and decontamination equipment."

The Executioner waved Radtke and his men forward from their covering positions.

The German captain lowered his machine pistol and peered quickly in the back of the truck as Schwarz closed the canvas flaps. "The containers are empty."

Bolan nodded. "Yeah, but we've determined that they were full."

"So, the plutonium has been moved."

Schwarz flicked off his radiation detector. "It would seem so."

Radtke frowned. "The retaining straps were cut and the containers left open. It appears the plutonium was moved in a hurry. The plutonium would be dangerous outside of the containers, would it not?"

Schwarz looked up. "Yes, it would. The plutonium we found in Russia was in pellet form. The trace dust I detected here tells me that this load was in pellet form, as well. Even in good containers the pellets grind against one another in transport. You would have to be very careful with it. The pellets would make you sick if you were exposed to them for long, and breathing in any of the dust would be unpleasantly lethal. It would require radiation-hazard suits and special loading and unloading equipment to move it."

The German scratched his chin. "Perhaps that is an angle we could use. Such things cannot be so readily available. Maybe we can trace them to here."

An icy thought came to the Executioner's mind. "I don't think so. If our friends were in a hurry, I don't think they'd want to waste time with it."

"What do you mean?" Radtke asked.

The Executioner's voice was grim. "I mean they probably hired some poor bastards to move the stuff and didn't tell them what it was. Captain, I think you should alert all hospitals in the east Berlin area to be on the alert for people displaying symptoms of radiation sickness."

Radtke spun about on his heel and began shouting orders in rapid-fire German to his men.

The two Americans looked at each other.

Schwarz shrugged. "What do you think?"

Bolan looked back at the truck. "Well, it looks like our friends bugged out."

"You're not totally convinced, are you?"

"No, I'm not. I think we may have stuck our necks out coming out here."

"You think we're being watched?"

Bolan nodded. "If you wanted to draw us out, that anonymous tip we got was the fastest way. We came over here and laid siege to the warehouse. If they're looking for us, they have us now."

Schwarz chewed his lip. "You think there might be an ambush?"

"Not right here or right now, and not when we've got half a platoon of GSG-9 with us. But if we're being watched now, then they can follow us and attack us when we're not ready and not armed to the teeth." Bolan folded his arms. "But if it's coming, it'll be quick—I'd bet tonight."

Schwarz folded his arms across his chest in return. "So?"

"So, I think we should take a few precautions."

KEMAL KOSE WAS PLEASED. "We have them."

Heidi Hochrein peered out the window through the binoculars. "Your men are prepared to follow them?"

"My street network is highly effective. I have people on every street corner and dozens of men in cars, on scooters, on bicycles and on foot. Unless a helicopter comes and picks them up, we will not lose them."

"Good. Your strike team is ready?"

"Indeed they are."

Hochrein frowned as Kose ran a hand over the seat of her jeans, but she didn't flinch away. She kept her binoculars trained on the gaggle of armed and armored men milling about the warehouse. "The GSG-9 man, Radtke, is a highly trained soldier. We know nothing about the Americans other than they are extremely dangerous. I hope you are using something more than your street thugs against them."

It was impudence, but Kose didn't mind. He liked the woman. He was particularly fond of the five million dollars in U.S. currency now in his possession in a Swiss bank account. He looked forward to another five million, and he looked forward to using the woman's body again. He smiled confidently.

"I have chosen twenty men, and all of them have served their eighteen-month conscription in the Turkish army. Two of them were sergeants." Kose casually cracked the knuckles of his massive fists. "All of them have killed men for me."

Hochrein nodded but didn't reply. Kose shrugged carelessly. "They are all armed with automatic rifles, and I have acquired a quantity of rifle grenades just for this occasion. We have surprise, we outnumber them and we will have superior firepower. They are dead men."

Hochrein lowered the field glasses and looked at Kose speculatively. "You are sure?"

Kose's smile turned feral. "I will kill the American myself."

BOLAN GLANCED across the table at Radtke. "How are we doing?"

The captain took a sip of his coffee and scowled at it. "Everything is in position."

The Executioner stared out into the night out of the diner window. The truck stop was a run-down affair just outside of Berlin. From the outside, the diner looked like little more than a shack beside the gas pumps. The captain had called ahead and had the place cleared. Two of his men were now dressed in coveralls. A tall blond man named Hans with a face like an anvil stood outside by the pumps. A shorter, darker soldier named Arnold stood behind the counter in the diner. Bolan and his team sat around one of the three small tables looking at a map. To anyone watching them out in the darkness, it would appear as if Bolan had taken his team outside of Berlin for some kind of private conference with the GSG-9 captain. The windows of the diner were wide, and the interior was lit with the sterile glare of overhead fluorescent lighting. Sitting in the tiny truck-stop, they presented almost ideal targets for an attack.

An occasional car drove by or stopped for gasoline, but luckily no one had stopped in for coffee or one of the unpleasant-looking plastic-wrapped sandwiches dispensed by a machine in the corner.

McCarter and Schwarz sat with Bolan and Radtke around the table. They were wearing street clothes, and none of them appeared to be armed. Looks were deceiving. Everyone wore Kevlar body armor under his jacket and each man was armed to the teeth. Gary Manning was on the roof with his M-21 sniper rifle for company. His voice spoke quietly in Bolan's earpiece.

"Motorcycle. Appears to be alone."

A moment later a BMW touring bike pulled into the station, and a rider dressed in motorcycle leathers parked and began to put gas in his tank. He left the nozzle in and walked toward the diner. The men around the table gave no visible sign as they went into a high state of alert. The biker removed his helmet as he walked in, went straight to the sandwich machine, slipped in some coins and pulled out a sandwich. Bolan watched as he walked back outside and paid Hans. Hans pocketed the money and looked back toward the diner with a shrug as the biker climbed onto his motorcycle and pulled out onto the road.

Bolan spoke into the microphone in the collar of his leather jacket. "Anything?"

The Executioner knew Gary Manning would be watching the rider drive away through the scope of sniper rifle. There was a slight pause on the radio link.

"Our boy is circling toward the freeway. He's stuck his sandwich inside his jacket. I don't think—" Manning stopped short. "Wait a minute. He's pulled up his visor. He has something in his hand. I think he's talking into it. I... He's out of range now."

The Executioner's eyes narrowed. "A radio?"

Manning's voice sounded positive. "A small black something, but yeah, I'd bet it was a radio."

Radtke put down his coffee. "We have something?"

Bolan nodded. "I think we've just been positively identified, and trouble is on the way."

Almost on cue, Manning said, "A van is pulling off the freeway and heading in."

Bolan slid his eyes sideways and saw the headlights. Manning spoke again. "Panel truck, coming in your direction."

Bolan watched a second pair of lights pull in. The van came to a stop at the parking area by the far set of pumps. A green panel truck pulled onto the lot and parked near the rest rooms.

The Executioner smiled thinly. The tiny diner was now in a cross fire between the two vehicles. Manning spoke again. "Car. Four passengers visible."

A BMW sedan pulled off the road and braked to a halt by the pumps. A thin man got out with a map in his hands and walked up to Hans. Another man got out and began to pump gas. A third grabbed the squeegee out of a bucket by the pumps and started to wipe down the windows. Bolan's gaze slid from vehicle to vehicle. His instincts spoke to him like an icy breeze down his back.

The attack would happen any second now.

At the pumps one man was still engaging Hans in conversation and pointing at a map. The man wiping the windows was using awkward strokes. Bolan's eyes slitted. The man was using his left hand. His right hand slid under his windbreaker.

The Executioner drew his .44 Magnum Desert Eagle and spoke into his collar. "The pumps!"

A small silenced automatic had appeared in the window-washer's hand, and he twisted around with practiced speed to point it at Hans.

A high-powered rifle cracked the night from the roof of the diner, and the man with the silenced pistol was hammered across the hood of the BMW. He slid off the hood and collapsed to the pavement. Hans and the man with the map both drew pistols and shot each other simultaneously. Hans was wearing body armor under his coverall. His attacker wasn't, and he collapsed as Hans shot him with his 9 mm P-7 pistol once in the chest and once in the head. Manning's rifle took out the man pumping gas as he drew a pistol, and a second later the windshield pebbled as he took out the driver.

The sliding door of the van and the panel truck flew open, and Manning's voice roared in Bolan's earpiece. "Grenades!"

"Shields!" Bolan reached behind him, and his hand closed around a metal handle. The heavy German police riot shield was made of nearly an inch of Lexan plastic sandwiched between sheets of steel, and it was rated to stop bullets from .30-caliber rifles. It was made to be used by policemen marching in lines as they approached armed mobs. The shield was much too heavy to be used in a running firefight, but in the static defense of the little diner it was the best life insurance they had other than personal body armor and the skill they had with their weapons.

Bolan kicked away his chair and he and his team crouched under the heavy shields. Outside, loud thumps rattled the windows of the diner. A second later the windows shattered and the interior of the diner exploded into armageddon.

He grimaced as the concussions of the grenades pounded his eardrums and rattled his bones. The shield Bolan held rattled and vibrated as razor-sharp bits of flying metal shrieked and sparked off its steel surface in a lethal storm. The overhead lighting shattered, and the interior of the diner suddenly darkened. Bolan smiled grimly. The enemy was using frags. If they had incendiaries or gas, it would get ugly very quickly.

A second salvo of rifle grenades flew through the shattered windows and detonated overhead. Metal fragments hissed down and scored the surface of their shields. Bolan forced himself to yawn and clear the ringing in his ears. He could dimly perceive the sound of many boots hitting the concrete outside. The sound of automatic-rifle fire was all too clear.

"I need you, Jack!" Bolan shouted into the microphone in his collar.

The pilot's voice sounded reassuringly near. "Inbound, Striker!"

The Executioner quickly scanned his team. No one was hurt. His voice rose above the din of rifle fire with the unmistakable thunder of command. "Now!"

The team rose. The heavy shields had a vision-and-firing slit cut into them, and it was guarded by a heavy steel shutter. Bolan shot the shutter back and slid through the barrel of the Desert Eagle. He grimaced and braced himself as the shield immediately began to take hits. The enemy was armed with German army Heckler & Koch assault rifles. The shields were rated against .30-caliber weapons, but holding the shield against multiple impacts from the powerful rifles wasn't an easy task, and the shield shuddered and vibrated in his grip as it was rocked by rifle fire. Bolan spread his feet into a wide, stable stance and pulled the shield tightly against his shoulder.

Through the slit Bolan could see well over a dozen men running forward with their rifles snarling on full automatic. He put the front sight of the Desert Eagle squarely on the leading man and fired. The rifle spun out of the gunner's hands, and he tumbled to the ground in a heap.

McCarter edged sideways and overlapped the edge of his shield with Bolan's. The Briton opened fire with his 9 mm Browning Hi-Power pistol, and a second later Schwarz slid the edge of his shield over McCarter's, as well. He began to unload his Beretta in a steady stream of aimed, semiautomatic fire through his firing slit.

Since ancient Rome the shield wall had been the foremost of defensive fighting formations. With iron discipline the Roman armies had withstood the charge of howling barbarian hordes and forged an empire. Several thousand years later, the men from Stony Man Farm stood with shields locked and fought shoulder to shoulder as bullets flew and the enemy swarmed forward in a human wave.

Dieter Radtke couldn't stand and hold his shield with his injured arm, but he knelt behind it and the muzzle of his VP-70 machine pistol spit burst after burst through the diner's shattered glass doorway. The other GSG-9 man, Arnold, stood behind the counter with his shield in his hand and fired his pistol through the window by the register.

The Stony Man team cut the enemy down as the gunners came. The interior of the diner was now darkened, but outside, the gas station was brightly lit and there was no cover for the charging men. More than half of the enemy was already down. If they'd had twice the manpower, they might have swamped the diner with their numbers before the Stony Man team could shoot them all. They didn't have enough men, and the men from Stony Man were some of the best fighters in the world.

The Desert Eagle clacked open on an empty chamber, and Bolan dropped it and drew his Beretta. He heard a voice outside roar, then there was a twin thumping sound. Some of the attackers had stayed back, and they were firing more rifle grenades. Bolan didn't have to shout a command. His team smoothly knelt together and raised their shields over their heads.

McCarter grimaced as the grenades detonated, and shouted in Bolan's ear, "They're trying to break contact!"

Bolan had already suspected this and spoke into his mike. "They're bolting, Jack!"

"They're not going anywhere."

The three men rose as one and locked their shields again. Outside, the surviving attackers had split into two retreating groups and were piling into the van and the panel truck. Over the sporadic gunfire Bolan could discern a steady vibration. A spotlight blazed into life overhead and lit up the gas station with an incandescent glare. A helicopter swooped low, and twin jets of flickering fire erupted with a sound like canvas being torn.

The German army BO 105 helicopter was a specially designed special-forces version. A powerful searchlight was mounted under its chin, and a pair of fixed 20 mm automatic cannons was mounted on each side of the landing skid. The doors on both sides of the helicopter were open, and a

GSG-9 soldier hung in each doorway on a chicken strap behind a .50-caliber machine gun.

The twin cannons drew a line of torn concrete in front of the panel truck while one of the door gunners swung his machine gun on its mount and drew a warning line in front of the van.

Manning's voice shouted over the line to Grimaldi. "Look out, Jack! On your six!"

From Grimaldi's position in the pilot's seat, the van was in the six o'clock position. Two men had leaped out and were bringing their rifles to bear on the hovering helicopter. Both weapons had grenades mounted on their muzzles.

Bolan, McCarter and Schwarz fired their pistols simultaneously, and on the roof Manning's rifle roared with them. The two men staggered in the withering cross fire, and the helicopter dipped its nose and surged forward with a roar from its turbocharged engines. One of the men fired his grenade before he fell to the ground, and the projectile shot upward past the helicopter. At hundred yards the grenade's fuse detonated, and there was a pulse of orange fire.

The van's tires squealed on the pavement as the driver floored it.

McCarter shook his head. "Jack isn't going to like that."

Bolan nodded. It seemed Jack Grimaldi didn't. The BO 105 helicopter suddenly spun on its axis and faced the van as it accelerated across the lot toward the road. The twin 20 mm Oerlikon cannons erupted into life, and the twin green lines of the tracers streaked directly into the van. The vehicle shuddered and came apart as high-explosive shells exploded into it at seven hundred rounds per second. Within moments the van was little more than a burning frame.

Figures desperately leaped out of the panel truck as the helicopter whirled about and turned the angry eye of its searchlight on it. Flames shot from the 20 mm muzzles of the cannons, and the panel truck rose up on its chassis as the HE shells blew it apart from the inside.

Bolan looked out across the truck-stop lot. Bodies littered the pavement, and the fluorescent lights competed with the fire from the burning vehicles. He glanced at Radtke and his man Arnold. Both of the Germans were unhurt and grimly surveying the scene. Outside, Radtke's other man, Hans, rose from behind the bumper of the BMW. He gave his commander the thumbs-up and covered the scene with his pistol.

"Let's see what we have," Bolan suggested to the captain.

KEMAL KOSE CRAWLED across the pavement. His head rang from the explosions, and he was bleeding from numerous small wounds where bits of the disintegrating panel truck had struck him. His rifle was a few feet away, and he reached for it.

A black boot kicked it away from his hand.

Kose looked up dazedly. A short, powerful man in a dark green uniform stood above him. One of the man's arms was strapped to his chest with a sling. In his other hand he held a machine pistol with an attached shoulder stock. The muzzle was casually pointed between Kose's eyes. The Turk recognized the man as Dieter Radtke, the GSG-9 captain he had been hired to kill. The German looked into Kose's face, and he suddenly grinned at Kose happily and then spoke in English to someone else.

"Why, it is the Turk himself!"

A man loomed over Kose. He was as large as Kose himself, and backlit by the flames of the burning truck he took on an almost inhuman appearance. In one hand he easily gripped a massive steel shield. In the other he held a pistol as if it were an extension of himself. From a smoke-streaked face, unblinking blue eyes looked down on Kose and regarded him with a gaze as cold as judgment.

Dieter Radtke smiled in a friendly fashion and spoke to Kose in German as the man gaped up at the Executioner. "Mr. Kose, if you do not give us your full and immediate cooperation, I will not be responsible for what this man does to you."

14

The German special-forces BO 105 helicopter streaked across the Berlin skyline. Jack Grimaldi banked the aircraft low over the German city in a race against time. Beside him Captain Dieter Radtke sat in the copilot's seat and spoke rapidly into the radio. Back in the cabin, McCarter, Schwarz and Manning sat with a pair of GSG-9 troopers. All five of them cradled their weapons and waited as the helicopter roared across the sky.

The only person in the helicopter who didn't look grimly determined was Kemal Kose, who sat shackled to one of the folding seats. Kose sat unhappily and tried to avoid looking into Mack Bolan's gaze.

The Executioner spoke to Manning without moving his eyes. "Ask him again."

Manning's mother had been born in Munich. When Manning had managed to infuriate his mother as a child, she had frequently reverted to German when dealing with his youthful transgressions. Manning turned his best angry German on Kose.

The Turk looked close to losing it. In Berlin he had been a master criminal. He had owned the streets, and his web had extended throughout Germany and the Mediterranean. In one night his empire had crumbled. His best men littered the ground in a truck stop outside of Berlin. No fancy lawyer could get him out of this one, and no one knew where he was. He wasn't under arrest. He wasn't even a prisoner of war. He had personally attacked members of the GSG-9 and a group of the most frightening Americans he had ever met. At the moment he happened to be alive. Kose desperately wanted to maintain that status. He chose to blame Heidi Hochrein for his present situation.

Kose turned belly-up on her like a fish.

Manning gazed without expression as Kose reiterated his story, then cut him off with a wave of his hand. He turned to Bolan. "Our friend's story isn't changing. He says he had some recent Turkish immigrants move the plutonium. They didn't know what it was. They were just glad to get work. He didn't give them any kind of protective gear. The men were then blindfolded, and a truck transported the plutonium in sacks to another warehouse. The men reloaded it into a new pair of containment vessels. The men were blindfolded again and then released back in the Turkish quarter."

Radtke shouted back above the rotor noise. "I have had local police and military units converge on the warehouse. Some units are almost on the scene. What do you want to do?"

Bolan considered. They were still five minutes from the warehouse. Kose maintained that no signal had been sent from the truck stop back to Berlin when his attack had failed. If that was true, they should catch Heidi Hochrein and her group flatfooted. If he had gotten off a signal, then twelve hundred pounds of plutonium could be pulling out and disappearing into the winding maze of East Berlin.

Every second could make the difference. Bolan sliced his hand through the air. "Have them attack! Now!"

Radtke nodded and shouted into his headset.

A sudden thought entered the Executioner's mind. He turned to Manning. "Ask Kose if there is a tunnel beneath the warehouse."

Manning fired off the question in German. Kose blinked uncomprehendingly, and Bolan frowned. "Ask if the sewers run beneath the warehouse."

Manning rephrased the question. The Turk stuttered back some kind of vaguery. "He doesn't know."

Schwarz scratched his chin. "Hochrein might not have told him about her escape route."

Bolan knew this was all too likely. Radtke shouted back from the cockpit. "Police units are meeting heavy resistance at the warehouse—multiple defenders with heavy automatic rifles."

Bolan shouted back at Grimaldi. "What's our ETA?"

The helicopter banked sharply. "One minute!"

The Executioner came to a decision. The local German units could storm the warehouse. It was up to the Stony Man team to make sure that Heidi Hochrein wasn't escaping beneath their feet. Bolan rose and leaned over the pilot's chair. "Take us down in the closest open area you can find near the warehouse."

Grimaldi nodded as the helicopter skimmed at nearly roof level over Berlin. "Roger that."

Radtke pointed. "There!"

Along a row of warehouses, one near the end of a street was under siege. The strobing fire of automatic weapons flew from the upper story windows. Below, German police units returned fire from the cover of their vehicles. Bolan pointed past the warehouse. A small park was dimly lit by a few lampposts.

"Put her down there!"

Grimaldi swept the helicopter over the battle scene and swooped down on the park. The BO 105 suddenly dropped like a stone, and with a last-second surge of the engines, touched down on a small grassy area. Bolan and his team leaped from the helicopter. Radtke and one of his men jumped out with them. Grimaldi stayed with the chopper, and the other GSG-9 trooper kept his MP-5 submachine gun pointed between Kose's eyes.

The Executioner swept his gaze across the park. In a small concrete circle was a set of swings and the iron skeleton of a climbing structure. Past the play area the concrete sloped downward slightly. At the bottom of the slope a metal grille was set against a berm.

The men from Stony Man converged on it. Manning and McCarter gave the grille one powerful heave, then shook their heads when the rusty iron didn't budge. Bolan jerked his head at Schwarz. "Blow it!"

Schwarz reached into his webbing and produced a small gray cube of C-4 plastic explosive. He stuck a remote detonator into it and packed it in between the bars as the team stepped back and crouched with their weapons. Schwarz produced a small black box with several buttons and retreated back to the team.

"Fire in the hole!"

A loud thump echoed through the park, and the grille shot upward on a ball of orange fire. Bolan and the team watched the twisted grille land a dozen yards away with a clang. The Executioner strode up to the smoking hole. Below the smell of burned high explosive, the stench of the Berlin sewer system asserted itself. He drew a small flashlight from his belt and played the beam into the hole. The sewer was a dozen feet below.

The Executioner grimaced and leaped into the breach.

Slowly moving, watery muck splashed up to Bolan's calves as he landed. He moved forward slightly and played his flashlight down the sewer tunnel as he swung his M-4 carbine on its sling and took the pistol grip in his hand. The rest of the team began to splash into the filth behind him and unsling their weapons. Bolan glanced at his watch. The luminescent dial had a built-in compass. The park had been directly north of the warehouse. As he stared down the sewer tunnel, his compass told him he was facing due south.

Unless it turned, the tunnel should lead straight to the warehouse.

Bolan clicked off the flashlight and pulled his night-vision goggles over his eyes. "Let's move."

The team moved swiftly down the ancient brick corridor. As they drew closer they could hear gunfire and shouting as it echoed through the grilles of the sewer drains above them. The sewer curved slightly, and the team paused as light spilled around it. Bolan, Radtke and Manning came around the corner with their weapons leveled.

In the view of their night-vision goggles, light seemed to pour down in a rectangular column from a six-foot shaft that had been cut through the floor of the warehouse into the ceiling of the sewer. A knotted rope dangled from the shaft and almost reached the floor.

The Executioner snapped his carbine to his shoulder as the light was abruptly blocked off and a figure dropped into the sewer without using the rope. A man in a sleeveless T-shirt looked about wildly as he rose up from one knee and brought up a German army G-3 automatic rifle.

The Executioner toppled the man into the muck with a long burst from his carbine. Manning and Radtke immediately stepped forward and began to fire their weapons up through the trapdoor to suppress any return fire. Bolan switched the carbine to his left hand as he reached for the bandolier slung across one shoulder. He decided it would be best if he threw a grenade through the trapdoor before someone upstairs got the bright idea to drop one down it.

Bolan pulled a flash-stun grenade from its loop. He didn't know what exactly was in the warehouse. He didn't want anything he couldn't see upstairs to suddenly blow up, and if Heidi Hochrein was still up there, he wanted to take her alive. The Executioner pulled the grenade's pin and strode forward. As Radtke's and Manning's cycled dry, Bolan heaved the grenade underhand up through the vertical shaft.

A second later a massive pulse of white light strobed down the shaft, accompanied by a sound like a thunderclap. Bolan squeezed his eyes shut as his night-vision goggles almost polarized from the magnesium flash.

"Down!" Dieter Radtke shouted at the top of his lungs and shoved Bolan.

Rifle fire erupted from farther down the tunnel. Bolan grimaced as he went to one knee and shouldered his carbine. There were men in the tunnel ahead of them. Radtke staggered as a bullet hit the frontal plate of his armor. With only one good arm the German hadn't been able to reload his machine pistol quickly enough. A second and third bullet smashed into his armor and pushed him backward as he attempted to draw his snub-nosed revolver from his hip. A fourth bullet tugged at the sleeve of his right arm, and the .44 Magnum weapon slipped out of his suddenly nerveless fingers.

Manning and Bolan fired at the same time and sent a hail of gunfire down the tunnel. The gunman had dropped back behind a curve in the sewer wall. Bolan pulled a fragmentation grenade from his belt and yanked out the pin. "Cover me!"

Manning began to fire his weapon against the bend in the tunnel. Sparks shrieked off the concrete, and ricochets whined down the ancient brick sewer. Bolan moved forward at a crouch and closed as Manning's shots cracked supersonic over his head. At ten yards the Executioner lobbed the grenade against the far wall of the curve and watched it bounce out of sight.

The grenade detonated, and down the corridor men screamed. Bolan brought up his M-4 carbine and went around the corner. Two badly wounded men lay twisting in the fetid sewer water. Ahead the corridor bent sharply, and Bolan could hear the echoes of splashing feet.

"David!" he shouted back over his shoulder. "You and Gadgets get Radtke back. Get beyond the range of any falling grenades, then keep the trapdoor in a cross fire! I don't want anyone else coming down until the Germans take the warehouse! Gary! You're with me!"

Manning splashed forward as Bolan began to move toward the bend. The Executioner tossed another frag around the corner, which detonated, and the two men took the corner in a crouch.

They found themselves in waist-deep water as a rifle fired at them from farther down the tunnel. Bolan could barely make out three dim figures, but he fired several bursts to keep them down. Manning raised his sniper rifle and fired. The weapon down the tunnel fell silent, and a figure crumpled.

Manning's voice rose as he looked down the ten-power view of the night-vision scope mounted on his rifle. "They're doing something! Satchel charge!"

Bolan fired the M-203 grenade launcher mounted on his carbine and yanked Manning down with him into the sewer water. The grenade detonated with a yellow flash. For one second the soldier thought he might have stopped them, then the entire tunnel lit up in a wave of orange fire. The slimy concrete beneath them shuddered, and bricks from the ceiling fell into the water.

A second later Bolan and Manning rose from the water. Both of them stayed in a crouch with only their heads and shoulders exposed as they pointed their weapons down the smoke-filled corridor.

Bolan spit foulness out of his mouth. "Your scope still operating?"

Manning brought the rifle to his shoulder and sighted. "Yeah."

"What do we have?"

Manning lowered the rifle and sighed heavily. "The sewer ahead has collapsed."

The two of them sloshed down the corridor and examined the heap of rubble. As they got close, they could see the roof of the sewer had collapsed. Several people from the street above peered down into the hole in road in wonder. Bolan frowned.

Manning looked at the blocked sewer with a professional's eye. "You think anyone could have survived that?"

Bolan thought about Heidi Hochrein and shook his head wearily. "I don't doubt it for a second."

DIETER RADTKE STARED DOWN at himself for the tenth time in disgust. The rifle bullet in the sewer had chipped the bone of his right elbow, and now both of his arms were in slings and bound across his chest. A short, older woman came into the briefing room and poured coffee for everyone present. The GSG-9 captain's injuries had apparently become common knowledge at headquarters. As the woman poured his coffee, she took a bright pink straw that looped and curved in on itself crazily out of her blouse pocket. In the middle of the straw was a red plastic heart emblazoned with the words Little Sweetheart. The woman smiled at the captain sunnily as she put the straw in his coffee cup.

She waggled her eyebrows at Bolan as she left the room.

The captain scowled down at the happy straw, then glared at his immobilized arms. "This is ridiculous."

Bolan nodded sympathetically.

The German shook his head grimly. "I am not going to drink out of that straw."

Bolan grinned. "Maybe someone could hold your cup for you."

Radtke glowered.

Bolan diplomatically changed the subject. "What did your police teams find in the tunnel?"

It had been twenty-four hours since the raid, and German local and state police units had swarmed over the scene. The captain glanced down at an open file that had been set before him. "The Berlin bomb unit has been sifting through the rubble. Chemical analysis shows that Amatol was the explosive used. They believe approximately twenty pounds were used in a satchel-charge configuration to cave in the sewer corridor."

Bolan nodded. Amatol was the basic Russian military explosive and was still in widespread use throughout almost all the former Warsaw Pact countries. "Did you recover any of the detonator components?"

Detonator components often survived the explosions they set off. "Yes, several fragments of the detonator were recovered from the debris. The bomb unit believes the detonator was of former East German military manufacture."

"It sounds like our friend Heidi still has matériel left over from the Grenztruppen she was using the first time I was here." Bolan frowned. "Were any former Grenztruppen captured or killed in the warehouse?"

"No, there were over twenty men in the warehouse. Every one of them was a Turkish national, except for the pieces of the unidentified man in the sewer. It seems that Miss Hochrein decided to switch security personnel."

"She knew that we would be watching for any kind of movement from former border guards, so she decided to hire the services of Kemal Kose. There was no way we could see that coming. If her attack at the truck stop had succeeded, she would have been free and clear to go on with her operation unhindered."

The captain stared longingly at his coffee but maintained his discipline. "That is my belief also."

"Were any bodies recovered from the rubble?"

Radtke nodded. "Two were discovered. One, according to his identification papers, was a Turkish national. He was armed with a G-3 automatic rifle that we have ascertained was stolen from the German army. The weapons used by the rest of the individuals in the warehouse, as well as for the attack on the truck stop, were of similar origin. The other body was literally blown apart, but we believe he was a Caucasian male. We found no identification. Our forensics experts believe he was shot and fell on top of his explosive device after he had activated the fuse."

Bolan knew Manning had gotten a hit with his rifle. It had just been a second to late. "What about Heidi Hochrein?"

The captain sighed. "The forensics team found bits of a

blood trail leading some twenty meters away from the other side of the cave-in. Several were handprints, and they were consistent with a woman's hand. The blood type also matches that of Heidi Hochrein's in the police files. As I said, the blood trail ended twenty meters from the cave-in. Another fifty meters down the corridor the sewer splits. There was no indication what direction she may have gone."

Bolan folded his arms. "And what of Mr. Kose?"

Radtke considered the matter of the Turk for a moment, then looked at Bolan philosophically. "We must all strive to overcome the inner *schweinhund*." The captain shrugged. "Mr. Kose has failed to do so."

"Did you get any more information out of him?"

Radtke frowned. "Not much. Miss Hochrein secured his services with five million U.S. dollars up front and with sexual favors. He was promised five million more and a safe escape route out of Germany. What this escape route was and who would help him was not made clear. Who his real employers were is not known. He had no information about any kind of operation going on in East Africa. He was hired to assassinate you and I and act as security for the plutonium."

"What's going to become of him?"

The captain shrugged again. With his arms immobilized it was one of the few gestures he was capable of. "He attempted to murder GSG-9 soldiers in the performance of their duties, as well as murder American guests of the German government, and he violated German weapons laws with the stolen rifles and the black-market rifle grenades. He was also was involved in the transportation and traffic of illegal nuclear materials within German borders, he exposed individuals to toxic materials without their knowledge and without taking proper safety precautions and he violated Berlin public-health codes by creating an unauthorized sewer entrance in property that has been zoned for residential and commercial use." Radtke suddenly grinned. "Mr. Kose will have an interesting variety of charges brought against him in German court. I do not think he will see daylight until he is a very old man.''

Bolan knew the answer to his next question in his gut, but he asked anyway. ''Was there a truck in the warehouse?''

''Yes. A small commercial Mercedes covered flatbed. It contained two shielded containment vessels. Each vessel contained approximately six hundred pounds of low-grade plutonium. The plutonium matched samples you brought with you from the Russian Republic.''

Bolan sighed with some relief. According to what they had found on scene and what Kurtzman had managed to decipher from the Libyan disk, there had been three consignments of nuclear materials. They had struck fast enough in Moscow and Berlin, and now two of them were accounted for. A line creased between the Executioner's eyebrows. Twelve hundred pounds of low-grade plutonium was still out there, unaccounted for, and they still had no idea who had it and what they wanted it for.

All they knew for certain was that someone with millions of dollars to spend was willing to kill to keep it.

Radtke looked at Bolan. ''What will you do now?''

There was very little for Bolan to do in Berlin, and they both knew it. They had won a battle in Berlin, but the results were inconclusive. The war was still on, and the enemy remained unknown and still held all the cards.

The Executioner rose. ''I'm going to check in and report what we have to my people.''

Radtke nodded. ''The investigation will continue in Berlin. I will make sure any information we uncover here will be forwarded to you immediately.''

''Thanks. I appreciate that.'' Bolan nodded at Grimaldi and Schwarz, and the men from Stony Man filed out of the briefing room. Bolan hid his frustration, but it was mounting. Too much of what they had accomplished had relied on luck, and only their skill had kept them alive. He considered the call he was about to make.

Kurtzman had to start making some real progress, or sooner or later their unknown enemy was going to win.

"WHAT CAN YOU give me, Bear?"

Kurtzman sounded unhappy over the satellite link. "This is the damnedest code I ever worked on, Mack, and we don't have the whole thing to work with. It's not easy, believe me. I've had the entire cybernetic team on it around the clock. We've even sent a copy of the disk to the National Security Agency, and even the NSA boys say they've never seen anything so sophisticated."

"I'm out of leads, Aaron. I have nothing. The trail is cold, and someone out there intends to do something with over half a ton of radioactive material. I'm willing to take hunches and wild guesses at this point, but give me something, anything."

Kurtzman's voice was hesitant. "Hunt and Akira have an idea, but we can't substantiate yet. Not by a long shot."

Bolan felt a glimmer of hope. Huntington Wethers and Akira Tokaido were two of the most brilliant cybernetic engineers on the planet. Kurtzman had recruited them himself. Mack Bolan would take an even unsubstantiated idea from those two men with extreme seriousness.

"Lay it on me."

"All right. Remember we managed to pull 'Moscow' out of the code. I had Akira and Hunt take that and try to decipher any kind of geographic location out of the code. When you found the plutonium in Moscow, and the manifest in the truck, we knew that there were three loads of plutonium. Now that you've been attacked in Berlin and you found the second load, we have more matches to work with."

"What have you got?"

"We might—*might*, that is—have a geographic link," Kurtzman replied.

"Where?"

"Hunt thinks he can relate the English Channel as a route the plutonium may have taken. Since the plutonium came west out of Moscow, he wants to assume it's going into England. But we've also still got over a dozen different scenarios that fit as—''

Bolan cut him off. "I'll call you from London."

15

London, England

Heidi Hochrein stood naked in her hotel room and examined herself critically in the full-length mirror. She had dyed her shoulder-length hair a deep coppery red and permed it so that it curled around her head in auburn waves. She smiled with satisfaction. Matched with her light complexion, the new hair made her look every inch the flower of English womanhood. Judicious application of lipstick subtly changed the shape of her mouth, and with makeup she had accentuated different lines and curves of her face. She glanced down at her chest.

Those curves had proved very useful to her on more than one occasion, but they were more difficult to hide.

She winced as she wrapped her chest in a compressing elastic bandage. The elastic band just met the tape that bound her ribs. The explosion in the sewer had thrown her against the wall and broken a number of her ribs, and she'd had to artfully sculpt her new hairdo to hide where her head had been split open. She'd been forced to sneak into an east Berlin gas station late in the night and tell the lone attendant her boyfriend had beaten her. The teenage boy working there had been very nice. He had helped her clean herself up and tape her ribs. His eyes had bugged out of his head when she had removed her shirt to show him how mean her boyfriend was. The boy had actually shown some talent with his hands when he had expertly taped her split scalp closed with butterfly bandages from the gas station's first-aid kit. When he was finished, she had cried and gushed and pulled his face and hands to her. His reward for his kindness had been an ecstatic moment with her bosoms, then her knife slashed across his Adam's apple once he'd become oblivious to all else.

Hochrein scowled at the pulsing ache between her eyes as it seemed to march in time to her heartbeat. She was fairly sure she had a concussion.

Her lips twisted into a silent snarl. The American bastard would pay for that. So would his friends. The snarl rearranged itself on her face and set into an ugly smile. Soon his entire people would pay. They would fall to their knees, weeping in despair at the vengeance wreaked upon them. But first there was the present business to attend to.

She pulled over her head an oversize gray athletic sweatshirt that was almost big enough to be a minidress and put a pair of dark wraparound sunglasses over her eyes. She smiled at herself again. Even someone with her photograph who was looking for her wouldn't immediately recognize her as Heidi Hochrein.

Even someone who had taken aim and shot at her wouldn't recognize her.

She looked over at the small end table by bed. On it lay a Ruger Mark II .22-caliber automatic loaded with ten rounds of high-velocity hollowpoint ammunition. The pistol's four-and-three-quarter-inch barrel was slightly thickened by the integral sound suppressor that ran its length. The suppressor left the pistol with a report barely louder than someone smothering a cough in the bottom of his or her throat. Hochrein's smile became almost beatific. No, no one would recognize her.

Not until it was much too late.

Outside, Big Ben tolled the ten o'clock hour in long peals. She glanced out the open window of her hotel room at the great face of London's magnificent landmark clock tower.

It was time to check in.

THE OLD MAN WAS as close to livid as the young man had ever seen him. They had both known that something had gone wrong in Berlin. Now the full impact of the catastrophe was clear. The old man's black eyes regarded him like a piece of meat on a stick.

"The operation is falling apart."

When the young man had gotten the report from Berlin, he had known full well that he would assume responsibility for the failure, and he would probably pay for it with his life. He looked back at the old man with almost supernatural calm. He was surprised to find himself almost without worry. It was extremely liberating to have almost nothing to lose.

The young man shrugged casually. "Aspects of the operation have been compromised."

The old man blinked. "Aspects?"

"Yes. Aspects of the operation have been compromised."

The old man nearly sneered with contempt. "Ah, I understand completely. There is nothing to be upset about. You have everything under control. Everything is well and good. I will report that to the board members. They will be pleased."

The young man knew the apparent contempt was a shield to hide the old man's fear. While the old man was unlikely to be killed for the failure of the operation, it would at the very least irreparably stain his reputation and his standing. At the end of a long and successful life spent acquiring power, he would be left with nothing but the ashes of his career. He would do almost anything to avoid that eventuality, and the young man knew it.

"What we have lost is two of our consignments of plutonium. They can be replaced, but that will take some time."

"The board will not be pleased with any more delays in the timetable."

The young man nodded. "Understood. Therefore, I suggest we go ahead with the operation. It is too bad that two of the targets must be ignored, or at least tabled, but we both know, and so does the board, who our primary target in Europe was.

The other two targets were secondary. The effect of all three acts would have been more powerful, but a successful strike against the primary target will still have much the same effect.''

The old man looked at him with an unforgiving gaze. ''That is assuming a successful strike can be launched. Since you have taken command, the entire operation has encountered...difficulties.''

A phrase the younger man had learned came to mind. ''Good help is hard to find.''

The old man's expression didn't change. ''A good worker does not blame his tools.''

The young man almost smiled. The old man hadn't always been a fixture behind his massive oak desk like a spider in its web. He had traveled, fought, stolen, dealed and killed around the world in his younger years. He had earned his position the old-fashioned way. It was good to keep that in mind when looking at the wizened old creature behind the desk.

The young man appealed to the old man's expertise. ''That is true, but your own field work has been extensive. Truly, have you ever had such a strange assortment to tools to work with?''

The old man grunted. ''I will grant you that, but it does not excuse failure.''

The young man pressed. ''We are using an international assortment of religious fanatics, political lunatics and criminals. Their reliability is questionable.''

The old man's voice hardened. ''It is their very nature that makes them useful to us—indeed, it is vital to our operation. The use of terrorists gives us a ready cadre of dedicated operatives in all the countries in question. They are also ideal cutouts. As long as we provide them with money and materials they are only too glad not to ask questions. Their acts cannot be traced back to us.''

The young man nodded. ''It is not their loyalty or political reliability that I object to. It is their operational reliability, which the reports from Moscow and Berlin show all too clearly, that is questionable.''

The old man paused. The words *operational reliability* had struck home. If the operation was to continue, they would have to make the next strike count. He steepled his fingers meditatively on the table before him. "What do you suggest be done to increase our operational reliability?"

The younger man drew himself up. "I was put in operational command by your recommendation to the board."

"Yes, that is true."

"Then I suggest you give me permission to take personal command in the field. I cannot operate by receiving reports and then taking action after the fact. Our operatives will require someone who can make decisions for them moment by moment. Particularly in dealing with the counterterrorist operatives we have been encountering. Allow me to take command in the field, and I will personally see to the downfall of our enemies."

The old man stared at him without expression. "The consequences of your capture would be astronomical."

The younger man steeled himself. He had entered this room with the knowledge that he might not leave the building alive. "I am prepared to take whatever precautions are necessary to ensure that I will not be captured alive."

The old man stared at him for a long moment. The young man stood unflinching as he was reappraised by his mentor. The old man nodded curtly. "I will put your suggestion before the board."

LIAM O'LAUGHLIN RAN his eyes over Heidi Hochrein's body, and he liked what he saw. He was very impressed with the way she tossed around American money. He had been even more impressed at how easily she had arranged for him to be smuggled into London. That showed professionalism, which in O'Laughlin's line of work was in too short a supply.

Hochrein looked Liam O'Laughlin up and down with the same frank appraisal.

The man looked like a huge redheaded ape. Big arms hung from his impossibly wide shoulders and ended in massive fists. His neck was nearly as wide as his square head, and his naturally auburn hair almost matched the dye job she had done on herself. His fiery hair tightly curled around his head like a helmet. He wasn't a very handsome man at all, and his broken nose and cauliflowered ears didn't improve his appearance. If someone wanted to draw a cartoon of an IRA terrorist to frighten schoolchildren, one really couldn't have a better model.

Hochrein liked everything about him.

O'Laughlin's brutal appearance belied a well-won reputation for cleverness, but his intelligence glittered in his dark green eyes. He had earned a degree in Irish history and language at the prestigious Irish-language college of Fal Carrach, and afterward had enlisted in the Irish Defense Force. He had risen to the rank of sergeant in the elite, fast-reaction Ranger Battalion. O'Laughlin had been honorably discharged, and then taken his hard-earned skills and education to the IRA. He had immediately joined the Provisionals. The Provisional Irish Republican Army was one of the most fanatical IRA splinter groups, and just as quickly O'Laughlin had risen to the higher levels of command. Even among the Provisionals, he and the men who joined him were renowned for their dedication and brutal violence. When Hochrein had first contacted O'Laughlin about the operation and told him what was planned, he had been almost ecstatic.

His hatred of the English was the consuming passion of his life, and with skill and willpower he had groomed himself for the role he now played.

This operation would be the crowning achievement of his life.

Hochrein smiled at the big man warmly. She liked a dedicated terrorist. In her opinion the ex-KGB men and the Grenztruppen had simply been frustrated and out-of-work murderers. Useful, but not to her liking. The Turks had simply been highly organized criminals. The IRA, particularly the Provisionals, were the real thing. She considered them to be in the same morally superior class in which she considered herself.

She also enjoyed sleeping with powerful, dangerous men. More than once she had considered what it would be like to seduce the American commando and then kill him in throes of passion. It was too bad that he had seen her face. She smiled up as she took in O'Laughlin's powerful frame and ugly face. Seducing the man who would murder the American would suffice elegantly.

Her face turned serious as she pulled a photograph out of her rucksack and handed it to the Irishman. "There have been complications."

O'Laughlin reached for the photo. "What sort of complications?"

"The man in the photograph, and his friends."

The Irishman peered at the photo long and hard. "An American?"

The woman nodded. "How did you know?"

O'Laughlin grunted and his nostrils flared. "He smells like an American. He smells like trouble, too."

"He is. Parts of our operation took place in Moscow and Berlin. On both occasions this man has shown up and made a mess of everything. In Moscow he received the help of the GRU. In Berlin he acted in concert with the GSG-9."

The big man raised an eyebrow at the mention of the GSG-9. In the circles O'Laughlin traveled in, the elite German antiterrorist unit was the equivalent of the bogeyman. "I don't rightly like the idea of some American commando who can travel anywhere in the world and call on the local special forces. It's unnatural, and it means you've attracted unhealthy attention to yourselves."

"That is true, but our enemies still do not know what is going on." Her blue eyes looked deeply into the Irishman's.

"From our side, the operation is still a go. Are you willing to go ahead?"

O'Laughlin glanced at the photo again. "This mysterious American, he is here in England?"

"We do not yet know, but we are operating under the assumption that if he is not, he soon will be."

The Irishman shrugged. "Then it would be best if this man were dead."

Hochrein's smile lit up brilliantly. "Excellent. How will you accomplish it?"

O'Laughlin allowed himself a grin. "I know a few likely lads here in London. This Yank seems to get along famously with other people's special forces. If he is here, and looking about for what we're up to, sooner or later he'll show up around MI-5 headquarters. We'll see if we can pick up his trail there."

Hochrein strode over to O'Laughlin's chair and straddled his lap. "And if you locate him?"

The big man grinned from ear to ear as his hands slid up onto the woman's hips. "Then we'll see just how tough this Yank of yours really is."

16

The Executioner walked through the streets of London and knew he was being followed.

He spoke quietly into the microphone in the collar of the leather jacket he wore. "What have you got?"

Gary Manning's voice spoke back into Bolan's earpiece. "The same guy is still following you. Dark pants, green jacket, knit cap. He's not doing too bad a tail job, but I think you'll get handed off once you're in the Underground."

Bolan headed for the subway entrance across the street. Once he was down the steps, David McCarter would pick him up. The soldier knew that from the actions he had taken in Libya and Moscow, and now particularly in Berlin, where they had been followed to the truck stop, the enemy had to have a fairly decent description of him floating around. He had no leads in London, and once again he and his team were playing catch-up ball. It was an ugly way to play the game, and Bolan knew he couldn't keep rolling the dice and exposing himself without finding himself locking gazes with snake-eyes.

They did have one advantage, though it was a gamble. Bolan was betting they would watch his movements carefully before they struck. The key would be to reel in the tail, and do it in a place where he couldn't escape or dump a weapon if he had one. London's underground train system would be ideal. Bolan grinned at himself wryly.

Of course, if they intended to take him out in a quick, preemptive strike, the subway would also make an excellent site for an ambush.

Bolan walked down the steps. It was midafternoon, and the crowd wasn't too bad. McCarter's voice spoke in his ear. "I have you, Striker."

"Acknowledged."

Bolan scanned the crowd from behind a pair of dark aviator's glasses and spoke to Manning. "What's happening with our boy topside?"

"He watched you go into the Underground, then he stepped into the pub across the street from your stop. I no longer have him in sight."

On arriving in London, Bolan had gone to MI-5 headquarters twice, and both times he hadn't been very secretive about it or about going back to his hotel room. Within the past forty-eight hours he had come to this subway station three times. Each time he had taken different, circuitous routes. Difficult routes, but not impossible for a dedicated tail job to follow. Each time he had come here he had taken a fifteen-minute meeting with Gadgets Schwarz. To anyone following him, it would appear something was definitely going on. With any luck, someone was having him followed, and by now that someone knew to have a lookout posted at this train station whenever Bolan left his hotel room.

They would also know that Bolan almost ritually went to the bathroom before Schwarz's train arrived. Bolan glanced around the station again and then at his watch. Schwarz's train would be arriving in about five minutes. "All right, I'm going to hit the head."

"Roger that." Down at the far end of the station David McCarter sat on a bench with his nose buried in a newspaper. His dark suit was impeccably tailored and a folded umbrella leaned by his side. He looked every inch an upper-class English businessman waiting for a train.

Bolan headed to the washroom, and McCarter's voice immediately spoke up across the radio. "You may have company."

Bolan kept walking. "Who?"

"A short, stout fellow. Brown hair in a short ponytail. Baggy brown leather jacket."

The Executioner went through the bathroom door. There was a pair of feet in dress shoes in one of the stalls, but other than that the washroom seemed deserted. Bolan plastered himself against the wall beside the doorframe. "What's happening?"

"He's on his way in to join you, he—" McCarter's voice rose in warning. "His hand is going into his jacket. He's almost in."

Bolan lunged as the door started to open. A short, powerful-looking man with a brown leather jacket blinked in surprise. The man's right hand was inside his jacket. The Executioner grabbed the man's leather jacket by both lapels and yanked with all of his strength.

Bolan's attacker had almost no time to resist. The man lurched forward, and as he did Bolan twisted and knelt. The man's feet left the ground, and he sailed over the big American's right shoulder.

The second the man was airborne, the Executioner rose and drew the Beretta 93-R from his shoulder holster. The man thudded to the washroom floor, and the pistol he had been drawing clattered onto the tiles. Despite the heavy fall, the man bounced back up to his feet like a rubber ball and twisted around desperately.

Bolan took two long strides forward. A switchblade clicked open and glittered in the attacker's left hand as he turned. As he came around, the Executioner snapped the ball of his foot into his adversary's solar plexus. The knife dropped from the man's hand as his whole body seemed to fold in two around Bolan's boot. Seized by the throat and yanked upright, the assassin retched and wheezed as Bolan's left hand held his larynx in a viselike grip. The soldier rapped the Beretta smartly across his opponent's temple.

The man collapsed to the bathroom floor like he'd been shot.

McCarter's voice spoke quickly. "Two more, Striker, coming at the run! I'm on it!"

Bolan moved back to the door. There was a louvered grille at the bottom of the door, and the Executioner kept his eyes on it as he listened to the sound of approaching feet outside. The second he saw a shadow cross the grille he drove the heel of his boot into the edge of the door with every ounce of his 220-pound frame. The door began to fly open as Bolan's foot hit it, and it shuddered on its frame as it rebounded off the man coming in.

The soldier yanked open the vibrating door. A tall man stood tottering in the doorway, bleeding from his split-open forehead. Bolan stepped in and drove his elbow upward into the point of the man's chin.

The new arrival sagged backward into his partner. The second man was reaching for a weapon as his partner fell against him. Bolan kicked the sagging man in the chest with the same force he had used on the door, and both men spilled backward out into the train station.

Bolan leveled the Beretta at the third man's forehead as he struggled under his partner's unconscious body. McCarter seemed to materialize out of thin air, and his voice was very calm. "I'd listen to the man if I were you."

The man glared up at McCarter with palpable hatred. "Sod off, black dog!"

McCarter's eyes narrowed, and Bolan recognized the man's thick brogue and the insult he spit out in it. The soldier cocked his head and spoke to the man conversationally. "You're Irish, aren't you?"

BOLAN STOOD in the MI-5 briefing room and examined the tagged evidence on the table. British Intelligence was broken into two main sections, MI-5 and MI-6. MI-5 was the branch that dealt primarily with military and terrorist threats. There had been some doubt among the higher-ups in British Intelligence when they had been informed of the possibility of low-grade plutonium being smuggled into Britain for unknown reasons. To them the whole idea had seemed somewhat far-fetched. Bolan glanced again at the confiscated equipment on the table.

He had just become an MI-5 priority.

Each of the men who had attacked him in the subway station had been identically equipped. Three small personal radio rigs with earpieces and concealed transmitters lay on the table. Scotland Yard had been able to trace their serial numbers and determine that they had been stolen from an electronics store in London's Chelsea district. Bolan took in the three assassination weapons beside the radio rigs.

Three big Webley revolvers lay on the table. The old pistols were nearly antiques, and Bolan had few hopes that Scotland Yard would be able to trace them. The massive revolvers were well used, but obviously well oiled and maintained. The muzzle of each pistol had been snaked through the neck of an empty plastic one-liter tonic water bottle, then the bottles had been securely taped into place. The result was somewhat bulky, and looked incredibly crude, but Bolan had to admire the "whatever works" ingenuity of it.

The Webley revolver fired a huge .455-caliber slug, but it did so at barely over 600 feet per second. By modern standards of ballistics, the Webley bullet moved almost at a crawl, but the brutal stopping power of the huge, soft-lead, 265-grain bullet was undeniable. The combination of the subsonic low-pressure round and the sealed chamber of the bottle over the muzzle would give an assassin a weapon that would be virtually silent for the first one or two shots. Bolan shook his head as he looked at the massive old pistols with the tonic bottles taped over their barrels.

With surprise on his side, Bolan had no doubt that an assassin could easily blow someone's head off in a men's room and no one would hear a thing.

Someone had put some serious thought into rendering Bolan dead.

McCarter looked at the three pistols speculatively. Before he had been recruited into Phoenix Force, he had served in the British regular army's crack Gloucestershire regiment in Northern Ireland and then transferred to the elite SAS regiment. In that time, he had developed a deep and abiding dislike for the IRA. He scratched his chin.

"The Irish Volunteer Army Reserves are mostly equipped with old, cast-off British army weapons. Hell, some of those blokes are still equipped with old, bolt-action Lee-Enfield rifles. I'd be willing to bet that these pistols have gone missing from an Irish Volunteer arsenal."

Bolan nodded. "It's a place to start."

The Englishman's face was stone as he glanced downward. "I know a better place to start."

Bolan glanced down, as well. On the floor below them two of the three Irishmen were being held in holding cells. The man Bolan had first encountered in the subway station was in the hospital under military guard with a ruptured spleen and a concussion. Bolan was very aware that McCarter would be more than happy to go downstairs and begin ripping the two healthier suspects limb from limb.

"We'll have none of that." The MI-5 antiterrorist subsector chief was a thin, almost bookish-looking man, and he looked at McCarter as officiously as possible. He knew who McCarter was; McCarter's exemplary military-service records with the Territorial Army and the SAS were in MI-5 files. The subsector chief frowned. Captain McCarter's activities since his discharge from the active-duty SAS weren't in his files. All there was about his current activities was an extremely short blurb about "a need-to-know basis," and then nothing.

The subsector chief had been informed from on high that other than the fact that he was required to render all assistance to McCarter and the men he was working with, he didn't need to know anything about them.

Bolan turned to the subsector chief. "What can you tell us about the men you have in custody?"

The Englishman scanned a file in front of him. "All of the suspects were carrying false pieces of identification. None of the men are talking, and we haven't been able to immediately identify the two men below, other than the fact that they appear to be Irish in origin."

The chief cleared his throat and glanced at Bolan with an arched eyebrow. "The man you put in hospital, however, we have on file. His name is Timothy O'Leary, an Irish Republic national with suspected links to the Provisionals of the Irish Republican Army. He was arrested seven years ago in London while driving a stolen vehicle. He had fifty thousand British pounds in a suitcase in the trunk for which he could give no valid explanation. The money was confiscated, and he was sentenced to five years for vehicular theft. He was a model prisoner and released after three and a half. The judge didn't see fit to deport him back to Ireland. We believe he is an IRA courier, but we can't prove it."

"How long can you hold them for?"

The chief's shoulders sank. "The weapons possession and their illegal modification are serious charges. However, it is you who initiated the attack upon Mr. O'Leary, and they may not be admissible as evidence. His barrister is already clamoring for his release. I doubt whether we can hold him more than another twenty-four hours, if that."

Bolan nodded. "You believe he'll be released?"

"If he can make bail. However, his barrister is a very high-profile character. Someone had to have hired the man for Mr. O'Leary, and if they have that much money to spend, I'm certain that they can afford his bail, as well."

Bolan had no doubt that whoever it was could afford Mr. O'Leary's bail. "Whoever it was" was undoubtedly Sinn Fein, the respectable, "political" branch of the IRA, and they had a considerable war chest devoted to the legal defense of arrested IRA members.

The Executioner shrugged. "Well, we'll just have to let him go, then."

The chief looked vexed. "I'm sorry, but it is much harder to get wiretaps and surveillance on people here in England than in the United States. Even if we can put a tight watch on O'Leary, I don't believe he'd be fool enough to lead us to his superiors."

What the MI-5 chief said was essentially correct, but it wasn't relevant. "He's not the one we need to follow," Bolan replied.

The chief raised an eyebrow. "Oh, who then?"

"The other man in the washroom."

The Englishman's face went blank. "The other man in the washroom?"

"Yes, I saw a pair of feet in one of the stalls." Bolan shrugged. "Understandably their owner didn't make an appearance during the fight, but he didn't come out when the police arrived, either."

"Why was I not informed about this?"

Bolan spread his hands. "I'm sorry, but I figured your men or the police on the scene would have questioned him, and if they'd found him suspicious, probably arrested him."

The Englishman's studied composure was slowly eroding. "You're bloody well right we would have."

"And then we would have had four men in custody, and none of them talking."

The MI-5 man looked at Bolan for a long moment and then sighed. The chief was in British Military Intelligence, but he wasn't a soldier. However, MI-5 was a sharp outfit, and he wouldn't have risen to his rank if he wasn't a capable man. "I gather you have a man following our mysterious man."

"As you know, I was staging meetings with one of my men at the train station to attract attention. I contacted him by radio after we dragged out the bodies and had him wait for whoever came out of the bathroom. He followed him. I'm expecting my man to contact me when our suspect goes to ground. It's who he contacts that I'm interested in.''

The chief folded his arms. "And what if he turns out to be just a frightened man who happened to be in the wrong place at the wrong time?"

"Well, we still have Mr. O'Leary, and I'll probably have to go for another walk and see who tries to kill me."

"I suppose I can count on your keeping me informed of developments as they occur," the chief said.

"I'll be counting heavily on your support."

A flustered-looking woman entered the briefing room and glanced at the chief. "Sir, you have visitors."

"Visitors?"

The secretary cleared her throat and gestured between the chief and Bolan. "Official visitors. I was told to direct them to you and the American gentleman."

The chief shook his head helplessly. "Well, show them in, please."

Bolan folded his arms across his chest and couldn't help but grin as the door opened. A tall striking blonde in a well-tailored dark green military dress uniform entered the room, removed her service cap and saluted sharply. "I am Captain Valentina Svarzkova of Russian Military Intelligence. I am here to act as official liaison for my government, and assist in any manner required to capture plutonium that has been stolen from Russian Republic and smuggled onto soil of United Kingdom."

The chief's eyes bugged at the Russian woman, and then he blinked as a fire hydrant of a man in a light green uniform with one arm slung across his chest stepped in from behind the Russian captain. He winced as he raised his right arm, but he managed to fire off a crisp salute.

"I am Captain Dieter Radtke of the GSG-9. The plutonium was smuggled through my country and with the aid of a wanted German terrorist. I am here to assist you in the recapture of both in any way possible.''

Bolan admired the subsection chief as he reined in his confusion and took refuge in the only defense left to him. He relied on English upper-class dignity. He stood and saluted back. ''I am very pleased to welcome you both to Great Britain, and I look forward to working successfully with both of you and your respective governments.'' He gestured to the secretary. ''Please, see to the captains' needs. I will be with them in a moment.''

The chief watched as the German and Russian captains turned and followed the secretary into the outer room. He turned and looked from Bolan to McCarter, and then back again. ''It goes without saying that this is highly irregular.''

17

Liam O'Laughlin's massive frame lay spread out on the bed as he talked on the phone. He loved cellular phones. He had quite a collection of them. He had a small army of children in London and Dublin who stole them for him at every opportunity. He literally used a fresh phone for almost each phone call he made, which made it almost impossible to intercept his calls.

He clicked the phone shut as Heidi Hochrein ran a finger through the red hair of his chest. She purred up at him. "What is the situation?"

The massive Irishman grunted. "The Brits have Timothy and Finn in custody. O'Leary is in hospital under guard."

Hochrein shot upright. "What!"

O'Laughlin stretched out his arms casually. "It's no matter. They won't crack, and our lawyers should have them out soon enough. If not, they're good men. They can do their time standing on their heads. They'll keep their mouths shut."

"How has this happened?"

The Irishman shrugged. "I had the Yank followed. I told the men to be cool about it, but if they saw an opportunity to take him out, then to do so. The lads saw an opportunity, and…"

"And?"

"And it seems the Yank took all three of them out, and bare-handed, too, I might add." O'Laughlin sighed. "This Yank of yours, he seems to be quite a likely lad."

"He is a threat. He needs to be killed."

O'Laughlin's knuckles cracked like the sound of someone else's bones breaking as he idly clenched his hamlike fists and then relaxed them. "In due time."

She relaxed back down onto the Irishman's chest and began to trace the hard ridges of his stomach. "And what are you doing now?"

"I'm having men I trust sneak into London one by one. All of them are veterans of the Provisionals. Some of them have already arrived, and when I have them all assembled, I'll tell them exactly what we have planned." He reached down and touched Hochrein's hair. "What about the plutonium?"

"I've had it moved from your safehouse to the final staging area. It is nearby, and it is in a safe place. I have arranged for the rest of the materials to arrive in the next forty-eight hours."

"Excellent. My man who observed the fight in the train station will report to me when the men are assembled and ready." O'Laughlin's face split into a huge grin. "Then we'll see about your Yank friend."

SCHWARZ SOUNDED PLEASED with himself over the radio. "I have him."

"Where are you?" Bolan asked.

"Somewhere east of Regent's Park, I believe."

Bolan listened and then repeated the address to McCarter, who sat in the driver's seat of the unmarked van.

The Briton nodded. "I vaguely know where that is. It's about a fifteen-minute ride from here."

"Then let's do it." Bolan paused and craned his neck around to face the back of the van. "With your permission, Chief."

"By all means," said Jack Rawlins, MI-5 subsector chief.

In the back in the van, Svarzkova, Radtke, Manning and Rawlins sat on the bench seats and checked their equipment as the van pulled out.

All of them were now in civilian clothes, and all of them wore concealed radio rigs and body armor under baggy jackets. They had other items under their baggy jackets, as well. Under her jacket, Svarzkova carried a silenced 9 mm Stechkin machine pistol with a collapsible wire shoulder stock clipped to its grip. The German captain had brought his VP-70 Heckler & Koch machine pistol, and its plastic stock and sound suppressor were also attached. Bolan's own Beretta 93-R pistol was in a silenced and wire-stocked configuration, too.

McCarter and Manning were much more prosaically armed. Both had stockless Remington 12-gauge pump shotguns with the barrels brutally shortened to twelve inches.

The MI-5 chief unconsciously patted the Browning Hi-Power pistol concealed in his shoulder holster. He seemed to be feeling somewhat out of his element among a German special-forces captain, a blond Russian Military Intelligence agent and heavily armed Americans who should have been in his files but weren't.

Bolan looked up out of his window. Somewhere above London, Jack Grimaldi would be circling in a borrowed Westland Scout helicopter. The Scout was an old bird and nearing retirement, but it was reliable and had done yeoman's service in the United Kingdom since the 1960s. The Stony Man pilot had a London police helicopter pilot acting as a navigator for him and an SAS corporal manning the .30-caliber door machine gun to keep him company.

"How are we doing up there, Jack?" Bolan prompted.

The pilot's voice came through loud and clear. "Have you in sight, Striker. Will follow your lead."

The trip through London was uneventful. As they passed Regent's Park, London began to sprawl out into the upper-class homes and town houses of the west end and out into the suburbs.

Bolan was surprised as the van pulled down a long, well-manicured row of ancient Victorian town houses and he saw Schwarz sitting on a bench chatting amiably with an old woman and her immense yellow cat. He looked up and waved at Bolan as the van passed by. The old woman smiled and waved a white-gloved hand, as well.

The Executioner had McCarter pull the van to a halt. The Briton raised a questioning eyebrow, and Bolan shook his head. You never quite knew what Gadgets Schwarz's antics might lead up to. "All right, let's see what he's up to now."

The soldier jumped out of the vehicle and walked up to the happy couple on the bench. Schwarz grinned at Bolan, then turned to the old woman. "There's my friend, Mr. Belasko." He nodded at Bolan. "This is Mrs. Smythe."

The old woman beamed up at Bolan with a look of gratitude. "I am so glad to meet you, Mr. Belasko."

Bolan smiled and took the woman's hand. "I'm very pleased to make your acquaintance, Mrs. Smythe."

The woman continued to beam at the polite American and scratched her cat between the ears. "This is Smithers."

The Executioner smiled down at Smithers, who peered up at Bolan noncommittally.

Schwarz looked extremely pleased with himself. "I've just been telling Mrs. Smythe about our mutual interest."

Bolan's smile stayed fixed. "Oh?"

Mrs. Smythe nodded her head vigorously. "Oh, yes. I can't believe those—" her voiced dropped conspiratorially "—Irish want to tear down any of these beautiful old houses. Can you?"

"Well, ma'am, that is the rumor."

Schwarz nodded. "I've been telling Mrs. Smythe about our firm's plan to buy some of the older, more run-down town houses and have them restored, and how our Irish competitors intend to tear them down and put in modern condominiums."

Bolan glanced at Schwarz. Sometimes the man's genius was vaguely disturbing.

The old woman's eyes flared with indignation. "It's a sin! That's what it is!"

"Oh, indeed," Bolan agreed solemnly.

The old woman shook her head. "And that Mr. Barnes seemed like such a nice man. Hard to believe that he and his friends are plotting to tear up our neighborhood."

Bolan cocked his head. "Mr. Barnes's friends?"

"Oh, yes. He has four or five houseguests. I'm his neighbor, and he told me not to be concerned if I saw people I didn't know coming in and out of the house. Says they're business partners of his."

Bolan had little doubt that Mr. Barnes and his friends were in the same business. Mrs. Smythe looked up at Bolan almost pleadingly. "You aren't going to let those men do anything bad, are you?"

The Executioner's smile was utterly sincere. "No, ma'am. We're not."

SCHWARZ SAT IN THE BACK of the van and looked smug. "So, what do you think?"

Bolan shook his head. "You know no shame, Gadgets. Exploiting the fears of old women as intelligence resources."

"Yes, and given the situation, her fears are not unfounded. Her neighborhood may actually be in a great deal of danger."

Arguing with Gadgets Schwarz was generally a losing proposition. Bolan turned to the MI-5 chief. "What do you think?"

Rawlins frowned. "It smells very fishy to me, and I agree with your friend. I believe Mrs. Smythe's neighborhood may indeed be in danger. I can have a listening post set up on the town house in a matter of hours, and I can have a full SAS counterterrorist team assembled to back it up."

Bolan considered the chief's offer. It was very tempting. A listening post might come up with some real information they could use, and the British SAS was in the same league as the German GSG-9 and America's Delta Force.

Time, however, was a luxury they didn't have. They had no idea what the enemy was planning or what the timetable was. Every minute that passed drew them closer to whatever the terrorists planned to do with over twelve hundred pounds of plutonium.

Bolan locked eyes with Rawlins. "Chief, how do you feel about going in now?"

The chief blinked. "Now?"

Bolan nodded. "Now."

"Highly irregular. We aren't cleared for any action other than surveillance at the moment."

Bolan grimaced. This sort of situation was always a danger when dealing with civilian operators. However, the man seemed capable. Bolan decided to rely on that. "Chief, this is a quiet neighborhood. Setting up a full, round the clock surveillance team will be difficult to do without their being noticed. We don't know what, if any, kind of intelligence-gathering resources our friend Mr. Barnes may have in the neighborhood of his own. Right now he's home and not expecting us. I defer to your authority in the matter, but I strongly urge you to move now, while we have the chance."

The wheels turned in Rawlins's mind. It was obvious he was in over his head in a field-operation situation. Almost against his will he turned to McCarter, who was English and a reserve SAS officer. "Captain McCarter, what do you think?"

"We don't know what they're planning. I believe every second counts." McCarter's face was grave. "I think we should hit them, and I think we should do it now."

The chief took a deep breath, then turned back to Bolan. "Very well. You know more about this kind of operation than I do. I believe you should be in command while we are taking a military action." A grim smile set across Rawlins's face as he decided on action. "Let's see what these bastards are up to."

The Executioner's smile was equally grim. "All right. This is how I want to run it."

BOLAN EASED HIMSELF through the hedge and into the side yard of the town house, and Svarzkova followed as he held open the break in the foliage. He whispered into the microphone in his collar. "We're on the grounds."

McCarter's voice came back. "Check. We're moving in."

Bolan knew his description was known to the opposition, so the two Englishmen would take the front door in case they needed a distraction. Schwarz, Manning and the German were working their way around to the back of the town house to close off the rear. Bolan and Svarzkova would make the initial penetration.

The Executioner eased the Beretta 93-R from under his jacket. He clicked the metal shoulder stock into place and pulled down the folding metal foregrip from under the slide. He gave the sound suppressor a twist to make sure it was firmly in place, then glanced back at the Russian. Svarzkova's own Russian-made Stechkin machine pistol was stocked and silenced, as well. She nodded her readiness.

Bolan whispered into his collar again. "How are you doing, Gary?"

"In position." Manning paused for a moment. "All clear back here, waiting on your signal."

"Roger that." Bolan glanced upward. "Hold on." He tugged Svarzkova's sleeve and pointed. Almost directly above their heads, a second-story window was open. Svarzkova glanced at it, then nodded in silent agreement. Bolan whispered. "We are going to make our penetration through an upstairs window. Hold for my signal."

"Roger that," Manning replied.

McCarter's voice came back a second later. "Check, Striker. Waiting on your signal."

Bolan clipped the Beretta to a strap under his jacket, then formed a stirrup with both hands as he leaned against the wall. Svarzkova stepped into Bolan's hands, then up to his shoulders. He stuck his hands rigidly over his head and tensed as he took the Russian agent's full weight in the palms of his hands. He felt her legs flex, then she pushed off and her weight was gone. Bolan turned and peered up in time to see the Russian woman's legs disappear into the window. Her voice whispered in his earpiece a moment later.

"Room is clear."

Bolan ran a hand over the rough stone exterior of the old town house.

He'd climbed up worse.

His hands probed between the stones and found purchase. He shoved the rubber edges of the soles of his boots into the mortar, and they gripped. Bolan plastered himself against the wall and began to climb. The second-story window wasn't far, and after six handholds Bolan shoved himself upward and grabbed the window ledge. With one smooth motion he did a pull-up, then pushed himself over the sill and rolled silently into the room.

Svarzkova stood by the door with her machine pistol at the ready. Her eyes suddenly flared and her voice dropped into a hiss. "Someone is coming!"

Bolan spoke into his mike. "David, I need a distraction."

"Understood."

Bolan and Svarzkova leveled their weapons at the door as footsteps on the wooden floor outside became audible. Just as the steps came to a halt on the other side of the door, the doorbell downstairs rang.

An exasperated voice spoke in an Irish accent outside the door. "Oh, bloody hell." The footsteps receded again.

Svarzkova's eyes narrowed as she listened intently with her ear pressed to the door. "He is going down steps."

"Let's not be here when he comes back."

Bolan strode to the door and cracked it open. The upstairs hallway was narrow and high ceilinged and apparently deserted. Reggae music came softly through one of the doors opposite the stairs. The Executioner eased into the hallway with his machine pistol preceding him. He jerked his head toward the stairwell, and Svarzkova silently moved to cover the stairs with her weapon. Bolan moved to the door and listened.

There was a fascinating conversation going on.

The music was playing softly. The voices speaking in the room were much more animated.

"It's going to be the biggest bloody blowup London's ever seen! I'm telling you, the Royals will be finished."

The Royal Family would be finished. Bolan thought that both Rawlins and McCarter would be very interested to hear that bit of news.

Another, gruffer voice spoke unhappily. "Yeah, I know, I know. It's the biggest thing we've ever done. But I don't mind saying it, I'm not happy working with all that radioactive stuff. I hear there's a bloody truckload of it, and it gives me the willies."

The evidence was quickly piling up against Mr. Barnes.

Bolan tensed as someone yelled downstairs. "Now, I told you! Bugger off!"

A door slammed below, and upstairs the voices in the room fell silent. A second voice downstairs spoke in question. "Who was that?"

The first voice was still perturbed. "Oh, some bloody real-estate bastards, talking rubbish about restoration and resale values."

The second voice was steely calm. "Do me a favor."

"What's that?"

The crack of flesh on flesh sounded almost like a gunshot on the floor below. There was a howl of pain, then the first voice rose in amazed indignation. "Jesus! What'd you do that for?"

The second voice remained icily level. "The next time you answer the door, you're going to be polite, do you understand me? Telling the locals to 'bugger off' is unfriendly and attracts attention. You aren't back in Belfast, boyo. This is a nice neighborhood. You'll learn to mind your manners, or I'll teach them to you."

"All right, all right! Jesus, Joseph and Mary! You don't have to be like that about it!"

The second voice wasn't mollified. "Quit your bleating. If Liam was here, he'd have done a lot worse than slap your stupid face."

The second man had no reply to that. Bolan filed away the name Liam in his mind as he spoke into his throat mike. "Do me a favor. Ring the doorbell again. Be irritated."

McCarter's voice spoke back. "Right. Ringing it again in ten seconds."

Bolan jerked his head, and Svarzkova retreated back from the stairwell to cover him. A moment later the doorbell rang. Bolan could hear the door open, and McCarter's voice sounded irate.

"Listen, mate! I don't know where you bloody well get off talking to me and my associate like that, but I'll have you know—"

Bolan recognized the voice of the man who had been slapped as he cut in desperately.

"Listen, I'm awfully sorry. I've had a very bad day. Why don't you gentlemen give me your business phone number?"

McCarter made mollified noises. Bolan silently tried the knob of the door in front of him. It was unlocked. He swiftly entered the room.

Three men looked up as Bolan entered. Two of the men sat on small twin beds facing each other with glasses of dark beer in their hands. The third man sat at a small writing desk looking over what appeared to be a thin ledger. All three of them gaped openmouthed at the silenced muzzle of the Beretta. Bolan raised a finger to his lips. The three men looked intently at the Beretta and sat frozen.

"I want you to close the ledger, and quietly slide it over to me across the floor," Bolan told the man at the desk.

The man's eyes narrowed, then suddenly flared wide. "Good God! It's the bloody Yank!"

Bolan whipped the machine pistol to his shoulder and sighted at the man's forehead. "I said quietly."

The Beretta never wavered as the man slid the ledger across the floor. Bolan didn't stoop to pick it up. "How many of you are up here?"

One of the men sitting on the bed shrugged. "Just us three, really!"

Bolan's head moved almost imperceptibly as the sound of a toilet flushing sounded through the walls. Svarzkova made a strangled noise of consternation out in the hallway, then quickly retreated into the room and closed the door.

The man on the bed roared at the top of his lungs and lunged at Bolan. "It's a raid! The Yank is—"

Bolan cut him off with a shot through the forehead. Svarzkova flung the door back open and whipped the muzzle of her weapon into the hallway. The other two men lunged up from their seats with murder in their eyes. Bolan put two rounds into the one at the desk, then two into the man lunging from the bed. The second man fell across his comrade. The third man didn't stop as the 9 mm hollowpoints slammed into him.

Bolan heard the suppressed hiss of Svarzkova's machine pistol and the Russian woman's matching snarl as she engaged someone in the hallway. The Executioner had put six rounds into the third man in less than a second, but the man bore into him with inhuman drive. The soldier staggered backward under the brunt of the man's charge and felt his back slam into the wall. He twisted his head away as the Irishman clawed at his face. With one hand he grabbed the man by the hair and twisted his head upward and back. The Executioner shoved the silenced muzzle of the Beretta 93-R under the terrorist's chin and fired. The man went limp and collapsed to the floor.

As Bolan moved into the hallway weapons began to fire downstairs. The flat cracking of 9 mm pistols rang off the wooden walls, then the unmistakable roar of a sawed-off 12-gauge shotgun thundered through the town house. Svarzkova crouched while she slipped a fresh magazine into her machine pistol. A man holding a Sterling submachine gun lay twisted and bullet ridden at her feet.

Bolan slapped a fresh 20-round magazine into the Beretta and moved to the staircase. At the bottom of the landing, a man lay dead in a spreading pool of blood. The front door was open, and a blast from a shotgun roared around the jamb into the house. Pistol fire from deeper within the building answered back.

"McCarter!" Bolan said from the top of the stairs.

The Briton's voice came across the radio. "I'm at the doorway, Striker!"

"Where's your opponent?"

"In the kitchen."

Bolan nodded and pulled a grenade out of his jacket. "Stay put. I'm going to frag them."

"Check."

He pulled the grenade's pin and held down the safety lever as he moved halfway down the staircase. From this angle he could see the open doorway into the kitchen. A hand holding an automatic pistol snaked around the jamb and fired three quick rounds toward the front door, then retreated out of sight again.

Bolan released the safety lever, silently counted down the numbers, then tossed the grenade and watched it bounce off the floor and skitter out of sight into the kitchen. The grenade detonated with an earsplitting crack, and the kitchen windows shattered under the lethal hail of metal fragments.

McCarter bounded through the doorway with his shotgun leveled, with Rawlins close on his heels holding his Browning Hi-Power.

Bolan took the stairs three at a time with Svarzkova right behind him. He spoke into his microphone. "Gary, how are we in back?"

"No movement here, Striker!"

McCarter called out from the kitchen. "Clear! One terrorist down!"

Bolan nodded. "All right, Gary, you and Radtke close in. Gadgets, cover the outside."

"Roger, Striker."

Wood suddenly crashed in the kitchen, and McCarter swore. The Briton fired his shotgun once, and a shotgun blast answered it. McCarter tumbled backward out of the kitchen and fell heavily to the floor at Svarzkova's feet.

Rawlins lunged forward and bodychecked the Russian woman sideways as an automatic rifle snarled off a long burst from the kitchen. The chief rose up and fired his pistol in return. The rifle fell silent, but the unseen shotgun roared again and the chief flew backward as if some invisible giant had swatted him in the chest.

Bolan pulled the pin from a flash-stun grenade and hurled the bomb into the kitchen. He squeezed his eyes shut as the walls of the house shuddered under the sudden thunderclap and a wall of blinding white light pulsed out of the kitchen. The Executioner opened his eyes and moved. He seized the two Englishmen by their collars and dragged them out of the line of fire as Svarzkova rose to her knees and sprayed an entire magazine from her machine pistol into the kitchen. She dived behind the opposite doorjamb and slapped a fresh magazine into her weapon.

McCarter grimaced and sat up. "Damn it!"

There were six holes in the lower left side of his jacket just above his belt-line. He had taken half a pattern of buckshot, but his body armor had held. Bolan shook Rawlins. "How are you, Chief?"

The man coughed and rolled his eyes. He had taken an entire pattern of buck directly in the chest. His armor had held, as well, but Bolan knew from bitter experience that the next day the chief would feel as if he had been beaten with a hammer. Bolan pulled him up into a sitting position as the man gaped and wheezed. "Just concentrate on breathing, Chief. You're going to be fine."

McCarter drew his Browning pistol from his shoulder holster and grimaced. "There's a door to the basement in the kitchen. It's been papered to match the wall. I didn't notice until they came crashing through it."

Bolan could hear muffled voices speaking at one another from somewhere around the kitchen. "There's more of them." He spoke into his throat mike. "Gary, what's your situation?"

"I'm at the back door. Entering hard, now." From beyond the kitchen wood splintered and crashed as Manning kicked the door. "Living room, clear!" Another door crashed. "Downstairs bath, clear!"

There was a slight pause, and Bolan could hear Manning and Radtke moving through the house. "Downstairs bedroom, clear! Striker, I see a hallway that I believe leads into the other end of the kitchen."

Bolan nodded. "Hold position." He pulled his remaining frag and yelled, "Grenade!"

He could hear the sound of feet hitting a wooden staircase as he tossed the grenade into the kitchen. The bomb detonated with a crack, and Bolan was up and into the kitchen. Another terrorist lay dead with a bullet through his head, and an AK-47 rifle lay just out of the dead terrorist's fingers. Bolan nodded. The MI-5 chief had probably saved Svarzkova's and McCarter's lives. The soft body armor they wore wouldn't have stopped the assault rifle's high-velocity bullets. Bolan glanced past the bodies at the fractured wall. A six-foot panel had been broken outward, and Bolan could see the wooden landing of the basement stairs beyond. The Executioner fired several bursts into the landing to keep his opponents downstairs.

He spoke into his radio. "Move in!"

Manning and Radtke came through the opposite door, and Bolan pointed at the basement stairs. "Keep firing down the stairs. I don't want anyone coming up."

The two men began to put suppressive fire down the staircase as Svarzkova and McCarter entered the kitchen. Bolan pointed at the floor. "I think they're right below us." He turned to Manning. "Gary, give me a fun hole, right there."

Manning nodded and pulled a small coil of what looked like triangular metal tubing out of his jacket. He cut a twenty-inch length of the flexible linear-shaped charge and formed it into a hoop. Radtke and Svarzkova fired bursts from their weapons down the staircase while the big Canadian produced a roll of tape and quickly began to tape the hoop tightly against the kitchen floor. Bolan pulled out his remaining flash-stun grenade while Manning attached a detonator to the charge.

Answering shots came back up the narrow stairs as the demolitions man pulled what looked like a miniature TV remote out of his pocket and grinned. "Here we go."

He pushed a button, and the hoop lit up with yellow fire and hissed and cracked as it blew. The shaped charge sent its blast directly into the wooden floor, and a second later a perfect ten-inch circle of flooring fell into the basement.

Bolan released the safety lever and dropped his flash-stun grenade into the hole.

The floor shuddered, and white light strobed upward like a telephoto flash. Bolan turned to McCarter. "Drop another one. Drop two."

McCarter smiled. His side was still aching from the hammering his armor had taken, and he enjoyed dropping flash-stun grenades on terrorists.

The Briton produced two grenades and pulled the pins. He dropped one bomb and waited for the flash and roar of its detonation and then dropped the second one.

The flash-stun grenade wasn't lethal. Its explosive element was designed to produce a stunning shock wave and a deafening concussion. The incandescent brilliance of its magnesium flare would produce temporary blindness. The combination of its shock and flare was designed to temporarily incapacitate armed and determined opponents nonlethally. In the narrow confines of a basement, three flash-stun grenades one on top of the other had to have seemed like the end of the world.

Bolan brought his Beretta to his shoulder and pulled a mini-flashlight from his pocket. "All right, let's take them."

The stairs to the basement were riddled with bullet holes, and the shock waves from the grenades had shattered the bare bulbs that illuminated the area. Bolan and McCarter flicked on their flashlights as the sound of coughing and moaning rose up the narrow stair among wisps of smoke. The beleaguered stairs creaked under Bolan's weight as he descended.

The Executioner played his flashlight into the basement, which was larger than he expected. Nearly ten cots were laid side by side, and a portable toilet had been set up in a corner. It would be cramped quarters, but the basement could easily conceal nearly a squad of armed men from a cursory police search.

McCarter grunted. "Tidy little barracks they've got here."

Bolan swept the basement with the muzzle of his Beretta, but the resistance had been smashed. Men lay all about on the basement floor, twitching and groaning, blinded and deafened from the repeated blasts of the flash-stun grenades.

The two men moved among the disabled terrorists and began to disarm them. They were heavily armed with a hodgepodge of automatic rifles and police-model shotguns. Most had knives and handguns, as well. Svarzkova came down the stairs with a pair of long extension cords she had looted from the kitchen and began to tie up the downed terrorists.

Rawlins came down the stairs holding his chest and observed the scene in the glare of the flashlights. He glanced at Bolan and smiled shakily. "Well, it seems you were right, Mr. Belasko. Something was indeed going on in here."

"Chief, can you expedite getting a forensics team in here?"

Rawlins nodded. "I'll see to it immediately."

The Executioner glanced around at the men they had captured and the hidden barracks under the house. Something was indeed going on, and it was time to figure out exactly what the something was.

A creeping suspicion told Bolan that they were running out of time.

18

The MI-5 briefing room was a buzz of activity. Secretaries rushed in and out with files. Everyone around the table looked grimly pleased.

The raid had been the break they were looking for.

Many of the captured men were known Provisional IRA members, and several were actively wanted by the police. The arrests alone were quite a break in England's war with the IRA. It was up to forensics and the MI-5 intelligence crew to see what they could make of the evidence.

Rawlins looked immensely pleased. His first field action had been a monumental success. He was already receiving commendations for his quick thinking and initiative, and he had been given direct command in the operation against the IRA terrorists. Another secretary whirled in and placed the ledger they had captured from the town house in front of the chief and put a file on top of it.

Rawlins opened the file and looked at it grimly for some moments. "It was as we suspected." He passed the file to Bolan. "The ledger was coded, but it was a code we have run into before. The IRA is very fond of old Irish culture, and they like to incorporate it into their missions. The code on this ledger is a simple cipher. What was boggling about it was that it seemed to translate into gibberish until we figured out it was in old Gaelic. After that it was fairly simple to break. We've been very careful about not letting on we know about it."

The Executioner scanned the file. It simply accounted for

deliveries and weights, and it indicated that someone, presumably the IRA, was accumulating very large amounts of ammonium-nitrate fertilizer.

Bolan grimaced and looked up at the chief. "A truck bomb."

Rawlins nodded. "So it would seem."

Bolan glanced over the translated invoice. "They've acquired almost eight thousand pounds of it."

"Yes, almost enough ammonium nitrate for two large truck bombs, I would say."

"Can you run a check on who's been buying?"

"That will be difficult. There is a great deal of farm land outside of London, and that's assuming the fertilizer was acquired locally. Also we have very little regulation on that sort of thing here in the UK. For that matter, anyone who buys fertilizer generally buys it by the truckload, and I'm sure the IRA was clever enough to use false names and fronts."

Bolan knew the chief was probably all too right. Rawlins shrugged. "Of course we'll run a check anyway with every available resource. Perhaps our friends slipped up someplace."

The Executioner frowned down at the file. "They'll need diesel fuel to soak the ammonium fertilizer, and if they want a really big bang, they'll bury propane tanks in the fertilizer, as well, to augment the explosion. The diesel fuel they can probably get at any gas station, but I'd run a check on propane dealers in the UK. Propane is an explosive flammable, and I suspect licensed dealers must keep fairly sharp records." Bolan looked up from the file. "What did you get on the name Liam?"

The chief handed Bolan another file. "That one was fairly easy. I'm willing to bet they meant Liam O'Laughlin, one of the IRA Provisional's most notorious leaders. If the IRA was going to make a truck-bomb attack here in London, he's the man for the job." The chief paused. A certain bit of conversation Bolan had overheard in the town house hadn't gone over very well in MI-5 headquarters. "And if one intended to

finish off the Royals, as you say you overheard, Liam
O'Laughlin is just the fanatic to do it."

Bolan looked at the man's photo. He was big, as tall as
Bolan himself and heavier built. His file said he was classically
educated and had the equivalent of special-forces training with
the Irish army's fast-reaction Rangers. Bolan frowned and the
chief read his mind.

"Yes, he is extremely intelligent. Very capable and very
dangerous. He may be the most dangerous element of the IRA
at the moment. If he is here, and in charge of this operation,
it will be a very professionally run affair."

Bolan nodded and stared down at the file. Knowing one's
enemy was half of the battle. The chief looked over another
file. "We have some other evidence, as well. Of the weapons
found in the town house, the shotguns and pistols were stolen
police-issue, as we expected. However, as it turns out, the
automatic rifles found on the scene were Bulgarian AK-47s,
and we also found a pair of Bulgarian manufacture RPG-7
antitank weapons with half a dozen rocket grenade projectiles
in the basement. We believe they passed through Libyan hands
and were then smuggled into Ireland before being brought into
the UK." The chief frowned. "Colonel Khaddafi has always
been a staunch supporter of the IRA, and you have said before,
your hunt initially began in a Libyan training camp."

The Executioner paused in thought. It seemed they had a
good idea who their opponent was, and what he intended to
do. IRA terrorist Liam O'Laughlin intended to kill the British
Royal Family, presumably with a truck bomb, and he was
getting Libyan help to do it.

But the twelve hundred pounds of smuggled Russian low-
grade plutonium was still a mystery, and something in the back
of Bolan's mind told him that Colonel Moammar Khaddafi
wasn't the mastermind behind this operation.

There was something larger going on.

Bolan drummed his fingers on the tabletop. "You had your
forensics team run a radiation sweep on the town house?"

The chief nodded. "Yes, and minute traces of radioactive material were found in one of the men's clothing in the upstairs bedroom. The traces were consistent with the low-grade plutonium captured in Moscow."

"That fits. One of the men upstairs was complaining about working with radioactive materials." Bolan turned things over in his mind. "What's being done about guarding the Royal Family?"

The chief's frown deepened. "Her Royal Majesty, of course, has been informed of the situation."

Bolan could see what was coming. "And?"

The Chief sighed. "Buckingham Palace receives thousands of visitors from all over the world every day. It isn't as if we can just shut it down or surround it with tanks and orbiting gunships."

"And?"

"And…" Rawlins straightened in his chair. "Her Royal Majesty says that she will not shut down Buckingham Palace, nor will she go into hiding because the IRA has decided to target her. She's rather adamant about it."

The queen of England wasn't about to be intimidated by terrorists. Bolan had suspected as much. "So what's being done?"

The chief flipped at a file. "Well, all that can be done, given the circumstances. We've already doubled the guards around the palace, and we're stationing a fully equipped SAS antiterrorist team within the palace grounds. Several .50-caliber machine guns with telescopic sights are being mounted behind concealment from positions that overlook roads with straight-line approaches to the walls of the palace." The chief shrugged. "If MI-5 had its way, the entire Guards Division would be standing shoulder to shoulder around the palace fence, and on the grounds there would be a Ghurka rifleman hiding behind every tree and shrub. However, Her Majesty intends to keep at least a semblance of normalcy."

The wheels turned in Bolan's mind. Things simply didn't

add up. A truck bomb launched against Britain's Royal Family would be a terrible blow. If it succeeded and the palace was devastated and members of the Royal Family killed, the reigning British government would fall to a vote of no confidence. What it would do to the United Kingdom politically, economically and socially was beyond foretelling.

Bolan scowled. It was just too uncertain. The potential to miss the queen, or her being there and surviving the blast was high, and even if successful, there were three royal princes in line to become king, and they would almost certainly call for bloody vengeance against the perpetrators. Of course, the IRA, particularly the branch of it Liam O'Laughlin seemed to represent, were fanatics, and the idea of striking against the Royals so powerfully might be more temptation than they could bear.

But again, something, somehow didn't add up.

Bolan straightened in his chair. "Chief, I believe you may have to allow for the possibility that the truck bombs may be a feint."

Everyone at the table looked at Bolan as if he were mad. They had spent the past few hours feverishly debating what to be done about the truck-bomb threat to the Royal Family.

Rawlins glanced at Bolan. "I respect your opinion, Mr. Belasko, but I beg to differ. In one week and a half there is to be a state ceremony at Buckingham Palace. The Queen and the Prince of Wales are scheduled to be in attendance. I believe it is too great an opportunity for our opponents to pass up."

Bolan folded his arms across his chest. "How would you explain the plutonium?"

The chief shrugged. "Perhaps you yourself have explained it. Perhaps the plutonium itself is a feint. France, Germany, the Russian Republic and the United Kingdom all have their intelligence agencies and their top scientists trying to figure out how a bunch of terrorists could make a nuclear weapon out of low-grade plutonium. The answer is, they can't. But we're wasting vast resources trying to figure out how they could or what nuclear facility in Europe they could be using in this mythical process. In the meantime they're simply going to make their attack with a simple, powerful chemical-fertilizer bomb." The chief nodded. "Very clever actually."

Bolan stared at the chief without blinking, and Rawlins glanced back uncomfortably. "You don't buy it."

The Executioner's expression didn't change. "No, I don't."

The chief sighed. "Well, I'm afraid you're in the minority. However, your service in the matter has been invaluable, and I greatly respect your input. Can you tell me what you think might be our enemy's alternative plan?"

Bolan shook his head. "No, I can't."

"Very well, we shall proceed on the assumption that they intend to kill the Royal Family with a truck bomb during the ceremony. We know who our enemy is, and I think we have a good grasp on what they intend to do. Let's get cracking."

LIAM O'LAUGHLIN WASN'T happy. The taking of the town house was almost inconceivable. O'Laughlin considered himself a brave man, and if he could kill the Royals, he might well go along with a suicide attack, but with the plan almost undoubtedly blown by now, the idea of going ahead with it regardless was more than just suicidal. It would be a failure.

The man standing before him disagreed.

O'Laughlin again tried to place the man. There was something odd about his face. The man's tone of voice was carefully modulated, and his English was perfect and betrayed no accent whatsoever. It was almost his lack of distinguishing features that made him distinct. Other than the fact that he seemed to be over thirty years old and had dark hair, there was almost nothing to him. He was of average height, and the cut of his dark suit was immaculate. Only his carriage betrayed him. The Irishman recognized the upright carriage and ease of gesture that bespoke long training.

He had no idea who the man in the dark suit was or whom exactly he represented, but the Irishman had no doubt whatsoever that the man who stood before him was a stone-cold killer.

He was also a representative of the organization that Heidi Hochrein represented. Whoever he was, the man had money and resources that O'Laughlin could only dream about. Still, the fact remained. It would be insane to go ahead.

"They have the ledger from the town house. You know they must have broken the code."

The man nodded. "Yes, that is too bad. If you had used one of our codes, they would certainly still be puzzling over it as we speak." The man's lips tightened for a moment. "Still, we did not issue you any of our advanced codes. It was a tactical error on our part. You cannot be blamed for that particular mistake."

O'Laughlin bridled. "And as for other mistakes?"

The man's agreeable tone didn't change. "Of course. Attacking the American in the train station was foolish. Failing to kill him was unforgivable. Allowing him to track one of your bases of operations and allowing sensitive materials to fall in his hands was even worse."

O'Laughlin struggled to retain his composure. It was the mission that mattered, and whether it could be salvaged. The cause was all. Keeping that in mind had kept him from making mistakes in the past, and he held on to it now.

The man before him seemed to read O'Laughlin's mind. "What matters most is the operation. It is not a question of salvaging it. I believe we can go ahead with it. What matters now is are you willing to go through with it and can I rely on you?"

"They'll be expecting us."

The man nodded. "I am counting on it."

The Irishman blinked. "They must know we intend to hit the Royals at the state ceremony. They have the entire place surrounded, and they'll be expecting a truck bomb. They'll have snipers and antitank weapons. We'll never even get close."

The man nodded again with irritating calm. "Yes, that is undoubtedly so."

O'Laughlin folded his arms across his chest. "You have a plan?"

"Indeed. I believe that we can actually make our recent mishap work in our favor. They think they know what we intend to do, and they are partially right. This will be their undoing." The man allowed himself a small smile. "The plan will remain essentially the same with a few small differences. Listen carefully."

O'Laughlin's eyes widened slightly as the man laid out the changes in the plan. They were subtle, and they were clever. The Irishman grudgingly admitted to himself that the man was a genius.

The man looked deeply into the Irishman's eyes. "Do you believe that you and your remaining men can carry this out?"

"I believe your plan will work, and I believe my men and I can carry it out."

The man stared at O'Laughlin for a long, judging moment. He finally nodded. "Good."

The Irishman suddenly frowned. "What about the American and his friends?"

"An excellent question. However, do not worry about them. I will see that he is taken care of, personally."

19

The five assassins moved silently through the night.

Each one was highly trained, and each had numerous kills under his belt. Their lead weapon was a highly modified Calico 100 .22-caliber carbine. The Calico's claim to fame was its revolutionary 100-round-capacity helical magazine that rested on top of the receiver. During trials in World War II, the Allies had given a great deal of thought to assassination weapons, as the Nazis held almost all of Western Europe in their grip.

The Allied intelligence services had tested almost all firearms and calibers of bullets available at the time. After testing numerous high-powered weapons, a simple discovery was made. Someone who was shot in his center body mass with the typical 7-to-10-shot magazine load of a .22-caliber pistol was a dead man. The .22 was a naturally quiet caliber to begin with, and its soft, all-lead bullet often broke apart and ricocheted within the victim, creating multiple wound channels. A highly trained gunman could dump all ten rounds of a .22-caliber pistol into an opponent in two seconds. Given the barest moment of surprise, the target would never be able to draw his weapon before he had been gunned down, and more often than not, the target would be dead before he hit the ground. Not surprisingly, .22-caliber semiautomatic target pistols became the Allies' preferred assassination weapon of the war, and in many wars to come.

This lesson hadn't been lost on others in the killing profession.

The assassins' carbines had been highly modified. Their barrels had been cut down to five inches, and the muzzles were shrouded with short sound-suppressing sleeves. Each weapon was capable of full-automatic fire, and that fire was guided by a laser-dot sighting device slaved to the weapon's barrel. With its stock folded, each carbine was barely a foot and a half long and weighed only three pounds. The weapon had almost no perceivable recoil and, fired on full-auto, it could dump one hundred rounds into a target in five seconds.

Modified as it was, the Calico was a .22-caliber buzz saw.

The five killers were highly proficient with their weapons, and their objective was clear. They split as they approached the hotel. Their target had been tracked, and observers reported that he was on the third floor and currently in his room. When the assassins attacked it would be from all angles. All possible routes of escape would be covered. Their target would be caught in a lethal cross-fire that he wouldn't survive.

This night the American would die.

VALENTINA SVARZKOVA rested her chin in her palm as she lazily traced a pattern across the slablike muscles of the Executioner's chest. Her finger suddenly stopped and tapped irritatedly.

"I cannot believe we are to be simply liaisons now."

Bolan sighed in the dark. He wasn't exactly pleased about it, either, but they were in England, and the British were calling the shots. It wasn't as though they were indispensable. The combination of British Intelligence backed by the antiterrorist teams of the SAS was a formidable defense.

"The MI-5 chief seems capable, and he did save your life."

"Yes, this is true. He hurled himself into the line of fire to save myself and Captain McCarter. I intend to put him up for a medal."

Bolan raised an eyebrow. "Oh?"

"Yes, the Russian Republic Medal of Valor. It is made of silver, it is very nice. Medal of Valor comes with ten-ruble-per-month pension and lifetime pass for Moscow railway. I have one of my own. My senior officer recommended me for it after my actions in the former Yugoslavia and the United States. Apparently my senior officer was influenced by letter of commendation from the United States Justice Department."

Bolan allowed himself a grin in the dark. He remembered drafting that letter, though it didn't bear his name. "I'm sure the chief will appreciate it. Foreign commendations always look good on your service record."

Svarzkova sighed. "Yes, but still, I do not like being—how do you say?—sidelined like this. It is our investigation. It is we who have made it happen."

Bolan shrugged. "It's their show, and now that they have their plan of action, they probably figure foreign operators would just be in the way. I'm surprised we haven't been thanked profusely and sent home already." He reached out a hand and ran it along the small of the Russian agent's back. "Besides, being demoted to observers does give us time for other things."

He felt Svarzkova's lips smile against his ear, and she threw a leg over his thighs. "Yes, this is true." She snuggled closer.

The Executioner suddenly tensed. "What?" Svarzkova breathed in his ear.

Bolan's eyes were fixed on the bedstand. The small black box that sat there was invisible in the darkness, but a tiny red light on its miniature console blinked insistently. Gadgets Schwarz had designed that box, and it was intimately linked to the security measures that Bolan had set up in his hotel room.

He reached out to the bedstand and closed his hand around the grips of his Beretta 93-R pistol. His thumb pushed the selector switch to 3-round-burst mode. "We may have company."

Svarzkova disentangled herself and rolled over to her side

of the bed. Her Stechkin machine pistol was in her own room, but her 9 mm CZ-75 and her knife accompanied her wherever she went, including Bolan's bed. The Czech pistol's safety came off with an almost inaudible click.

The Executioner rolled out the bed and scooped Schwarz's black box off of the bedstand. The blinking light told him that the doorknob had been tried. The London hotel had gone over to the modern system of computer-controlled card keys that were swiped through the lock like a credit card. The black box was equipped to deal with their peculiarities. Bolan flicked a switch on the box and sent an override signal pulsing into the microchip that ruled the door lock. The signal scrambled the card-swipe's input so that neither Bolan's card, the Hotel master-key nor a faked signal would unlock the door.

He smiled coldly in the dark as he watched the lights on the tiny console. A second red light blinked as an attempt was made to signal the door lock to open. The attempt failed, and the warning light blinked a second and third time as someone tried to electronically pick the lock twice more.

Someone was definitely trying to get in.

Bolan pressed another button and sent a warning signal to the black boxes in the rooms where the rest of the Stony Man team were staying. "Watch the balcony," he whispered to Svarzkova.

The Russian GRU agent took a two handed hold on her 9 mm pistol and crouched by the bed as she trained her weapon on the draperies.

Bolan suspected what the next ploy would be, and his opponents didn't let him down. Someone rapped on the door with a short, professional-sounding knock.

The Executioner waited several long seconds before asking, "What is it?"

"Room service!" a woman's voice called out cheerily in an English accent.

"For God's sake! It's two o'clock in the morning!"

The voice sounded very apologetic. "I'm sorry to disturb

you, sir, but we've suffered an electrical fire in our security room, and we're experiencing some technical difficulties. The door locks are jamming on the first three floors. We would like you to manually open your door, and if the problem is extensive, we may have to give you a new room on the upper floors.''

It was almost plausible, and it would almost explain the signals sent to his black box.

Almost.

Bolan sighed loud enough to be heard. "Just a minute."

The Executioner turned on the light on the bedstand, then picked up his .44 Magnum Desert Eagle. He moved to the door, then stepped to one side of the jamb. A peephole was mounted in the door at shoulder level. From the outside, all someone could see would be a tiny circle of light in the lens, but to a killer, that would be signal enough. When someone put his eye up to the lens to see who was at the door, that tiny circle of light would disappear.

Bolan rapidly passed the massive slide of the Desert Eagle automatic in front of the peephole, then whipped his arm back quickly.

There was no sound of gunfire, but the door instantly began to vibrate on its hinges as if it were being hit by a hailstorm. The hail tore through the door at chest level and sent splinters of wood flying in all directions.

Bolan leaned away and shouted at Svarzkova, "The door!"

He turned to cover the balcony as the Russian swiveled to aim her weapon at the disintegrating door. Her pistol wasn't silenced, and its roar in the enclosed room was deafening as she began unloading 9 mm hollowpoints through the wood.

Bolan crouched as the sliding glass door of the balcony shattered inward. A ragged line of holes erupted along the wall and snaked toward Bolan as they followed the red dot of a laser sight.

"Goggles!" he snarled at Svarzkova as he leveled his Beretta at the lamp on the bedstand.

The Executioner squeezed off a 3-round burst, and the lamp shattered in a shower of sparks. The room plunged back into darkness.

He rolled back toward the bed and snaked his hand into the kit bag near the headboard. His hands closed around his night-vision goggles, and he yanked them over his head and flicked the power switch. The room lit up in green-and-gray tones.

On the balcony a man clutching a weapon was yanking his own goggles down over his eyes.

Bolan raised the Desert Eagle and put the front sight on the man's chest. The massive .44 Magnum thundered, and the man jerked backward. His weapon let out a long hiss, and plaster rained from the ceiling as the burst went high. Bolan's second shot tumbled the man backward and toppled him over the balcony railing.

Svarzkova had pulled on her own night-vision goggles, and her weapon stayed trained on the door. She began to fire again as the door shattered inward off its hinges.

Three figures burst into the room, wearing night-vision goggles, and fired their weapons on full-auto like firehoses. They charged into Svarzkova's fire fearlessly. Her shots hit, but the gunners didn't stop, and Bolan knew they were wearing body armor. The Russian's weapon clacked open on empty, and she dropped out of sight behind the bed. The comforter rippled and snaked as if something were alive beneath it as extended bursts of fire ripped into the bed.

The assassins apparently hadn't known that there was a second person in the room. The Executioner used that split-second advantage. The Desert Eagle packed a punch that wasn't stopped by soft body armor.

The big Magnum pistol roared and recoiled in Bolan's hand. He swung the heavy muzzle from target to target, and the big .44 Magnum bullets took a terrible toll. Two of the killers tumbled to the carpet. The third whirled on Bolan as the Desert Eagle cycled through to an empty chamber. The Executioner fired the Beretta in his other hand as his opponent fired his own weapon.

The 9 mm bullets struck the assassin in the chest, but the man didn't go down and the plaster behind Bolan's shoulder stripped off the wall under a hail of returning .22 bullets. A second burst drilled into the man, then the soldier raised the Beretta for a head shot.

The red dot of the assassin's laser sight swung onto Bolan's chest.

Svarzkova dived into the assassin's knees with a high-pitched yell of rage. The Russian agent and the assassin fell in a tangle to the floor. Steel glinted in Svarzkova's hand as she plunged her knife into her opponent. The killer beneath her tried to bring up the muzzle of his gun between them, then gasped as the knife punched through his armor. The Russian agent sat up on top of the killer, then thrust her knife into his throat and slashed sideways.

The assassin's body relaxed, and the weapon slipped out of his hands.

The Executioner whirled back on the open doorway. The thin hiss of suppressed automatic fire whispered through the doorway, and Svarzkova yelped as she fell backward. Bolan loosed a 3-round burst into the assassin in the doorway. The killer was dressed in a maid's outfit, but the weapon in her hand and the night-vision goggles over her face betrayed her. The assassin staggered, but her armor held as she swung his laser sight on to Bolan.

Out in the hallway a 12-gauge shotgun roared. The assassin stumbled sideways under the buckshot's impact, and her burst flew high and wide. Bolan raised his weapon and took an extra fraction of a second to align his sights. The Beretta rattled in his hand, and the 3-round burst shattered the lenses of the killer's night-vision goggles and snapped her head back. A second shotgun blast from out in the hallway hammered the already dead assassin to the ground.

For a moment everything was quiet except for muffled

screaming coming from other rooms on the floor. "Striker!" Manning called out.

"I'm all right. Svarzkova's hit. I've got three down in the room, one on the balcony and one in the hallway."

"We're coming in, Striker."

Bolan lowered his pistols. "Come ahead." He moved to the wall switch and flicked on the overhead light. He stripped off his night-vision goggles and moved around the bed as Svarzkova stood up.

Manning and McCarter entered the room with their shotguns ready. Schwarz and Radtke stayed in sentry positions in the hallway. Bolan could already hear Grimaldi starting to smooth-talk frightened and angry people outside. McCarter moved to the shattered balcony window and quickly peered around the jamb.

"Not much of an angle on this window for a sniper. I think we're all right." He held up a dangling black rope and nudged the fallen assassin it was attached to with his foot. "This one rappeled off the roof."

Bolan moved to Svarzkova. "Are you all right?"

The Russian agent's face screwed into an irritated frown. She pointed to the fallen assassin at her feet with her knife. "Yes, I am fine. Most of the blood is his."

Manning was staring at Svarzkova with deep admiration. Bolan's eyes narrowed as he watched Svarzkova's blood-covered chest heave. Both he and the Russian woman were nearly naked. "Hey, Gary. Why don't you go to the bathroom and get the lady a robe."

"Oh, right. You got it."

Svarzkova suddenly turned pale, and the bloody AK-47 bayonet blade slipped from her fingers and fell to the floor. Bolan grabbed her as her knees buckled. "Gadgets! Break out the medical kit!"

The Russian agent let out a rasping wheeze as Bolan examined her. Her chest was splashed with the arterial spray from the man she had killed, but he quickly found two pinpoint wounds just below her right clavicle. He turned to Schwarz as he knelt beside them and broke open an emergency field kit. "She's taken two rounds through the right lung." Bolan ran his fingers under her back and felt sticky wetness. "I've got two exit wounds. The bullets went through her. I'm betting they're .22 solids."

Gadgets nodded and began to apply a field dressing to keep her from bleeding from the back. Bolan turned to McCarter. "David, get an ambulance!"

Bolan glanced around at the dead assassins as he pressed his hand over the two entry wounds in Svarzkova's chest to maintain an air seal. The killers' attack had been highly professional, and their laser-sighted .22-caliber silenced submachine guns were very sophisticated pieces of ordnance. If it had not been for Schwarz's security measures, they would have silently triggered the door lock and cut both Bolan and Svarzkova to pieces with hardly more sound than a whisper. They would have been in and out in little more than seconds, and left no evidence other the pair's bullet-ridden bodies. Even when they had been stymied by the black-box countermeasures, they had barely skipped a beat in their attack.

Bolan's smile was cold and grim. The attackers hadn't been IRA terrorists. They had been highly trained, first-class, professional assassins.

It confirmed what Bolan already believed. The IRA wouldn't send assassins to kill Bolan after he had been relegated to observer status. Not unless they still considered him a threat somehow. The game was still afoot, and there was still something going on that neither Bolan nor British Intelligence knew about.

The Executioner had no doubt in his mind that whatever it was involved twelve hundred pounds of stolen plutonium.

20

"How many men have you recruited?"

Liam O'Laughlin grinned. He'd no lack of volunteers, and he had been able to pick and choose from among the most reliable men in the Provisionals. "Twenty, many of them with military experience, all of them with experience in this sort of thing."

"They know what is expected of them?"

"Indeed they do, and they are eager to be about it." The huge Irishman folded his arms. "You have the gear we'll be needing?"

"Of course."

"And the vehicles?"

"All is in readiness."

O'Laughlin cocked his head and peered at his mysterious benefactor. "My sources tell me that the Yank is still alive."

"The American is alive, that is true."

The Irishman raised an eyebrow. "And I also am informed that five of your best professional boyos were killed in the attempt, with the result of one wounded Russian GRU agent who is expected to make a full recovery."

The man peered at O'Laughlin expressionlessly. "That is essentially correct." His eyes narrowed almost imperceptibly. "You have a point?"

O'Laughlin didn't blink. "Only that the Yank is still alive, and as long as he is, he's a threat to us."

The man nodded slowly in thought. "Yes, the American is

remarkably persistent. However, it is that very persistence that will kill him. Now that we have made this attempt on his life, I am sure he will stay close to the scene. Too close, I suspect." The man shrugged slightly. "If you do your job correctly, Mr. O'Laughlin, the American will die as a matter of course, no matter how he tries to interfere with our operation. As a matter of fact, I am counting on it."

O'Laughlin unfolded his arms. "How soon do we launch the attack?"

"The equipment and the vehicles should be in position in the warehouse by now. See to having your men assembled and go over the plan with them a final time." The man in the dark suit checked his watch. "We attack in exactly twenty-four hours."

MACK BOLAN POINTED to the highly modified Calico carbine where it sat on the table. "Have you ever seen IRA hit men with this kind of equipment?" he asked Rawlins.

"Well, no." The MI-5 chief shifted in his seat uncomfortably. "No, I haven't. Nor have I ever heard of them using night-vision devices or using electronic countermeasures on hotel door locks. I'm not saying it's impossible, but I agree with you. The attack that was made upon yourself and Captain Svarzkova in the hotel seemed like a very professionally run affair." The chief paused. "How is the captain?"

Bolan frowned. "She'll be all right. She took two bullets in the chest, and her right lung collapsed. However, the bullets failed to deform and they entered and exited cleanly. With any luck she'll be able to return to full active duty."

"Excellent. I'll have to write her a letter of commendation for her outstanding performance here in London."

Bolan suppressed a smile. "She'll appreciate that."

The chief looked down at the weapon on the table again. "It is odd."

"Very odd." Bolan held Rawlins's gaze. "Can you think of a reason why they would make an attempt on me like that?"

"Revenge? You have been a thorn in their side."

Bolan's eyes narrowed slightly. "Revenge? When I and my team had been relegated to observers? Would you risk an attack like that against noncombatants so soon before a major terrorist operation?"

The chief saw Bolan's point all too clearly. "No. Not unless I thought killing you was absolutely necessary to accomplish the mission."

Bolan leaned back in his chair. "I was thinking along the same lines."

Rawlins sighed in exasperation. "Well, they will have the Royal Family all lined up to be blown to kingdom come in a few days. What else could they be planning?"

An unpleasant thought began to take shape in his mind. "Our enemies have to suspect that we're looking at the state ceremony next week as the primary target of their attack."

The chief nodded grudgingly. "One would think so. However, the IRA are fanatics. I would not rule out their willingness to launch a suicide attack."

"Neither would I, and if we were dealing with only the IRA I'd be tempted to agree with you. But I think there are larger forces at work, and there's still twelve hundred pounds of plutonium to be accounted for."

The chief sighed heavily. "Yes, you keep coming back to the plutonium. But our scientists, your scientists and the Russian scientists my government has contacted all agree that there is no way to convert the low-grade plutonium into a nuclear weapon. If they can't turn it into a weapon, what could they possibly be planning?"

The Executioner frowned in consternation. The thought in the back of his mind suddenly solidified, and it made his blood run cold.

Rawlins saw the look on Bolan's face. "What? What is it?"

Bolan turned to Captain Radtke. "Have you received any more reports from Berlin?"

"Nothing of much importance."

"What about the Turkish immigrants that Kemal Kose used to relocate the plutonium?"

A deep line drew down between the German GSG-9 captain's eyebrows. "Four of the men involved have died from acute radiation poisoning. The doctors say they breathed plutonium dust into their lungs. Two more are critical, and two are very ill but recovering."

Bolan turned to Schwarz. "How would you rate plutonium as a toxin?"

Schwarz frowned and shook his head slowly. "It's one of the most toxic substances known to man. It's worse than mercury. Once you're poisoned with it, there's very little that can be done for you. As Captain Radtke just informed us, if you breathe it into your lungs, there's no way to get it out, and each speck of it will emit lethal concentrations of radiation into your body. It burns the lung tissue it is in contact with and poisons your blood and internal organs. It's a very ugly way to die."

Bolan took a deep breath and let it out as he turned to Gary Manning. Of all the men who worked for Stony Man Farm, he had the most practical experience with explosives. "Gary, what do you think would happen if you took twelve hundred pounds of plutonium in pellet form and mixed it in with several thousand pounds of ammonium-nitrate fertilizer and diesel oil and loaded it into a truck?"

Manning gaped at the idea. "Jesus."

"My thoughts exactly." Bolan turned his gaze on the chief. "They're not going to turn the plutonium into a weapon. It already is a weapon, and they're going to mix it into a truck bomb to blow their weapon into dust and spread it around."

"But we know when they intend to attack. They'll still never get close enough to the Royal Family to make it work."

Bolan shook his head impatiently. "They won't attack during the ceremony. You yourself admitted that they must know we suspect an attack during the ceremony. So they won't. They'll attack Buckingham Palace before the ceremony."

Radtke scratched his head. "But the whole Royal Family will not be there. If killing them is their goal, they will fail."

"No. They will succeed." Bolan looked at Rawlins frankly. "Chief, what would the Royal Family do if a truck-bomb attack devastated Buckingham Palace?"

"Why they would..." Rawlins trailed off as he was dumbstruck by the idea.

Bolan nodded. "That's right. The queen would be seen on every television set in the world, standing among the rescue workers and the rubble, swearing that the United Kingdom would never bow before terrorism and promising swift vengeance against the perpetrators. Prince Charles and other members of the Royal Family would tour the wreckage."

The chief gaped as Bolan continued in a voice as cold as ice. "No one would know that the walls, the trees, the dirt, the rubble, the debris and the very air itself around Buckingham Palace was inundated with highly radioactive plutonium dust. No one would know until a day or two later, when the soldiers, the police, the medics, the rescue workers, the cleanup crews, the members of the press and the members of the Royal Family all began dying of radiation poisoning."

Rawlins sat thunderstruck. "Good...God."

Bolan sat back slightly in his chair. "No one would think to bring a Geiger counter to the scene of a truck-bomb blast. You were right, Chief. The idea of turning the plutonium into a nuclear weapon was a red herring. The stuff is lethal enough for their purposes just as it is."

Everyone around the table was silent for a long moment. Rawlins slowly nodded. "An incredible plan, but I believe it would work, and despite all of our preparations, it seems we have been playing right into our opponents' hands."

"It's worse than that. They had at least three initial lots of plutonium that we know about. We've managed to seize two of them. I suspect they intended the others for similar European targets, perhaps in Germany and France. I've told you before, I believe there are other forces at work here than the

IRA or the Libyans. I believe someone intends to take a serious stab at destabilizing Western Europe.''

The chief took a moment to mull over all he had just heard. "Who do you think is behind all of this?"

Bolan leaned back in his chair. "I don't know, but they have connections that seem to span the globe." The Executioner grimly looked at a map of London up on the wall. "Our main concern now is to make sure the truck bomb never goes off. I'm sure you and your SAS teams can defend the palace, but we have to make sure our friends don't detonate the bomb in downtown London as a last, retributive strike. Out in the open streets the blast would do less damage, but the fallout would still be very dangerous."

Schwarz sighed. "It would be worse than fallout. Fallout from a nuclear weapon is just dust and debris that is temporarily radioactive due to the blast. It's dangerous and can make you very sick, but it's only radioactive for a few weeks. The fallout from this kind of bomb won't be irradiated debris, but actual plutonium dust. In even tiny concentrations it'll be lethally radioactive for hundreds of years. If their blast gets a decent dispersal, or if the wind is blowing, no amount of cleanup procedures will be able to get it all. People will be turning up sick and dying in London for decades to come."

Rawlins stared up at the wall map without blinking. "The palace destroyed, the Royal Family killed and radiation sickness lurking in the streets of London for decades to come..." He trailed off as he contemplated the horror of it.

Bolan steepled his fingers before him. "We have one advantage. The enemy doesn't know that we've figured out what they're up to. The key will be to catch them at what they are doing and take them out before they can detonate the bomb."

The chief swiveled around in his chair. He was suddenly all business. "What do you suggest?"

Bolan glanced up at the map again and the red circles drawn on it. "I'm betting they go for Buckingham Palace, and if they really want to do the job right they'll try to breach the fence to get the truck right up onto the grounds. I believe they'll go for it before the ceremony to try and take us off guard, and that means from this minute on the attack could come at any time.''

The Executioner leaned forward. ''This is what I propose we do.''

21

The Executioner crouched on top of the Queen's Gallery in Buckingham Palace with a scope sighted .378 Magnum Weatherby rifle in his hands and surveyed the palace defenses. David McCarter crouched next to him, holding an M-16 rifle. A few yards away Gary Manning stood with his 7.62 mm M-21 semiautomatic sniper rifle, drinking coffee with Gadgets Schwarz. Captain Dieter Radtke was beside him, his stocked machine pistol in his hand. He had removed the sling from his other arm and was scanning the horizon through a pair of binoculars he held.

The palace was surrounded by heavy black wrought-iron fencing with highly carved stone stele every dozen yards or so. To the east the wide Mall road led up to the palace and the huge traffic circle that stood before the gates. Even at that early hour there were walkers and joggers on the Mall parkway, and cars came and went on palace business. The traffic circle was dominated in its center by the massive winged statue that had been dedicated to Queen Victoria, and beyond it lay Trafalgar square. To the south Buckingham Palace Road ran parallel to the palace. To the north was Constitution Hill, and the western end of the palace was surrounded by more than forty acres of secluded gardens.

Around the perimeter of the palace, the soldiers of the Grenadier Guards stood at ramrod attention in their red dress uniforms and tall bearskin hats. There were many more of them visible than on any standard day, and someone scrutinizing them closely would notice small differences in their equipment. Each guardsman had a personal radio fitted with a throat mike and earpiece, and his armament was different as well. The guardsmen normally carried the 5.56 mm British SA-80 assault rifles. This day all of the guardsmen carried the older, heavier .308-caliber automatic rifles with the thought of stopping a speeding truck.

A detachment of Ghurka riflemen prowled the gardens on the west side of the palace in full dress uniform. Ostensibly they were drilling for the impending state ceremony, but each Gurkha's M-16 rifle was loaded and his massive *kukri* fighting knife was honed to a razor's edge. The Gurkhas had been informed that the queen's life was in danger, and they took their duty with utmost seriousness. Parked out in the secluded gardens were six military trucks loaded with decontamination teams in full radiation suits in case the unthinkable were to occur.

Within the palace grounds lurked three heavily armed SAS antiterrorist teams, and on the roof, six SAS teams armed with scope-sighted .50-caliber Browning heavy machine guns loaded with armor-piercing ammunition watched the roads to and from the palace. Two more teams faced the east and west roads, manning wire-guided MILAN antitank missile launchers.

Bolan watched the early-morning traffic pass down Buckingham Palace Road.

The sun was just rising, and the city of London was amazingly quiet. A small army of pigeons had awakened to greet the new day, and they cooed and bobbed their heads as they marched about the roof in tangled formations and ignored the heavily armed soldiers that stood among them.

The teams had been deployed nearly twenty-four hours ago, and had been on continuous watch. The night had passed without any major incidents, though every commercial truck that passed within half a mile of the palace threw everyone into red alert.

Bolan glanced about at the red-eyed SAS troopers perched on the palace roof. Despite the long night and the very real possibility of being blown to bits or lethally irradiated, their morale was high.

Dieter Radtke grunted as he scanned the Mall road with his binoculars. "That car is riding very low on its tires."

Bolan whipped the Weatherby to his eye and sighted down the ten-power scope. "Where?"

The German kept his eyes fixed as he pointed with his machine pistol. "There. A white Citroën, with tinted windows, approaching the traffic circle."

Bolan quickly scanned the approaching vehicle through his scope. It was riding very low on its tires. Either its suspension was almost shot, or it was very heavily laden. The windows were tinted so dark that nothing could be seen of the interior. The Executioner spoke into his throat mike. "This is Striker. I have a suspicious vehicle approaching from the Mall. A white Citroën, tinted windows, riding low. I think you should have an officer flag it down."

"Roger that." The SAS controller inside the palace radioed the Military Police officers who were stationed at Queen Victoria's statue. Bolan watched through his scope as one of the officers stepped out into traffic and waved his baton for the Citroën to pull over.

With a squealing of tires the vehicle accelerated directly at the officer.

"We have contact!" Bolan yelled. "White Citroën! Coming toward the east gate! All units engage!"

The officer in the street hurled himself out of the way of the speeding car and clawed for his holstered pistol. All along the roof heavy machine-gun bolts clacked as the weapons were racked into action. Bolan, Manning and McCarter had already begun to fire their rifles at the speeding vehicle.

The Citroën's windows shattered under the repeated impact of high-powered rifle bullets. The Grenadier Guards stationed at the palace gate brought their rifles to their shoulders and dropped to one knee with parade-ground precision as they began to put short, rapid bursts of automatic-rifle fire into the speeding car. The two .50-caliber machine guns dedicated to the east side of the palace ripped into life as they put the French sedan into a lethal cross fire.

The Citroën was literally coming apart as it hurtled forward, but it wasn't stopping. Sparks flew outward from the shattered windshield, and Bolan realized that the car had been armored. The sparks flew from heavy welded-steel plating that protected the driver and probably the engine compartment of the car, as well. The tires shredded and tore as bullets hit them, but they didn't burst or deflate. Bolan knew that they had to take solid composite like those used on armored limousines.

Bullets wouldn't stop the car in time.

Bolan shouted above the sound of gunfire. "Team One! Hit them! Now!"

The SAS gunner of antitank missile Team One took a split second to lock on to the car through the MILAN missile's optical sight and fired. With a sizzling whoosh the antitank missile flew out of its launch tube trailing its guide wires. The SAS gunner unerringly kept his cross hairs on the Citroën as it approached the palace gates. Within a second the missile accelerated to half the speed of sound and flew directly through the vehicle's shattered windshield. The MILAN's six-and-a-half-pound shaped-charged warhead slammed into the steel plating and detonated. The shaped charge burned through the steel plating and sent a lethal stream of superheated gas and molten metal into the interior of the Citroën.

The sedan exploded with an immense thunderclap, and a huge ball of orange fire obscured the Mall. Many of the palace windows shattered, and Grenadier guardsmen were knocked off of their feet by the blast. Bolan squinted as the heat of the blast wave washed over the palace.

Bolan's nostrils flared. There was no characteristic smell of ammonium nitrate. The car had been filled with military high explosives. They were using car bombs to try to breach the palace gates.

He shouted across his radio. "Watch the road! They're going to hit us again!"

As Bolan spoke, a second Citroën sedan came screaming down the Mall, followed a second later by a Land Rover. Both vehicles hurtled toward the traffic circle, and both had tinted windows.

The big Browning .50s roared into life and hammered the oncoming vehicles. The Grenadier Guards poured in rifle fire, and Bolan and the Stony Man team fired their weapons with uncanny accuracy. Tracers streaked down into the vehicles in what seemed like solid streams.

It wasn't enough.

Both of the vehicles had been armored, and even as their exteriors flew apart under the firestorm, the heavy steel plating protected the engines and the drivers. The manned bombs hurtled on with single-minded determination.

Off to Bolan's right the MILAN team desperately fixed a new missile tube onto the launcher. The loader slapped the gunner on his shoulder. "Ready!"

The gunner fixed his cross hairs on the second Citroën and fired. The missile streaked out of its launch tube and struck the vehicle dead on. The sedan exploded in a ball of orange fire, and again the Mall was hammered by the shock wave of nearly a thousand pounds of detonating high explosive. The blast rolled over the speeding Land Rover, and the overloaded vehicle slewed sideways.

The Executioner stood his ground as the shock wave rolled up and over him, and he kept the big .378 Magnum rifle on target. As the Land Rover slewed, he raised his aim to put his cross hairs on the rear passenger's window. The rear window shattered as Bolan fired his last two rounds one on top of the other as fast as he could work his rifle's bolt. As he had suspected, only the top and front of the vehicles had been armored for a head-on attack on the palace gates.

Two 300-grain bullets slammed into nearly a thousand pounds of high explosive at almost three thousand feet per second.

The Land Rover launched into the air and came apart on a column of fire as its half-ton payload detonated. Bolan lowered his rifle and quickly began to reload as he squinted against the blast and scanned for more targets.

The traffic circle and the Mall were suddenly very still. Early-morning traffic had ground to a halt, and drivers crunched in their cars and looked about fearfully. Most of the windows fronting the palace were shattered. Fire alarms and sirens began to howl in the distance, and people who had been walking or jogging along the road huddled and held one another. The sounds of moaning and screaming dimly filtered through the Executioner's ringing ears. Black smoke rose from the burning wreckage of the three shattered vehicles. Grenadier guardsman rose up dazedly from the ground where they had been thrown by the repeated explosions. Some had been injured by flying debris, and some civilians appeared to have been injured, as well.

Bolan could hear the sirens of approaching police and fire units as McCarter and Manning stood beside him and slipped fresh magazines into their smoking rifles.

Radtke scanned the roads with his binoculars. "Nothing seems to be moving." He lowered the field glasses and raised an eyebrow at Bolan. "Do you think that was it?"

Bolan flicked his rifle's bolt home on a full magazine and scanned the roads. "I don't know. Maybe. They must have people watching. We scratched all three of their attempts to breach the gates. They might have decided to scrub the mission for today." Bolan grimaced as he took in the carnage in front of the east gate. "I don't know."

A police car screeched onto the scene, followed by several ambulances that had been on standby. A pair of fire engines quickly arrived and began to spray the burning wreckage. Moments later a British army jeep with a .50-caliber machine gun mounted came down the Mall preceding a pair of troop trucks. The trucks came to a halt outside the gates, and armed British soldiers in disruptive-pattern-camouflaged fatigues began to jump out of the back and deploy as their sergeant yelled orders at them.

Bolan spoke into his radio. "Control, what do we have on the west side?"

"Checking, Striker." The SAS controller came back. "West side reports no movement outside the gardens. All troops are holding their positions."

"Roger." Bolan glanced back at the traffic circle. McCarter scratched his chin as he watched. "Well, I'll be damned."

Bolan turned his gaze to where McCarter was looking. The soldiers were quickly deploying in a skirmish line in front of the east gate. "What?"

"Look at their insignia. Those lads are from the Gloucestershires, my old regiment. I wonder what the hell the Gloussters are doing here?"

"Where should they be?"

McCarter shrugged. "Last I heard they had been rotated to Northern Ire—"

The Executioner whipped his rifle to his shoulder and fired. A man in a British army uniform below twisted and fell before the east gate. His SA-80 assault rifle fell from his hands. A rifle grenade was fitted to its muzzle.

To Bolan's left an SAS commando roared as he tracked his .50-caliber machine gun onto Bolan. "What the bloody hell are you doing?"

Bolan roared. "Down!"

The thumping noise of a rifle grenade firing came from below as Bolan threw himself on the roof. A grenade slammed into the machine-gun emplacement, and the SAS gunner and his loader were hurled backward in bloody heaps.

Rifle fire erupted in front of the palace gates. Another grenade hit the second machine-gun emplacement that watched the Mall road. The two SAS commandos managed to hurl themselves down, but their weapon was smashed off its tripod and the loader twisted as he was hit with flying metal fragments. Below, a .50-caliber machine gun opened up with a hammering roar.

The Executioner rose.

On the street two-thirds of the Grenadier guardsmen were already down. With the stolen British army uniforms and equipment, the IRA terrorists had achieved total surprise. A man stood in the jeep behind the heavy machine gun and mercilessly cut down the Grenadiers. Bolan put his cross hairs on the gunner's chest and fired. The rifle roared, and the machine gunner was swatted away from his weapon and thrown off the jeep by the Magnum bullet's impact.

Beside Bolan, McCarter and Manning began to fire their weapons. The Executioner tracked his rifle's aim as two men leaped from the back of the second truck, both armed with an RPG-7 rocket grenade launcher. Bolan put one of the men in his sights, and the big Weatherby rifle boomed as the man was smashed to the ground. He swung his sights to his second target, but the man had already fired his weapon.

The RPG-7 rocket sizzled out of its launch tube and flew straight toward the east gate of the palace, trailing a long plume of gray smoke. The ancient wrought-iron box locks of the palace's twin gates were no match for the rocket-propelled grenade's five-pound shaped-charge payload. The gate locks twisted and blew apart as the antitank warhead detonated against them.

The perimeter had been breached.

Bolan squeezed the Weatherby's trigger, and the second RPG man fell dead to the ground. The diesel engines of the two military troop transports roared and snarled as the drivers shoved them back into gear.

Bolan slung his rifle and turned to Schwarz. "Hit the jammer! Now!"

The Executioner clipped a length of rope to the D-ring of

his web equipment and went over the side of Buckingham Palace in a face-forward rapel.

LIAM O'LAUGHLIN WAS nearly giddy with success. The hated Grenadier Guards lay dead all over the street. The machine-gun nests on the roof had been knocked out, as well as the missile launcher. The car bombs had been an excellent feint. Dressed as British soldiers rushing to the scene of the attack had been a sheer stroke of genius.

There was now one last great act to perform.

"Forward! Now!" O'Laughlin shouted.

The driver shoved the truck into gear, and the vehicle lurched forward. In the back of the truck in sealed plastic bags were eight thousand pounds of ammonium-nitrate fertilizer heavily soaked with diesel fuel. The diesel fuel reacted with the normally stable ammonium nitrate and made it highly sensitive to detonation and boosted its explosive power. Inserted among the bags were six-hundred-pound tanks of propane gas that had already leaked most of their charge into the sealed plastic tarps surrounding the bags. The gas would turn the already powerful detonation into a fuel-air explosion of massive power. In the very center was a small steel tube containing two pounds of lead stifyinate. When the detonator received its signal, a superheated jet of fire would stream out of one end of the tube into the mass of ammonium nitrate, diesel fuel and propane gas. The man in the dark suit had informed O'Laughlin that the resulting explosion would be the equivalent of twenty thousand pounds of TNT.

Spread throughout the thousand pound sacks of ammonium-nitrate explosive were twelve hundred pounds of lethally radioactive plutonium.

The truck surged through the gates as the driver floored the accelerator. In his hand, O'Laughlin held the dead man's switch. The switch was a plastic tube with a large red plastic button that he held down with his thumb. The mechanism was very simple. As long as he held his thumb down on the switch, the circuit was disconnected and nothing happened. If his thumb released the switch, the circuit was completed and the signal was sent to the detonator. Even if he was killed, the bomb would detonate.

The truck surged through the gates as the driver pressed the accelerator to the floor. Both O'Laughlin and the driver were totally prepared to die. This moment would live in the pages of history forever. Buckingham Palace would be destroyed, the Royal Family would die and London itself would be an abandoned ghost town as its residents fled the specter of radiation poisoning lurking in the air and water.

O'Laughlin started as a figure in black crawled down the front of the palace on a rope like a crazed spider. The figure slammed down at the top of the palace steps and whipped a long black rifle around on its sling and raised it to his shoulder.

With his free hand O'Laughlin brought up his stolen 9 mm Sterling submachine gun and shouted at his driver. "Keep going! Straight on—"

Flame shot from the muzzle of the black rifle facing them, and the front windshield shattered. O'Laughlin felt the wet spatter as the high-powered rifle took its terrible toll on his driver's skull. The truck swerved as the dead driver fell against the wheel. The Irishman grabbed for the wheel as more shots rang out, and the truck's engine shrieked in protest as heavy rifle bullets smashed into it.

O'Laughlin grinned. It made no difference. They were close enough, and nothing could stop fate now. The grin turned savage with triumph as he lifted his thumb from the dead man's switch. The switch clicked up into position and cheeped as the signal was sent.

The terrorist frowned as nothing happened.

The driverless truck lurched to a halt against the palace steps, and O'Laughlin was thrown against the dashboard. He pressed the button and released it several times. Each time it clicked back up into place, and the electric cheep told him the signal had been sent.

Still nothing happened.

O'Laughlin's face split into an ugly grimace. Somehow the signal had been jammed. That didn't matter. In the back of the truck he had eight thousand pounds of explosive surrounded by flammable gas. He twisted around in his seat and racked back the action of his Sterling submachine gun.

He would just have to detonate it by hand.

THE EXECUTIONER ROSE from his rifleman's crouch. The big Weatherby was empty. Through the shattered windshield he could see the nearly headless driver slumped over the wheel. In the passenger's seat a large man was bringing a submachine gun into action. Bolan couldn't afford to shoot into the truck. His taking the driver with a head shot had been a necessary risk. Now everything rested on keeping the man in the passenger's seat from firing his weapon into the back of the truck.

Bolan grabbed his rifle by the barrel and threw it as hard as he could.

The .378 Magnum Weatherby spun in the air and scythed through the truck's windshield. The heavy rifle thudded into the man with the submachine gun and knocked him against the back of the cabin. Even as the rifle flew, Bolan was taking the palace steps two at a time. He jumped and put one foot on the truck's bumper; his next step brought him up on the hood.

The Executioner dived through the shattered windshield headfirst.

Bolan's right hand seized the submachine gun's barrel, and flame shot forth as he rammed the muzzle skyward. Hot brass flew in the cabin as the weapon fired, and a line of holes punched through the roof of the cab. Bolan recognized Liam O'Laughlin's face from the MI-5 files even as he rammed his left fist into it.

O'Laughlin let out a bellow of rage and seized Bolan by the throat with his left hand. The Irishman's hands were huge, and the Executioner felt his windpipe pinch closed as powerful fingers dug like vise grips into his carotid arteries.

O'Laughlin ducked his head as Bolan's fingers stabbed at his eyes, and the soldier felt his blood hammer in his veins as his brain began to starve for oxygen. As his vision began to darken, Bolan's hand skidded down the side of O'Laughlin's head and he seized the Irishman's cauliflowered left ear and yanked with all his might.

O'Laughlin screamed and released his hold. Letting the ear fall from his hand as the Irishman dropped the submachine gun, the Executioner knocked the weapon to the floorboards with a sweep of his hand.

The Irishman's pupils condensed into pinpoints of fury as he seized his adversary by the throat again with both hands. Bolan felt the fingers sink into his neck and knew only killing the man would break his death grip. The Executioner ignored the grip and wrestled himself on top of O'Laughlin and shoved the man's head down. Fingers closed off Bolan's air and blood flow, and again he felt the blood start to thud in his temples. With another shove, the back of O'Laughlin's head was brutally jammed against the dashboard, then stuck fast. The Irishman's grip stayed fast, as well, and spots began to shimmer in Bolan's darkening vision.

The Executioner kicked upward and planted his feet against the roof of the truck, then he rammed his forearm against his opponent's throat and shoved off the roof with every ounce of strength in his legs.

For a long second the two men were locked in a jam as Bolan arched his body against the forearm he had barred against the Irishman's throat. O'Laughlin's bull-like neck held as his arms stayed flexed and his thumbs pressed in against Bolan's windpipe with crushing force. For a split second the soldier relaxed his legs and O'Laughlin's head shifted as the strain was lifted.

With desperate strength the Executioner shoved down again with all of his might.

The terrorist's neck broke with a gurgling snap, and his suddenly limp upper body suddenly slithered to the floorboards.

Bolan yanked the dead man's hands away from his throat and drew a ragged gasp of air into his tortured lungs. With a shaking hand he drew his Beretta and shoved the truck's door open.

Manning lowered his M-21 sniper rifle slightly and grinned.

Bolan managed a cough and took a moment or two to breathe. "What's the situation, Gary?"

Manning shrugged. "All the terrorists are dead. We count nineteen, and your two friends in the truck there make twenty-one. We've got a lot of casualties. The Grenadier Guards took the brunt of the attack. They got hit, and they got hit hard."

Bolan nodded and leaned back against the seat. "What about the second truck?"

"The fake troopers all jumped out of that one, so we figured it was safe to shoot into it."

The Executioner needed no further explanation of the fate of the second truck. "Get the bomb squad and the men in the radiation suits out here, ASAP. I think there's some very nasty stuff in the back of this truck, and I want it defused as quickly as possible."

"You got it, boss." Manning spoke into his throat mike.

Bolan reached up to his neck, and as he suspected, his own mike had been ripped away. He swallowed painfully. It felt as if his whole throat had been ripped away.

SAS troopers and Ghurka riflemen came swarming out of the palace and around its flanks. The wailing of sirens was constant, and in the truck's side mirror Bolan could see flashing lights and emergency vehicles coming down the Mall.

He coughed again and spoke. "Gary."

"Yeah, Mack?"

"What's the situation with the machine guns on the roof?"

Manning frowned. "They're off-line."

Bolan nodded. "There's a fifty on that jeep. Take it and a

detachment of riflemen to the queen's statue. Don't let any vehicles pass without checking them. All it would take is a man with a rifle to set this thing off.''

"Right away." Manning moved off and began shouting at the Ghurkas. The men quickly fell into formation around the jeep. Manning climbed behind the machine gun as two SAS men jumped in the front. The instant roadblock moved to intercept the incoming vehicles.

Bolan stepped out of the cab and sat on the palace steps. The sun had fully risen over the horizon, and the battleground was suffused with golden light. The battle was won.

He glanced back at the truck and Liam O'Laughlin's broken body. He hadn't planned this operation. Neither had the Libyans. There was a bigger force at work, with bigger plans than just England.

The battle was won.

Deep down in his bones, Mack Bolan knew the war was just beginning.

EPILOGUE

The man in the dark suit lowered his binoculars.

The old man wasn't going to be pleased.

He stood on the scaffolding of a massive soft drink sign that dominated part of Trafalgar Square's skyline. His view of the battle at Buckingham Palace had been nothing short of perfect.

The defeat had been total.

Everything had gone according to plan; how it had failed at the end was inexplicable. The failure was as monumental as it was inconceivable. The truck rested at the very steps of the palace, inert and intact. All of the IRA's best men lay dead. The man in the dark suit frowned and pressed the switch on the backup detonator several more times in vain. The signal was jammed. It was he himself who had suggested a radio-controlled detonation rather than using a cable in the truck. It had seemed safest. In battle, wires were notorious for being severed or disconnected. Now the signal had been jammed, and men in radiation suits were swarming all over the truck and defusing its lethal potential. The man sighed heavily and in an amazingly uncharacteristic display of emotion allowed his shoulders to sag as he vainly wished for an antitank missile.

The European phase of the operation was an unmitigated failure.

Beside the man in the dark suit, Heidi Hochrein lowered her binoculars. Liam O'Laughlin was dead. It was a shame that such a capable man had died in vain, but emotionally his death meant almost nothing to her. Buckingham Palace standing undemolished and mocking her, however, raised very ugly emotions in her. Deep in her gut she knew the American survived, as well, and that made her want to draw her pistol and begin randomly shooting people down on the street.

With an immense effort of will, Hochrein kept a tight rein on those emotions and let them seethe under the surface. She wouldn't allow them to show in front of the man. Her voice was carefully controlled as she spoke. "What do we do now?"

The man in the dark suit peered at her and considered her question. So far he had entertained no thoughts about the future. His only thought was that the old man was most likely to have him killed, and therefore thinking about the future was a useless pastime.

He considered the recent past.

Hiding behind terrorists had been a clever ploy, and he still doubted the American or any of his allies knew who their enemy really was. However, as their defeat in three different countries showed, terrorists were simply too unreliable. The old man and the board would have to be made aware of this. The defeat here in Europe was total, and there was nothing that could be done about that.

However, a fact remained.

Europe was only one phase of the operation, and he himself was still the most qualified man to lead the operation to its conclusion. The operation was still capable of success. If America fell, Europe could easily be taken in its wake. The man in the dark suit decided he could convince the old man— and the board, for that matter—of that simple fact.

The man in the dark suit turned to Heidi Hochrein and smiled. "I believe we will be going to the United States."

*The heart-stopping action continues
in the second book of* THE POWER TRILOGY:
PLAGUE WIND, coming in July.

Take
4 explosive books
plus a
mystery bonus
FREE

James Axler

OUTLANDERS™

PARALLAX RED

Kane and his colleagues stumble upon an ancient colony on Mars that housed a group of genetically altered humans, retained by the Archons to do their bidding. After making the mat-trans jump to Mars, the group finds itself faced with two challenges: a doomsday device that could destroy Earth, and a race of Transhumans desperate to steal human genetic material to make moving to Earth possible.

In the Outlands, the future is an eternity of hell....